The Osterlund Saga

*Two generations taking twentieth-century
America by storm*

It's 1933 and the Great Depression has left
heiress Jolie Cramer's family in ruin. A convenient
marriage to wealthy Randal Osterlund is her
only hope. But could this practical partnership
actually be a perfect match?

Find out in
Marriage or Ruin for the Heiress

Twenty-three years later... It's 1956 and Jolie
and Randal's daughter, Randi, is all grown up!
When she's reunited with her high school enemy,
sparks fly—this time of attraction! But their fiery
encounter has unexpected consequences...

Find out what happens in
The Heiress and the Baby Boom

Author Note

America was booming during the 1950s. The economy had a strong rebound after the war, suburbs exploded with newly built homes, hot rod cars and motorcycles filled the roadways, and rock and roll music filled the airways. Along with all that came the babies! During the "baby boom," nearly four million babies were born each year of the 1950s in the USA.

All of that made the '50s a memorable time, and writing a story set during this era was a lot of fun.

I hope you enjoy Randi and Jason's story as they encounter the baby boom firsthand.

Cheers!

LAURI ROBINSON

The Heiress and the Baby Boom

ISBN-13: 978-1-335-40766-5

The Heiress and the Baby Boom

Copyright © 2022 by Lauri Robinson

Harlequin Enterprises ULC
22 Adelaide St. West, 41st Floor
Toronto, Ontario M5H 4E3, Canada
www.Harlequin.com

Printed in U.S.A.

A lover of fairy tales and history, **Lauri Robinson** can't imagine a better profession than penning happily-ever-after stories about men and women in days gone past. Her favorite settings include World War II, the Roaring Twenties and the Old West. Lauri and her husband raised three sons in their rural Minnesota home and are now getting their just rewards by spoiling their grandchildren. Visit her at laurirobinson.blogspot.com, Facebook.com/lauri.robinson1 or Twitter.com/laurir.

Books by Lauri Robinson

Harlequin Historical

Diary of a War Bride
A Family for the Titanic Survivor

The Osterlund Saga

Marriage or Ruin for the Heiress
The Heiress and the Baby Boom

Twins of the Twenties

Scandal at the Speakeasy
A Proposal for the Unwed Mother

Sisters of the Roaring Twenties

The Flapper's Fake Fiancé
The Flapper's Baby Scandal
The Flapper's Scandalous Elopement

Brides of the Roaring Twenties

Baby on His Hollywood Doorstep
Stolen Kiss with the Hollywood Starlet

Visit the Author Profile page
at Harlequin.com for more titles.

To Jean. Thanks for the lunches,
road trips and laughs.

Chapter One

1956

The deep breath of fortitude that Randi Osterlund drew in was full of chilly January air, and she begged the brightness of the sun to give her strength as she ran her hands up and down the front of her red wool coat.

All she had to do was knock. Just knock.

Then say hello.

Then... Her entire body drooped.

Oh, good grief.

She squared her shoulders, nodded to herself and almost took the last step toward the front door, but then she envisioned the unopened letter. The one he'd written *Return to Sender* on.

Her hands began to shake and she balled them until her nails dug into her palms. That had been years ago. She'd thrown that letter away. Was over it. Over him. All she needed was his land.

She checked the double row of brass buttons on the front of her coat, made sure they were neatly fastened and flipped her hair off her shoulders.

Time to get this over with. Knock on the door.

It was just Jason Heim.

With a motorcycle, a hot-rod car, slicked-back sandy-brown hair, dark brown eyes and a physique that would make the greatest male movie star jealous, Jason had been the James Dean of Chicago long before the real James Dean had hit the big screen.

He was also the reason she'd locked up her heart and thrown away the key.

Her family and his had bad history, as her father had wanted to buy the one hundred sixty-acre plot of land Jason's father owned, but Heim had refused to sell.

That had been years ago, though. Now Jason owned that land, and she was going to acquire it. Prove she had what it took to be a woman in the corporate world. She might only be twenty-two, but she was ready, and fully capable. After all, the Queen of England was only thirty and had already been queen for three years.

Not that Randi wanted to be a queen, but she did want to prove that women could do more than get married and have children.

She took another deep breath in preparation to take that last step and knock on the door, but chose to make sure the big rhinestone R pinned on her coat was straight first.

"Are you going to stand there primping all morning, or are you going to knock on the door?"

Startled from her thoughts, her heels slipped on the concrete. She caught her footing, but seeing the man peering over the fence next to the house made her heart pound so hard it hurt and enough butterflies erupted in her stomach to make her take flight.

Jason's grin showed off the dimple in his right cheek, and his elbows propped on the gate were a sign that he'd been watching her for some time.

He was as handsome as ever.

Maybe this hadn't been a good idea.

No. She was no longer a schoolgirl. She was a grown woman. "No, I—" Quickly deciding that ignoring his comment would be a more mature choice, she lifted her chin. "I don't know if you remember—"

He laughed. "Everyone who ever stepped foot in Westward High School remembers *the* Randi Osterlund. The princess who would one day become queen."

The bitterness of his laugh sparked ire. She loved her family, loved her parents for all of their successes, but she was more than just Randal and Jolie Osterlund's daughter. Head up, she stepped off the concrete porch. "No more than they remember *the* Jason Heim."

"Aw, yeah, the rebel who was sent to reform school."

That was another thing that connected their families and not a subject she'd intended to bring up. "I would like to speak to you about—"

"Buying my land? It's not for sale."

And then he was gone, disappeared behind the fence.

She would not let him get away that easily. He'd not only walked away without an explanation years ago, he'd returned her letter of apology unread. This time he'd hear her out.

The snow crunched beneath her shoes as she stepped off the porch and was deeper than the low sides of her kitten-heeled black pumps, but she kept walking. She reached the gate and gave it a push. Then a second push, much harder. The snow on the other side gave way and she nearly fell through the opening. Catching herself, she let out a growl. "If you—"

"I said it's not for sale."

This time he disappeared around the house. Her pumps

were already snow packed, so she moved forward, stepping in his footprints as much as possible.

Rounding the corner of the house, she spied a concrete slab completely clear of snow and made her way to it. Her nylons were soaked through and her toes were becoming ice cubes. Shivering, she stood on one foot, emptied one shoe and then repeated the process with the other shoe.

"They're just going to get full again when you make your way back out the gate."

She would not let him affect her, in any way, and let her gaze start at his feet, which were covered with leather boots, before working upward. His pants were dark blue denim, cuffs rolled. The material hugged his thighs and hips. The jeans met a brown leather jacket that was zipped halfway up his chest, and the collar was turned up around the back of his neck. When her gaze met his, it took nearly all she had to keep it there, chin up. She wasn't sixteen and would not let her nerves get the best of her.

She had to get that land. Prove she was not only fully capable, but that nothing would get in her way from running Air America.

He was the first to look away, and that gave her an ounce of triumph. Something she needed greatly. Using it, she started, "The taxes alone on your prop—"

"Are none of your business. The land—"

"Isn't for sale." Holding up a hand, she continued. "You already said that. However, I would appreciate it if you'd let me get a complete sentence out before you interrupt."

He folded his arms across his chest.

"You are aware that your parcel of property is something Air America has been interested in purchasing, and I understand, from what you just said, that you are not interested in selling it."

He didn't so much as twitch.

She, however, was shivering from head to toe. Both from the cold and from being face-to-face with him. The dreams she'd had years ago kept trying to flash forward. Of her and him riding on his motorcycle, burning rubber in his hot-rod car and kissing. Blast it all, but that dream was stronger right now than ever. To the point it made her throat go dry. He'd matured. Was even better-looking, and the things she'd felt for him years ago were taking sprout all over again.

That couldn't be. Gathering her thoughts, she reminded herself that she had to get that land, despite all obstacles. Including those deep inside her. "I believe we could still come to an agreement, or arrangement of sorts, if you would give me the opportunity to explain."

Of all the people in the world who could have shown up on his front porch, Randi Osterlund was the last one Jason would have imagined. Well, he might have imagined it, but that would have been a fantasy. However, she was the last person he would ever make any sort of agreement or arrangement with in this lifetime. What was her father thinking, sending her over here to talk to him? Randal Osterlund was not the kind of man who would use his daughter— Jason's thought stopped right there.

"Does your father know you're here?"

Her entire body seemed to slump, but only for a moment before she caught herself and straightened her spine.

Bingo. Her father didn't know.

With her pert little chin lifted high, she said, "I am employed by Air America and have full authority to conduct business in their name and—"

He waved toward the fence as he walked over to collect the shovel and pail he'd left by the tree when he'd heard a car pull into the driveway. "You know where the gate is." She might claim to be employed by Air America, but there was more to it than that. She was an heir to Air America, and a multimillion-dollar lingerie company that her mother owned, JO's Dream Wear. Besides her mother, Randi Osterlund was one of, if not the, richest women in Chicago. He'd learned his lesson when it came to her years ago and didn't need a repeat. That was one thing his father had been right about. Thinking he would have ever had a chance with a girl like her had been stupid. Very, very stupid.

"Do you ever let someone finish a sentence?" she asked.

"I let you finish several." That had been a mistake. But not his first one. That had been speaking to her when she'd been preening on his front porch. As soon as he'd seen her climb out of her car, he'd known it was her. Other women may have chestnut hair like her, thick and long, but no one had the same shade of eyes. A pale blue, that captured and held attention. He should have kept his mouth shut, let her knock and believe he wasn't home. She would have left, but he'd opened his mouth and now she was standing on his back porch instead of his front one. He'd managed to steer clear of her for years and needed to continue to do so for the rest of his life.

He picked up the shovel, scooped a pile off the ground and dropped it in the bucket.

"Why are you shoveling snow into a bucket?"

He grabbed the bucket by the handle. "Why are you still here?"

"Because I'm not leaving until you hear me out."

Hands on her hips, arms akimbo, she continued. "I can wait until you get your bucket full of snow."

His jaw tightened. He'd worked hard to forget her. Forget the huge crush he'd had on her. He'd been a gangly teenager with pimples the first time he'd seen her. They had gone to different primary schools, but the same high school, and for two years he'd thought of little else than catching her attention. He finally had, and then had dug deep to find the confidence to ask her out. Bitterness filled him recalling how she'd laughed at him. His hands tightened on the shovel and the bucket handle. "It's shit, not snow."

"Excuse me?"

"I'm shoveling shit, not snow."

"Really?"

"Yes, really." He let out a whistle and a moment later, Tanner bounded out through the rubber flap installed in the back door for the yellow Lab to enter and exit at will.

As if taken aback by her beauty, Tanner slid to a stop at her side, plopped on his haunches and stared up at her with stars in his big brown dog eyes.

Letting out a cooing sound, she knelt down beside the dog and scratched him behind his ears. "Hello, big guy. You are a handsome one. What's his name?"

At that moment Jason figured *Traitor* would be a good name for the dog. "Tanner," Jason answered, growling out the name.

She leaned back and cupped the dog's head with both hands. "Tanner, is it?"

Tanner barked.

She laughed.

Jason carried the bucket to the back of the yard and dumped it over the fence, into the trash can placed there for just that purpose. After putting the bucket and shovel in the shed, he walked to the porch, where she and the dog were still fawning over each other. "Tanner, inside."

He could have sworn the dog curled a lip at him as he stood, turned and with his tail between his legs, reentered the house through his doggie door.

She stood, too. "You should take lessons from your dog. He listens."

"He's a dog."

Both of her finely arched brows lifted as she stared at him.

If he wasn't so irritated, he might have been impressed at her boldness. As things stood right now though, he wanted her gone. Needed her gone. He had tried, but the moment he'd seen her step out of her car, he'd known he'd never gotten her out of his system. "You need to leave."

"No. You ran away from me once. That won't happen again."

"Ran away? What the hell are you talking about?"

"I'm talking about the night you jumped on your motorcycle and sped away before I could—"

"Stop laughing?" He knew the night. It was forever scorched in his brain. An hour after she'd laughed in his face, he'd been arrested, and by the following Monday, he was in reform school.

"My toes are cold. I am going inside." With that, she turned, opened the door and marched straight into his house.

Chapter Two

Letting out a curse, Jason followed. "You're trespassing."

She stepped out of her shoes and walked to the table, unbuttoning her coat on the way. "Have me arrested."

With smooth, graceful movements, she removed her coat, laid it over the back of the chair and sat in one of his padded chrome chairs. His eyes betrayed him by refusing to pull his gaze off her white blouse, or how it was neatly tucked into a blue skirt at her narrow waist, or the way she crossed one leg over the other at the knee. Mad at his inability to stop staring, and at his dog who was at her side again, Jason turned around and shrugged out of his coat. "That's your family, not mine."

Her silence made him feel like an ass, and his statement made him sound childish.

Damn it. He'd made it through six years. Six! And in a matter of minutes, she'd brought back every thought he'd ever had about her. As well as some new ones.

He walked into the laundry room off the kitchen, hung his coat on the rack nailed to the wall and grabbed a pair of socks out of the pile of clean clothes he hadn't yet put away.

Back in the kitchen, he laid the socks on the table while walking past her on his way to the sink.

"Thank you."

"You're welcome." He washed his hands and then grabbed the electric percolator, emptied and refilled it to make coffee. As he set the pot back on the counter, something inside him flinched. The countertops were blue, as was the tabletop, and the chair cushions, appliances and walls. It was called turquoise, but it was a pastel shade of blue, much like the color of her eyes.

"Your kitchen is very nice, very modern," she said, as if reading his mind.

He opened a cupboard door, which he'd stained rather than painted, and lifted down the can of coffee. "Thanks."

"You built it, didn't you? The entire house?"

It was no surprise that she'd know that. Her father had probably been keeping track of him, especially since his father had died. He glanced over his shoulder, to voice that the land wasn't for sale again, but instantly realized he'd made a mistake when he saw how she was rolling one nylon down over her knee, down her shin. She must have reached under her dress to unhook the little plastic hooks that held it in place. The idea of watching her unhook the other silk stocking was what made him turn around. Not because he didn't want to see it, but because he did.

"Your craftsmanship is excellent," she said.

He spooned coffee grounds into the percolator, put on the top and plugged the cord into the wall, all while trying not to envision her taking off her second nylon.

"Do you live here alone?"

He chanced a glance and tried to convince himself that he was glad that she was pulling on the second sock of the pair that he'd given her. "No."

"So you had a woman's help," she said, sounding as if that explained everything.

"No." He opened another cupboard door and took down two cups and two saucers. They were white with blue rings around the edges. Light blue. Damn it. She'd been stuck in his head for years, but he hadn't realized just how deeply.

"Who lives here with you?"

He turned around, leaned his backside against the counter. "Tanner."

She smiled down at the dog, who, with his head on her lap, was looking up at her with pure devotion.

Damn dog.

"Poor puppy," she said.

The dog barked and Jason considered changing the dog's name to Traitor again. He pushed off the counter. "I'll go put your shoes near a furnace grate." With a nod toward the nylons as he crossed the room, he asked, "You want me to put those there, too?"

She picked up the nylons. "No, thank you. They have holes in them now. Where is your trash can?"

"Under the sink." He picked up her shoes, carried them into the laundry room and turned the grate all the way open after setting them in front of it. Her perfume filled his nose; had since he'd walked into the house. He'd been trying hard to ignore the soft, floral scent as much as he'd been trying to ignore the things going on inside him.

Chicago was full of women, good-looking chicks. He'd dated a good number of them. Why the hell couldn't one of them have affected him the way she did? Why the hell wasn't she married to Gus Albright? Living in some ivory tower, eating with silver spoons and throwing money out the windows.

Enough was enough. He needed to get rid of her. Out

of his house. Out of his life. Things were going well. His construction company was thriving, thanks to the housing boom, and there were four work sites he had to visit today. He would have already been gone if he hadn't spent a few hours this morning working on the plans for the racetrack. Drag racing was in his blood, and this summer he'd be building a real strip on the land she wanted.

There would be no arrangements, agreements, or anything else between the two of them. Not over the land or anything else.

He left the laundry room, ready to stand his ground, but stopped at the sight of her standing near the stove, running a hand over the handle on the oven door. It was as if he was seeing a dream that he hadn't known lived inside him, coming true before his eyes.

She completed the area. As if it had been built just for her.

Damn it. It had. She'd been the image in his mind the whole time he'd been designing and building the entire house.

Right down to her wearing his clothes.

It was only a pair of socks, but it made him want to claim her, to wrap his arms around her and kiss her as badly as he'd wanted to in high school when he used to imagine her wearing his jacket.

That had never happened, and he'd been a fool to think it ever would. He was older now, wiser, and more importantly, not the fool he'd been back then. Money divided people. Always would. He'd accepted that and the fact that the Randi Osterlunds of the world had no place in his life, or he in theirs.

Randi willed all the old feelings she'd had for Jason to go back down, deep inside her, where she'd kept them hidden for years. She should never have come here. Never thought she could face him and not remember how crushed she'd been when she'd ruined everything. He had reasons to hate her.

Swallowing hard, she reminded herself that she didn't have a choice. She needed that land. Had to have that under her belt when her father became a senator, otherwise, no one would respect her role at Air America. They'd go on believing she was only there because she was an Osterlund—the next in line to take over the helm because of her last name, not because she could truly do the job. Everyone thought she should be focused on taking over her mother's company. A woman could run a lingerie company, but not an airline. Never an airline. She should leave that for her brother.

Well, her mother wasn't running for senator and her brother was still in college. So that left her. She'd been soaring through the skyway in an Air America airplane since before she'd been born—while still in her mother's womb. Taking over the helm would prove she was more than just Randal and Jolie's daughter. She was her own woman.

"How's Gus these days?"

She blew the air out of her lungs and turned about. Jason was leaning one hand on the door frame that led into a laundry room. Her heart started racing all over again. Damn him for being even more handsome than ever. And damn him for being such a major hurdle in getting what she needed. "Good. He's out in California and loving it. Says he'll never move back." Gus Albright was a safe subject, so she continued. "He has a lot of family out there. Aunts and uncles, cousins, grandparents."

Jason pushed off the wall. "I figured the two of you would be married by now."

"Me and Gus?" She laughed. "Why would you think that?"

He shrugged. "The two of you were always together."

"Because he was my ride before I got my license. His parents and mine have been best friends since before either he or I were born. He's as much of a brother to me as Joey." She bit her lips together at the mention of her younger brother. Joey was another subject she wasn't going to bring up with Jason.

He stopped near the refrigerator. "Do you want cream or sugar in your coffee?"

"Both, please," she answered with a laugh. "I keep thinking I'll acquire a taste for it black someday, but it hasn't happened yet."

He nodded, and then shook his head.

Embarrassed because her joke failed, she turned back around to face the counter. That was what had happened years ago. She'd laughed. Not because he'd said something funny, but because she'd been so nervous and happy. He hadn't thought so, nor had he let her explain, and that had been the catalyst that had led to her never seeing him again, until today.

The days, weeks and months following that event had been the saddest in her life. Deep inside she'd felt that if she could just explain why she'd laughed, Jason might forgive her and her family for all that had happened afterward. She'd put out an olive branch in the letter she'd written to him, only to be heartbroken again when it had been returned unopened.

There had been no denying the inevitable then, so she'd tried to move on, and had. She'd put her focus on Air America. And that was where it had to stay.

The coffeepot was in front of her, perking. Assuming it was done by the color of the coffee in the glass bulb on top, she unplugged it from the wall and filled the two cups he'd set out. While he carried a bottle of cream out of the fridge and a sugar bowl from a cupboard, she carried the cups to the table in the center of the room.

He set the cream and sugar, and a spoon, in front of her and sat down across the table from her. She put both in her coffee and stirred, wondering what to say. "I—"

"Look—" he said at the same time.

"Sorry," they both said.

"You go ahead," they again said at the same time.

She shook her head and looked at him, waited for him to speak first. He didn't look exactly like she remembered. His hair was still sandy-brown, his eyes still as dark as the coffee in his cup and there was still that dimple in his cheek, but his features were more defined. His body, too. There was a power about him, a determination, that made him even more alluring. She used to stand in the hallways of the school just to get a glimpse of him, and she'd been on cloud nine the first time he'd said hello. She'd been in tenth grade and had been infatuated with him for almost an entire year by then. Everything she'd been so attracted to then was still there and fueling all of her old feelings for him tenfold.

"I have plans for my land," he said. "There is no sale, arrangement, or agreement that I'd be interested in."

So much for apologizing. That was what she'd been going to do. For the past. But he didn't want to hear it any more than he had back then. Accepting that, she took a sip of her coffee. "All of it? Forty acres is what I'm interested in. Possibly leasing it?"

"Leasing it?"

"Yes. Every one of our airplanes needs to be washed at least four times a year. Currently, we don't have space for that. Therefore, we pay other carriers to provide those services, which isn't cost-effective."

"You want to build a facility on land you *lease* from me to wash your planes?"

"No, I wouldn't build on leased property, but I would use it for storage, freeing up space that we currently own to build a washing station. The forty acres I'm interested in is the plot of land that butts up to the rear of our property." His acreage was in an L shape and her plan would still leave him one hundred and twenty acres for whatever plans he had.

He took a drink of coffee and set the cup down on the saucer before saying, "None of my property is available for sale or lease."

Growing frustrated by his stubbornness, she drew in a breath. "As I said—"

"I heard what you said, but you don't seem to have heard what *I* said. I'm not interested. Not in leasing or selling anything."

"Well, I think it would behoove you—"

"Behoove me?"

"Yes, it means—"

"I know what it means." He stood, picked up his cup and saucer. "I may not have gone to an Ivy League college, but I have a good grasp on the English language." He walked toward the sink.

"I didn't mean to insult you. If you would just listen to my offer, you'd see it would be beneficial. You'd have extra money and—"

"You didn't insult me." He set his cup and saucer in the sink and turned, looked at her with a somewhat scathing glare. "I'm used to your kind."

Her spine stiffened. "My kind?"

"Yes."

"And exactly what is my kind?"

He let out a bogus laugh. "The kind that believe I need your money. I don't."

"I wasn't implying—"

"Weren't you?"

Her last nerve was about to snap. "No. I wasn't." Unable to stop herself, she continued. "If you would have listened to me that night, maybe we'd be friends now."

He laughed again. "I'd rather be your enemy."

The response inside was so swift and unexpected, she pressed a hand to her breastbone, against the pain that sliced through her heart. No one had made her heart hurt, not like this, except for him. She wouldn't put herself through that again. "Fine, if that's the way you want it."

"It is."

She stood, grabbed her coat. Kept her chin up. "Thank you for the coffee, Mr. Heim."

"You're welcome, Miss Osterlund."

The living room and the front door were visible through the arched doorway of the kitchen, and she marched toward it, slipping on her coat as she walked through the living room and then out the front door. It wasn't until she stepped off the porch that she realized she didn't have any shoes on. Just his socks. She clamped her teeth together and kept moving. Walking through the snow stocking footed was better than facing him again.

She marched forward, along the shoveled walkway, to her car parked in the driveway. To her great distress, Jason arrived just as she opened her car door.

"You forgot your shoes." Holding out her pumps, he glanced at her feet. "You can keep the socks."

"I intend to." She grabbed her shoes and climbed in the car, slamming the door extra hard.

Chapter Three

Four days later Randi's temper was so close to the boiling point, she might actually break something. It was either that, or complain to her father, which she wouldn't do. Sam Wharton knew that, which was precisely why he was purposefully not providing her a copy of the profit and loss sheets for December. He was her main adversary in the company, because he knew, when—not if—she took over for her father, he'd be out the door. Or at least demoted. She wasn't so mean as to cause someone to completely lose their job.

Sam was one of the people who thought she couldn't do anything except spend her parents' money, and was trying his damnedest to make sure she failed. She wouldn't, but also had to be cautious because Sam would go to her father and complain. He already had. Several times over the years, against both her and her brother.

She understood that Sam had been working for the company for years, and that he was interested in taking over for her father, but he wasn't what the company needed. He took no initiative, had no drive to make changes that could grow the company. It was 1956, the world was changing and Air America had to, too, in order to remain on top.

Frustration had her slapping her desk with both hands, and she glanced out the window of her corner office, only to instantly pull her gaze away because her windows overlooked the very land that Jason wouldn't sell or lease to her.

He was stuck in her mind enough already.

She pushed her chair back. Without those P&L reports, she couldn't complete her reports, which were due by the end of the week. A deadline Sam didn't want her to meet.

Removing her shoes, she put them in a satchel and slid on her boots. They were black, heeled, lined with sheepskin and had black wool cuffs around the tops that stopped near her ankles. After getting her shoes wet at Jason's, she'd worn her boots every day and carried her shoes.

She put on her coat, slipped the satchel strap over her shoulder, picked up her purse and left her office.

"I'm leaving for the day, Carol," she told her secretary in the outer office. "Please inform Mr. Wharton, once again, that I expect those reports to be on my desk first thing in the morning."

Carol had been with the company for years, and knew what Sam was attempting to do. "I will, Miss Osterlund. Have a good evening."

"You, too." Once out the office door, while walking down the hall, Randi hooked her purse over her wrist to pull her gloves out of her pockets. Only to discover they weren't there. She dug in the satchel and pulled out a pair of socks rather than her gloves.

Jason's socks. She'd washed and dried them, and rolled them together like they'd been when he'd set them on the table.

Her insides sank at how that visit had gone. Everyone always wanted something from her, but not him. Jason didn't want anything to do with her.

She dropped the socks back in the bag and dug until she found both of her gloves and pulled them on as she walked down the steps to the front door of the big Air America office building.

It was spitting snow. Not a lot, just enough to leave a thin coating of the white flakes on the ground and on her car. There was also a sheet of ice covering her windshield from sitting in the elements since she'd arrived early this morning.

After putting her purse and bag in the car, and starting the engine, she grabbed the metal ice scraper and cleared the windshield, side windows and the rear one. By the time she climbed inside she was shivering from head to toe. Her gloves were wet, and she pulled them off, stuck them in her coat pockets and put her hands up on the dash, over the warm air blowing out.

She sat there until her fingers were warm, then shifted the car into First and drove out of the parking lot.

Her father hadn't yet announced who would be his successor when he was elected senator, because he claimed his bid was a long shot. In her mind, though, he was a shoo-in. He also claimed that he would continue to oversee the operation, even if he was elected, but everyone knew he'd need someone here on the day-to-day basis and she needed to be that person. Otherwise, besides being her mother's daughter, her father's daughter and her brother's sister, she'd also be the senator's daughter. Never her own person.

She had to get that land from Jason. That was all there was to it. The problem was facing him again. Seeing him had brought back more than memories. Just thinking about him made her heart beat faster. Dreams had formed again, and that scared her. He was so handsome. So fit. So iconic…

If only there was a way for them to be friends, so she could explain why she needed the land, not just for the washing bay, but for her. So she would be recognized as her own person. He'd done that. His construction company was very successful. He'd been his own person in high school, too, and she'd admired that.

She had to try. Had to do something. The socks were in her bag. She could drop them off to him.

That might work, and she already knew how he felt about her, so there was no reason for her to worry about having her heart broken again. She'd learned her lesson on that. No one would fall in love with someone who wanted to be their enemy. Furthermore, her focus was Air America, nothing more.

At one time Air America had been a distance from town, but the suburbs now extended farther out of the city, and in less than twenty minutes, she turned down Jason's street and wondered why he'd built his house here rather than on his land. That was where he'd lived when they were in high school, and as far as she knew, the house was still there.

She pulled into the driveway and took a moment to stare at the windows, looking for some sign of movement. It was only late afternoon. He might still be at work. The garage was on the far side of the backyard, in the alley, like the others in the neighborhood, so she couldn't tell if there was a vehicle here or not. She wasn't even sure what type of car Jason drove. He used to drive a motorcycle and a red hot-rod car with a ball of fire painted on the hood.

There was only one way to find out if he was home

or not. She shut off her car and pulled the socks out of the bag, stuffing them in her coat pocket while opening the car door.

There were no footprints in the thin coating of snow on the sidewalk, but there wouldn't be if he parked his car in the garage. Arriving at the door, she forced herself to not check her clothes like she had the other day and knocked.

A bark sounded and she smiled. Tanner's friendliness had already stolen her heart. He was much bigger than other Labs she'd seen and so very sweet.

When no one opened the door, she knocked again, heard Tanner bark again and waited until she had no choice but to believe Jason wasn't home.

She could leave the socks, but doubted he'd contact her to acknowledge their return. However, if she did leave them, she could stop by later to make sure he got them.

That was far more probable than him contacting her.

She lifted the door on the mail slot, but the slit was too narrow for one, let alone a pair of rolled socks. Closing the slot door, she glanced around, realizing he might not find them if she just left them on the porch.

Tanner barked again, and she smiled. The doggie door. Jason was sure to find the socks if she dropped them through it. Proud of her own ingenuity, she walked off the porch, proceeded to the gate and entered the backyard.

She was grateful she was wearing her boots because her feet were sinking into the snow, even though she was stepping into the footprints she'd left the other day.

On the back patio, she knelt down, pulled the socks out of her pocket and pushed open the doggie door to drop them in. The flap was made of rubber, and heavier than she'd expected. She held it open with one hand and, reaching in with the other, dropped the socks. As they fell, she realized one of her gloves had also been in her hand and tried to catch it, but it was too late. It had fallen inside the doggie door with the socks.

Shoot!

She tried to find the floor, feel her glove, but couldn't. Leaning closer, she shoved her entire arm inside the doggie door, right up to her shoulder, and then, able to feel the floor, searched for the glove, blindly, using only her fingers.

Not feeling anything—not the socks or glove—she pulled her arm back out and looked at the door. It was big. Big enough for Tanner, and therefore, big enough for her head.

With no other option, she got down on her hands and knees.

Jason shot a glare at Tanner, telling the dog to stay quiet as the slender hand, complete with manicured nails, painted pink, slipped back out of the doggie door. He'd been stepping out of the shower when he'd heard Tanner bark, but by the time he'd gotten dressed, no one was at the front door. However, he'd recognized the blue-and-white Bel Air parked in his driveway. Assuming Randi had walked around to the back, he'd entered the kitchen and had been about to open the door when a pair of socks and a woman's black leather glove had landed on the floor through the doggie door.

A moment later he'd bit back a smile and watched as the hand had slid through the door, searching for the glove.

He hadn't been able to help himself and had toed the glove and the socks out of her reach.

Eyes on the doggie door, he waited for the hand to return again. To his surprise, when the flap moved again, a full head of dark hair popped through the opening.

He knelt down, picked up the glove and dangled it where she'd see it as soon as she pushed the rubber flap up high enough.

As soon as that happened, he asked, "Is this what you're looking for?"

Her head snapped around so fast the rubber slapped the side of her face. Flinching from guilt at causing that to happen, and at her pain, he grabbed the flap, held it out of the way. "Are you okay?"

Light blue eyes blazing hot enough to light a good-sized fire glared at him.

He wanted to laugh at how adorable she looked, yet was concerned that she might be hurt and repeated, "Are you okay?"

"Why didn't you answer your front door?"

"I was in the shower."

"Oh." Her gaze went to his bare feet and then she glanced around, as if not sure what to say or do.

Still holding the flap with one hand, he balled the glove in his other hand, and used that one to reach up and turn the doorknob. "Hold still, I'm going to open the door."

She didn't answer, but did hold still as he slowly opened the door, until her head was no longer in the doggie door. He then released the flap and held out a hand to help her up.

There were still flames in her eyes, but she took his hand and gracefully rose to her feet.

His hand, where hers touched it, was on fire, shooting flames up his arms and igniting other flames.

She slowly pulled her hand away, ran it over her coat,

then, chin up, said, "Thank you. I—I'll take my glove, please."

The opportunity was too great to ignore. He dangled the glove. "This one?"

She reached for it.

He quickly pulled it out of her reach. "How do I know it's yours?"

"Because I have the other one right here." She pulled a matching glove out of her coat pocket.

"Oh, and here I was thinking it was yours because I watched you drop it through the doggie door."

"Because you didn't answer your front door."

Closing the door, he replied, "Because I was in the bathroom." He'd pulled on jeans and a white T-shirt, but was barefoot. "Didn't even have time to put on socks in my hurry to get to the door, but by then you were no longer at the door." He picked up the socks she'd just delivered and walked over to a kitchen chair, sat down and proceeded to put them on. "Your car was in my driveway, so I figured you'd walked around to the back, but I didn't expect to see you climbing through the doggie door. I wonder if that's considered breaking and entering?"

"I wasn't breaking and entering. I was returning your socks. Now, if you'll just give me my glove, I'll be leaving."

He should give her the glove, let her leave, but teasing her was so much fun. Little else had consumed his thoughts since she'd stormed out, wearing only his socks on her feet. Then again, she'd had a permanent place in his mind for years. "Nice boots," he said, nodding toward her feet. "You should have been wearing those other day."

"I hadn't planned on trudging through snow the other day."

"But you did today? Planning to come around to the back, to sneak in through the doggie door?"

"No. I—" She shook her head. Sighed. "What were you doing taking a shower at four in the afternoon?"

"If you must know, Miss Nosy—" he stood up, handed her the glove "—I just got off of work and need to be in Downers Grove by five."

"I wasn't being nosy. Just curious."

"What's the difference?"

She smoothed the fingers of the glove he'd given her with one hand. "There is a great difference."

"Do tell. I'm listening."

She rolled her eyes at him. "You know the difference."

He did indeed, and he was curious about her, even though he shouldn't be. "Came over to ask about the land again, did you? My answer hasn't changed."

"No, I didn't come to ask about the land," she said. "I heard your answer the other day. I just wanted to return your socks."

He wasn't sure he could believe that. "I said you could keep them."

"I don't have a need for a pair of men's socks."

"In that case, thank you." He wiggled his toes. "I do have need for them."

"Why do you have to be in Downers Grove?" She stuffed her glove in her coat pocket and shot him a saucy look. "I'm simply curious."

"A birthday party." He waited until she met his gaze before adding, "For a lovely young lady."

"Oh." She fidgeted, smoothed a hand over the front of her red coat that had the big rhinestone R pinned below one shoulder. "Well, then, I should be going so you can finish getting dressed."

His mouth moved before his brain engaged. "Would you like to go with me, meet her?"

"Oh, I couldn't, I—"

Had he just asked her on a date again? And been turned down again? Was he that stupid? "That's all right, I get it." Shaking his head at himself, he turned to lead her to the front door.

She caught his arm. "No, you don't understand. I would like to go, but I wouldn't want to impose."

Her touch was soft, yet he felt it as strongly as he had her hand earlier. "If it was an imposition, I wouldn't have asked."

They stood there for a moment, doing nothing but staring at each other, as if they were each trying to read the other's mind. At least, he was trying to read hers. His own was in too big of a jumble to make hide nor hair out of what he was doing. And his eyes kept flicking toward her lips, making him wonder what they tasted like.

"In that case, yes, I'd like to go with you."

His heart skipped several beats. So many he was damned near breathless. "All right, I have to put on my shirt and shoes and feed Tanner, then we can leave."

Stroking the dog's head, she offered, "I could feed Tanner for you."

Completely taken with her, the dog looked up at him with pleading eyes. "His dishes are by the door and there's a bag of dog food in the laundry room."

As she cooed over the dog, Jason hurried out of the room and down the hall. Within minutes he'd put on a blue-and-white button-up shirt, slipped his belt through the belt loops of his cuffed jeans and put on his shoes. On his way to the door, he grabbed his leather coat off the bed, all the while wondering what the hell he was doing.

This was Randi Osterlund—*the* Randi Osterlund—
and he was the rebel her father had sent to reform school.

He flinched, knowing that wasn't true. There was no
one to blame for his stint in reform school except for
himself. And that was another reason he needed to stay
clear of her. His past was more jaded now than it had
been back in high school.

She was still in the kitchen, petting Tanner as the dog
ate. "I wasn't sure how much to give him, so I filled the
bowl."

"That's fine." He nodded toward the back door. "We'll
take my car." His Buick was bigger, heavier, which meant
it would maneuver the snow-coated roads better than her
smaller Bel Air. Furthermore, the dollhouse and furniture he'd built for Rachelle were already in his car. "Unless you've changed your mind."

"I haven't changed my mind. Your car is fine."

He must have lost every last marble that he'd had, because he was excited to take her to the party. Then again,
he wanted the event to be a huge success. Rachelle deserved that after all she'd been through.

"I need to get my purse out of my car." She moved
away from Tanner, but on her way to the doorway, she
stopped and smiled at Jason. "Thank you for inviting
me to join you."

He nodded and fell into step beside her. "I hope it
didn't interfere with other plans." He didn't even sound
like himself.

"No. Just going home to an empty house. My parents
are in New York."

"What for?" he asked as they walked toward the front
door.

"A fashion show. Some of my mother's designs are
being showcased."

He'd seen some of her mother's designs and wasn't convinced that women's underwear would be a good topic to have floating around in his mind right now.

As if knowing his thoughts, she said, "She designs uniforms for several airlines."

He opened the front door. "I wasn't aware of that."

"Most people aren't."

He walked her out to her car, and then back through the house, the backyard and into the garage. They talked of several things, just small talk, but he found it interesting to learn more about her. That she found fashion shows tedious and that she'd never had a dog, but had had a cat for several years while growing up.

In the garage he held the passenger door open as she slid inside his car. Then he swung open the garage door before climbing in the driver's seat.

"How old is this lovely young lady?" she asked with a glance toward the backseat that said she'd noticed the two large wrapped boxes.

He grinned at her. "Six."

Chapter Four

Going out with Jason had been a dream of Randi's for years, and she was having a hard time convincing herself that this was not a date as he drove through the spitting snow. He looked so handsome, smelled so good, that every part of her body was alive, tingling with excitement.

"The party is at a café that my aunt works at," he said. "We'll eat there, if that's all right."

"Of course it's all right. What's the birthday girl's name?"

"Rachelle. She's my cousin's daughter."

"What are in the boxes?" Huge, they took up the backseat and were gaily wrapped and hosted big blue bows.

"You'll have to wait and see," he said.

He flashed her one of his grins that made her want to drop dead twice. That was a silly saying that had stuck with her since high school, but when it came to him, it held a whole different meaning. He could stop her heart with just one of those grins. If she let him. Which she would not do.

"I might need you to carry in the smaller one, if you don't mind. It's not too heavy."

"Aw, you had an ulterior motive in asking me to join you. You needed a helper."

"Free labor is nothing to scoff at."

She laughed. "How do you know it's free?" Embarrassed that he might take that the wrong way, she pointed to the radio. "Oh, I love this song."

He turned it up. "You're one of those?"

"Girls who love Elvis?" she asked. "Yes!" She then proceeded to sing along with the song about blue suede shoes.

He was tapping a hand on the top of the steering wheel, and she gave him a playful slap on the arm. "You like him, too."

"He has a few good songs."

"Like every one of them!"

He laughed and they talked about songs and performers for most of the drive, and her insides were nearly glowing when he pulled into a parking lot of a small café with a lighted sign in the shape of an arrow saying Mama's and pointing at the building.

She reached down and picked up her satchel. "I'm going to switch my boots for my shoes so my feet don't get hot."

"Oh, yes, hot feet would be a terrible thing."

"Very funny," she said while giggling because she was enjoying herself.

Perhaps too much, but it really couldn't be helped. He was fun and made her feel comfortable.

As they entered the café, with its black-and-white tiled floor and red-and-white booths, a tall blonde woman met them. "What's buzzin', Cuzzin?"

"Not much," Jason replied, carrying the large box that nearly covered the bottom of his face.

The woman lifted a brow. "Really?"

The woman was looking at her, grinning, and Randi, carrying the smaller box, smiled in return.

"Randi, this is Lottie, Rachelle's mom," he said.

"Yes, I am," Lottie said. "I'm also this cat's cool cousin."

"You wish you were as cool as me," he said.

Randi rolled her eyes toward Lottie, and teasingly asked, "Doesn't everyone wish they were as cool as him?"

"Ooh, I like you, Randi," Lottie said. "Someone who can rattle his cage is exactly what Jason needs."

"Ha ha," he said.

"Jason! Jason, I knew you'd come!"

Randi's attention was instantly drawn to a tiny, dark-haired girl moving toward them in a small wheelchair.

"I wouldn't miss this party for anything in the world," Jason replied.

Randi's heart swelled at how the little girl gazed up at Jason with adoration shimmering in her big brown eyes. It appeared that he still had the ability to steal a young girl's heart.

"Are both of those presents for me?" Rachelle asked, stopping her chair before them.

While holding the big box, Jason knelt down. "I don't know. Is someone else having a birthday party here to-night?"

"No!" Rachelle replied.

He kissed the girl's forehead. "Then they both must be for you, kiddo."

"Can I open them now?"

Lottie rested a hand on her daughter's shoulder. "Let's give Jason and Randi a chance to get their coats off first."

Not deterred in the least, Rachelle nodded. "Okay!" She quickly maneuvered the wheelchair around. "Follow me. You can sit at my table, and put the presents on it so I can open them right away."

Randi giggled at the girl's excitement.

"You heard her," Jason said, nodding for Randi to walk in front of him.

With her heart nearly flowing over, Randi followed the girl and said to Lottie, "Your daughter is adorable."

"Thank you. As you can tell, she adores Jason." Lottie glanced over her shoulder at Jason following them. "He visited her every day while she had been in the hospital with polio last year."

A deep sense of admiration for Jason grew inside Randi, at the same time empathy formed for Rachelle. "How long was she in the hospital?"

"Ten weeks," Lottie answered. "She was in an iron lung for over a month."

Randi knew the devastation polio caused and served as the chair of the local fundraiser to collect dimes to pay for every school-age child to get vaccinated, but mass inoculations had only started last year. They still had a long way to go before every child would receive the vaccination. "I'm glad she's recovering so wonderfully."

"Thank you. We are, too, and credit a lot of her healing to Jason. There were days that she wouldn't eat, like she was giving up." Lottie cleared her throat, as if choked up. "But Jason would find a way to get her to eat. To smile. I know it made a difference."

Randi's eyes stung, and she had to blink quickly to keep the tears inside.

"I need to stop," Lottie said. "Before I make myself cry again."

"Yes, you do, Cuz," Jason said. "And you need to step away from the table. This box is heavy."

Lottie laughed. "All right, you can put them right here on this table."

Rachelle had already wheeled her chair up to the end

of the table, and Randi stepped aside so Jason could put his package down first.

He set it in front of Rachelle and then took the package from Randi and set it near the back of the table.

"Can I open them now?" Rachelle asked.

"Not everyone is here yet," Lottie said.

"I arrived early, just so she could open these before everyone got here, then we can move it aside so it doesn't take up so much room," Jason said.

"Please?" Rachelle asked her mother.

"All right. Let me get Grandma," Lottie answered.

"I'm coming! Don't start without me!" a voice shouted from the kitchen area behind the long counter across the room from the booths.

"I'll take your coat," Jason said.

Randi was so enthralled, she hadn't even unbuttoned her coat yet, but did so quickly, and let him lift it off her shoulders.

He carried it over to hooks on the wall past the counter, where a jukebox sat, and hung up her coat and his. Before his return, a plump older woman with short, dark hair arrived at the booth and introduced herself as his aunt Marla.

After an exchange of greetings with his aunt, Randi slid into the booth, leaving room for Jason to sit on the edge, next to Rachelle.

Marla and Lottie slid in on the other side, and as soon as Jason sat, he said, "Go ahead, kiddo, rip it open."

Rachelle didn't waste a moment tearing away at the paper.

An adorable blue-and-white dollhouse was instantly revealed. Completely finished with shingles on the roof and shutters on the windows, tile and carpets on the floors, and each of the rooms was painted a different color.

Randi was in awe. The house was a work of art. Built with such skill and precision, it was truly extraordinary.

Jason stood and lifted the house. Seeing what he was doing, Randi slid the other box forward so there was room for him to set the dollhouse down behind the second present.

"Now this one?" Rachelle asked.

"Now this one," he answered.

Rachelle tore off the paper and opened a box full of miniature furniture that was handcrafted as perfectly as real furniture found in stores. The little chairs even had cushions attached to them, and the beds had mattresses. The amount of love Jason had put into the gifts had Randi's heart expanding, and her hands trembling. Her parents had showered her and Joe with their love, as well as each other, and she'd told herself she'd never settle for less. She'd been young, but there had been a time when she'd imagined Jason loving her like that.

He stood and lifted the house off the table. "Wheel your chair away from the table. I want to show you something."

Rachelle wheeled her chair backward, and he flipped down folded-up legs from the bottom of the house and locked them in place with metal brackets, and then set the dollhouse in front of her.

"I made it so you can wheel your chair right up to it," he said.

"This is the best present ever," Rachelle said. "Ever, ever, ever!"

"Oh, Jason, that is so perfect," his aunt said. "And so like you. You're amazing."

"Yes, he is." Realizing she'd said that aloud, Randi's cheeks burned when he looked at her, yet she couldn't look away. Nor could she deny that he was becoming the man of her dreams all over again.

* * *

Jason knew he should, but for the life of him, he couldn't pull his gaze off Randi, not with the way she was looking at him. It was causing a good case of chaos inside him. And desire. Strong desire to kiss her.

The ringing of the bell over the front door, signaling the arrivals of others, is what forced him to look away. He glanced down at Rachelle. "Let's move this over by the jukebox so it's not in the way."

"All right, but leave room so we can dance later," she said.

He ruffled her dark hair. "I will."

While he carried the dollhouse, Rachelle followed in her chair, as did Randi, carrying the box of dollhouse furniture. He set the house near the corner, where it wouldn't get bumped if there was dancing later, and made sure the legs were locked in tight.

Rachelle rolled up to the dollhouse, and as Randi handed the girl furniture, one piece at a time, Jason was once again questioning his sanity. He shouldn't have brought Randi with him. They were as opposite as night and day. No one in his family had ever had anything handed to them. They'd worked hard, and continued to, for every loaf of bread put on their table, whereas she'd probably never wanted for anything in her life.

He had. He'd wanted her and was wanting that again.

"This is a beautiful dollhouse," Randi told Rachelle.

"Jason could build one for you, too," Rachelle said.

"I might have to ask him," Randi replied.

She was wearing a red dress. Tailor made. Had to be. It enhanced every area of her body to perfection before it flowed into a wide skirt. Her hair was hanging loose, in soft curls, down her back. She looked eloquent, beautiful and had every part of his body alive, pounding with desires that he couldn't ignore. Couldn't control. Every fantasy he'd imagined about her seemed to float across his mind, filling his chest with abnormal sensations.

"He builds real houses, too," Rachelle said. "He could build you one of those, too."

"I'll remember that when I need a house," Randi said.

"He fixes houses, too," Rachelle said. "He fixed our house so my wheelchair can fit through the doors and he—"

"Hey, kid," he interrupted. "You have other guests arriving and should go say hello."

"Okay." She spun around and wheeled away.

Randi stepped in front of him, close enough he could smell her perfume, see the sparkles in her gorgeous blue eyes.

"I always knew your bad-boy persona was just an act," she said.

Needing to ground himself before he said or did something he'd regret, he pulled up the only reason for her to have agreed to come with him tonight. "The answer is still no."

She frowned. "Answer to what?"

"To buying my land."

Shaking her head, she said, "I wasn't thinking about your land, and I wish you weren't, either."

The sadness in her tone and in her eyes gutted him as she turned. He grasped her wrist. "I'm sorry. I was just teasing."

She glanced from him to where people were staring at them, walking in through the door two at a time. Everyone was sure to want to know who she was and why she was with him. For a moment he considered getting their coats and leaving, taking her to her car so she could go home. He couldn't do that to Rachelle. Didn't want to do that to Randi, either.

Rubbing the inside of her wrist with his thumb, he said, "Honestly, I was only teasing, and I'm sorry."

Her eyes fluttered closed for a moment. "I'm sorry, too." Sighing, she looked up at him. "I shouldn't be so prickly."

"Prickly?"

"Yes."

Of all the ways he could describe her, *prickly* wasn't what came to mind.

"I'm just nervous," she added.

"Why?"

Her one shoulder shrug was cute, charming. "Of meeting your family," she whispered. "I wouldn't want to embarrass you."

He had to laugh at that, which brought more curious stares from onlookers. "That will never happen." He took a hold of her hand and held on, even as his palm felt as if it was being licked by flames. "Come on, I'll introduce you to everyone."

Aunt Marla had worked at the diner for years, ever since her husband had died, and the owner, Elwood, who was also in attendance, had shut the diner down to the public tonight, so the entire family could celebrate Rachelle's birthday. And no one in the room was immune to Randi's charm, including him.

She was soon giving back one-liners about being with him as quickly as some of his cousins tossed them out. Her laughter, teasing comments and the way she'd touch his arm or dip her head against his shoulder, filled him with a lightheartedness that he hadn't felt in a long time.

Several family members worked for him, including

Stu, Rachelle's father, and Randi asked him about his company, appearing truly interested in his answers.

When the time came for Rachelle to open her gifts, he found seats for them on the stools at the counter to watch.

Randi leaned closer to him. "Rachelle is adorable. It had to have been hard, seeing her so sick. In an iron lung."

"It was." The past year had been hell, and tonight was an event that at times he'd worried might never happen. "She was so little, so sick, there were times I didn't know if she'd win."

Randi's fingers wrapped around his. "She did win. Tell me how you convinced her to eat."

The memory made him smile. "Ice cream. I took her milkshakes."

Randi giggled. "She must have loved that. What flavor was her favorite?"

Watching Rachelle rip open another present, he answered, "Strawberry, but chocolate was a close second."

"You took her one every day?"

"Yes."

As presents continued to be opened, Randi quietly asked more simple questions, and he ended up telling her things that he'd never told anyone about how concerned he'd been over Rachelle's illness and gradual climb to health. Ironically, talking about it to her felt right.

The last gift had been opened and he stood, pulled her off her stool. "What's your favorite milkshake?"

"I don't know. Why?"

He led her around the counter, toward the freezer and milkshake machine. "Because we'll make it."

"We can't go back there to make our own milkshake."

"Where do you think I got the milkshakes that I took to Rachelle?"

The smile on her face was reflected in her eyes. "You made them?"

"Yes."

A hint of challenge added to her expression. "Prove it."

He gently flicked the end of her nose, then grabbed a metal cup and slid open the top of the ice cream freezer.

A short time later, while eating hamburgers and French fries that Elwood had placed in front of their stools while they'd been making the strawberry milkshake, Randi let out an adorable sigh after taking another sip from one of the two straws sticking out of the glass.

Jason popped a French fry into his mouth, chewed and swallowed. "Still not going to admit it, are you?"

She gave him a cheeky grin. "I'm still deciding."

"If I should have made two?"

Giggling, she took another sip before setting the milkshake between them. "No, it's been so long since I've had a milkshake, I can't tell if it's that good, or if I'd just forgotten how tasty they are."

He picked up the glass, and not knowing which straw was hers and which was his, simply chose one and took a drink. "It's that good. I know. I have them all the time."

Her eyes were twinkling. "You do?"

"I do." He popped another French fry into his mouth.

She dipped a fry in ketchup and made a show of biting off the end. "I suppose you have hamburgers and French fries all the time, too."

He picked up his hamburger, said, "I do," and took a big bite.

The room was full of gaiety, laughter and music from the jukebox, but it was the sound of her giggle he liked the best. Her beauty had struck him years before, but tonight he'd discovered she was just as beautiful on the inside.

They continued eating and talking and laughing. He felt as if he'd been given a gift. A once-in-a-lifetime gift of her company, and wanted to make the most of it. "Want to dance?"

"Yes, I do." Eyes sparkling, she leaned closer. "But I'll wait."

"For what?"

"Until after you dance with Rachelle. It's her party."

It was Rachelle's party and he had promised her a dance, but it was the fact that she understood how much Rachelle's happiness meant to him that touched him deeply. "You won't mind?"

"Not in the least." Giggling, she picked up the glass. "I'll finish our milkshake."

Laughing, he stood. "I'll make you another one before we leave."

"I might hold you to that."

Giving her a wink, he spun around and crossed the room. To Rachelle's delight, he lifted her out of her chair.

Her arms latched around his neck as he carried her to the dance floor. "Thank you for the dollhouse. I really, really like it."

"I'm glad," he said, bumping his forehead to hers. "Because I really, really like you."

Her giggle floated on the air with the music about rocking around the clock. "I really, really like Randi, too. She's pretty."

"Yes, she is pretty."

"She's nice, too."

"Yes, she is nice."

"She likes you, too."

"How do you know that?"

"Because of the way she smiles at you. Like seeing you makes her happy."

As nice as that sounded, he wasn't going to hold much credence in what a six-year-old thought. "Seeing you makes me happy." He swung around quickly, making her laugh, and continued to do so until the music ended.

"Want to dance again?" he asked.

"No, you can dance with Randi now."

"Maybe she doesn't want to dance," he suggested while carrying her back to her chair.

"She will if you ask her," Rachelle said.

He set her in her chair, made sure her legs were straight and her feet on the little metal plates.

"Do you want me to ask her for you?" she offered. "I will."

"I'm sure you would, kiddo." He winked at her. "But I can manage on my own."

A short time later he wasn't overly sure if he could manage on his own. Randi was in his arms, swaying to the slow song about an earth angel and being a fool in love. He wasn't in love, would never be in love; his childhood had closed his heart to that ever happening. However, having her body pressed up against his had his mind nose-diving into what people called making love. That, with her, would be the ultimate.

He should have been glad when the song ended, but evidently, he hadn't tortured himself enough, because he stayed on the dance floor; kept her there, too.

Another record fell into place on the machine and began to play.

"I love this song!" She grasped one of his hands and started tap stepping to the beat of the music, making her skirt flip and flop around her knees.

He thought the fast beat of the song might clear his mind and so he matched her steps, twirled her beneath their clasped hands. "Every song is your favorite."

She laughed. "How can they not be?"

They danced several dances, some fast and fun, others slow and sensual. It was during one of those slow and sensual ones, where their bodies were touching from hips to shoulders and the singer was singing about being in paradise, that she lifted her face, looked at him with eyes glowing.

"I wasn't laughing at you that night, Jason, when you asked me out." She kept her gaze locked with his. "I was happy, so excited that all I could do was laugh because I'd thought you'd never notice me. Never ask me out. You walked away, got on your motorcycle and left, before I could explain."

He'd practiced, refined every single movement, on nearly every other girl in high school, all in order to build up the nerve to ask her. Yet, even though dozens of other girls had gone out with him, he'd expected her to say no, and had his escape route already set in his mind before he'd even approached her. They'd been from two different worlds then, and still were. He knew that, but it didn't stop him from admitting the truth. "I'd noticed you long before then."

Her arms tightened around his neck. "I'd noticed you long before then, too."

His resolve about not kissing her was dissolving like a sugar cube in hot coffee as the music played on, slow and low. She was looking up at him and dipping his head, touching his lips against hers, filled his thoughts.

She licked her lips, bit down on the bottom one, and every muscle in his body went tight. He'd wanted to kiss her for years, and at this moment knew without a doubt she wanted that, too.

He had to pull his gaze off her, look away. Had to,

because he couldn't kiss her. Not here. With his entire family in attendance.

He'd wait until the night ended, and then he'd kiss her because he had to experience that. Had to.

Randi's entire being was humming with such an all-encompassing excitement that she had to keep telling herself to breathe. The entire evening had been truly magical, as exciting as she'd imagined going out with him would be. However, he was more than she'd imagined. More charming. More kind and caring. From the time she'd been fourteen and seen him for the first time, she'd never looked at another boy because she'd known, somehow, deep inside, that he was the only one who would ever see her for herself. That her last name, her family's wealth, wouldn't make a difference to him.

She'd been nervous to meet his family. They all had to know it had been because of her family that he'd been sent to reform school, but right from the start, he'd made her feel comfortable. Hadn't even mentioned her last name, as if it didn't matter. She was just Randi, and she liked that. Liked him, so very much.

She'd never wanted to kiss someone so badly in her life. For a moment she'd thought he might kiss her, right here on the dance floor. He hadn't, but the way he'd looked at her gave her hope that it would happen before the night was over.

Heavens to Betsy, she hoped it did.

The music ended, and she slowly lifted her head, looked up him, and his smile sent a delectable tingle throughout her system.

"It—" he cleared his throat "—looks like the party girl is getting tired. I'm going to help Stu load up her presents."

The idea of leaving meant the kiss she wanted might happen sooner rather than later. Releasing her hold on his neck, she said, "I'll help, too."

"You don't have—"

"I want to."

With the help of so many, it didn't take long before the diner was put in order and the gifts all loaded in Stu and Lottie's car.

Jason retrieved their coats and as he was holding hers for her to slip her arms into the sleeves, Rachelle rolled in front of them.

"Thank you for coming to my party, Randi."

Kneeling down in front of the chair, Randi replied, "Thank you for having me. It was the best birthday party I've ever attended."

Rachelle touched the rhinestone pin on Randi's lapel. "Our names both start with an R."

"Yes, they do." After unpinning the pin, Randi removed it and pinned it on Rachelle's coat. "Happy birthday."

Rachelle's adorable eyes grew larger as she looked down at the pin. "I've never seen anything so pretty." She looked up at Jason. "Have you, Jason?"

"No, I haven't," he replied.

Randi's heart flipped at the way he was looking at her rather than Rachelle or the pin.

He held her elbow as she stood and then his hand slid down her arm, until their palms met and his fingers threaded between hers as they walked to the door. She was so giddy she could barely think.

The feeling continued long after they'd climbed into his car and were driving toward his house. She had to bite her lips together to keep the excitement inside her, and bit down harder as she wondered if he would kiss her in the car or at his house.

"Thank you for giving Rachelle your pin. She really liked that."

Trying to sound as normal as possible, she replied, "I'm glad she liked it, but nothing will ever compare to her dollhouse and furniture. That had to have taken you months to make."

"No, just a few weeks of evenings and weekends in my basement. I like working with wood."

"It shows, but I thought you liked cars and motorcycles."

"I do, but they are more of a summer hobby. I can't fit motorcycles and cars in my basement." He shot her a quick glance. "What about you? What do you do?"

"I work." She pinched her lips together, wishing she hadn't said that because she didn't want him to think she was thinking about work. She wasn't.

"What about for fun?"

"Tonight was fun." Oh, good grief. That made her sound like an idiot. A desperate idiot. Sighing, she searched her mind for an honest answer. She knew how to sew, that was a given considering her mother's company, but she wasn't very good at it and luckily her mother had never pressured her into getting better. "I like to bake, to cook." Shrugging, she went with the truth. "But mainly I work. I've worked at the airline since I was twelve."

"You have?"

"Yes, I started out cleaning my father's office and just kept moving into other jobs. Someday I will take over running the entire company." There was no one, especially not her parents, that she could tell about Sam, yet, for some reason, she felt comfortable telling Jason. "But I'm being sabotaged."

"Sabotaged?"

"Yes. By Sam Wharton. He's worked for my father

for several years and thinks that he should be the one who my father appoints to handle the day-to-day oversight of the company when my father is elected senator. He hasn't announced that he's running yet, but he is. For US Senator, not the state senate. Sam knows, and since learning about it, he's started to withhold reports that I need in order to complete my work, and other little things. Like claiming that he didn't get expense or wage reports from me on time and other things like that just to make me look bad. He's always wanted that—for me to look bad—but it's gotten worse lately."

"Have you told your father?"

"No."

"Why not?"

She twisted, just enough to be able to look at him. "Because that's what Sam wants me to do. He wants everyone to think that I run to my father with every little issue. Wants everyone to believe I only have a job there because of my last name. That I'm not capable of actually doing the work. I am, and I'm going to prove it. To everyone."

"You sound pretty determined."

"I am. I'll do anything I have to." Thinking about work was too irritating, and she didn't want that right now. Not tonight. It had been too wonderful. "Thank you for this evening. It was good to not even think about work. I really enjoyed that."

"Maybe you should do it more often." He slowed the car down to stop at a red light. "Go out and eat hamburgers and French fries."

"And drink milkshakes."

He looked at her, smiled.

Her toes curled inside her shoes at the bolt of excitement that shot through her at the connection she felt between them. One that grew the longer they looked at each other.

The sound of a horn honking had them both looking at the light that had turned green, but the connection was still there. She could feel it, and wished tonight would never have to end.

"And dance," he said.

The memory of dancing with him made her sigh with contentment. "How many other dollhouses have you built?" she asked as other memories of the night flowed through her mind.

"That was my first, but I have built a doghouse that a certain dog never uses."

She laughed. "Because he has a doggie door. That you built for him."

"I did."

They laughed, talked about Tanner and other things, until he pulled up next to his garage and climbed out to open the doors.

The headlights shone on a pickup truck, with Heim Construction painted on the door, and two motorcycles parked in front of it. "Why did you build your house here instead of on your land?" she asked once he climbed back in the car to pull it forward.

"Because I needed to make money. No one wants to live that far out of town, so I bought this entire block of land, one lot at a time, and built all six houses. Mine was the last one I built here, and if someone comes along and wants to buy it, I'll sell it."

"Where will you live then?"

He parked the car and shut it off. "Wherever. I have other houses I'm building, and an apartment complex."

"Where?"

"The apartment building is downtown, the houses in other suburbs." He opened the car door.

She collected her purse and satchel and opened her door.

They met in front of the car. He took a hold of her hand, and her heart started pounding again.

"Sounds like Tanner is at the door," he said.

She hadn't heard anything, but he was right. As soon as he opened the door on the side of the garage that led into the backyard, the dog was there to greet them, and walked ahead of them to the house.

"I don't have a milkshake maker, but I could make some coffee," he said while closing the door. "If you want."

She didn't want coffee, or a milkshake, but didn't know how to voice what she did want. Setting her purse and satchel on the table, she turned, looked at him. "Jason, I—"

"I'll go start your car. Clear off the windshield."

She looked at the hand he held out. If she gave him the keys, the night would be over. She didn't want that. Frustration and a hint of fear filled her. There was no experience that she could draw upon for this. She'd been kissed before, but had never initiated it, or wanted it to continue, because it had never been him who had been kissing her.

What if this was her only chance for that to happen? She'd regret not doing something. A need was pulsating inside her, a desire she'd never felt to this degree before, but it felt right. She took a hold of his hand and stepped closer.

He was looking at her, watching her. The heat between them was still there, making her feel as if the air was sizzling.

Taking a breath, she laid her other hand on his chest. "I don't want to leave yet."

His eyes landed on her lips.

Her heart was pounding, her body full of that magical electricity, and she couldn't wait any longer. She slid her hand to the back of his neck, stretched on her toes and pressed her lips against his.

The first touch made her knees go weak, then a surge ripped through her as their lips merged perfectly, naturally, and his arms encircled her. It was as if more than their lips were kissing. His entire body seemed to be kissing her. There was nothing even close to the way he made her insides feel. Crazy, and wild and wonderful.

He held her tighter, met her kisses over and over again, but she still wanted more. When his tongue slid across her lips, she opened her mouth, inviting him in.

A groan of pleasure rumbled in her throat. Tightening her hold on his neck, she held nothing back as their tongues met, twisted and teased each other's.

When their lips parted, they were both breathing hard, sucking in air. She tried to catch her bearings, but when their eyes met, she knew that wasn't going to happen.

The air between them was even more charged, sparking with an energy she'd never experienced.

Fervently, mutually, their lips met again, in a heated, nearly frantic way that somehow included getting rid of their coats. She'd never wanted to feel someone, to be so close to, so connected to, someone as she did him. All of her dreams about him were accumulating into this very moment, planting her in the place she'd wanted to be for years.

He let out a low, sexy-sounding groan and pulled his lips off hers, stared down at her.

A splash of fear rained upon her that he might say they had to stop before things went further. She wanted things to go further. Her heart was slamming against her breastbone with anticipation that it might. She could have had sex before but had never wanted to. Had never wanted anything like she did right now. Every part of her was alive, throbbing, begging for more, and she knew why.

Wanting him to know that she trusted him, and herself to continue, she touched the side of his face. "I still don't want to leave."

Chapter Five

Jason cupped her cheek. "Are you sure?"

She ran her hands down his upper arms, feeling the hard muscles beneath. He was leaving the choice up to her. She could leave now, knowing what it was like to kiss him, be kissed by him, but the want inside her had grown beyond kissing. The need to know what that would be like was growing by the second, making her toes curl. He was who she wanted to do that with, had always been who she'd wanted to do that with. "Very sure." She wanted a night to remember, even if it was just one night. With a boldness she didn't know she had, she pressed her hips against his. "We're adults, and both know what we want."

He let out a low growling sound as his arms tightened, holding her hard against him. "I've never wanted someone like I want you."

The thrill that shot through her was indescribable and confirmed she'd made the right choice. "Me neither," she admitted, and was instantly lost in another round of kissing.

She didn't have time to think about being nervous, not even when they made their way into his bedroom. It all felt too right, too perfect.

As he kissed a line down her neck, to the very top of the vee in her A-line dress, his hand slowly unzipped the zipper running down the back of the dress. She bit her bottom lip as every part of her body hummed, tingled. Her breasts grew heavy as her nipples hardened, and at this moment she was excited about the lingerie her mother designed. The bra and panties set beneath her dress was made of red lace, with a black silk under layer. So was the matching garter belt that held up her nylons.

She waited until the zipper had reached the very bottom, and then slowly slid her hands off his upper arms and took a step back, until she had enough space to shrug the dress off her shoulders.

He grasped the material as it reached her elbows, then guided it downward, until it slipped over her hands, and fell to the floor.

Randi held her breath as his gaze scanned her from head to toe, leaving a trail of heat that made her insides sizzle.

He trailed a hand down her arm, to her elbow. "You are so beautiful."

The heat swirling in her most private places increased; so did her confidence. He wanted her. She could see that in his eyes. This was her dream come true. "I'm glad you think so."

He threaded his fingers into her hair, combed it back, away from her face. "So beautiful."

Reaching up, she unbuttoned his shirt, all the way to the bottom, then pushed it off his shoulders. When that fell, she grasped the hem of his T-shirt and pulled it over his head. Her breath caught at her first sight of his chest, rippled with muscles and splattered with dark hair. "And you are extraordinarily handsome."

He let out a sexy-sounding laugh and grasped her waist, picked her up and pulled her tight against his body.

She looped her arms around his neck, and her legs around his hips, gasping at the sensations of her bare skin feeling the heat of his body. He buried his face between her breasts, and she was too focused on the pleasure to be self-conscious over the way a pleasure-filled moan rumbled in the back of her throat when he kissed her nipples through the material of her bra.

He laid her on the bed, and as he continued to kiss and touch her most sensitive areas, she knew all of her dreams about him didn't compare to the reality. The real Jason was far more consuming, far more enlightening, than her dream Jason.

As he slowly, teasingly removed her nylons, then garter belt, underwear and bra, Jason continuously watched her, making sure she was in agreement and enjoying everything he was doing.

She was. There was no doubt about that. She'd never known anything so exhilarating. It was like being on a carnival ride. Out of control, but loving every moment, and wanting more.

"Jason." It was hard to talk with so many sensations rippling through her body, making her muscles contract and her toes curl.

"Hmmm?" he asked, once again kissing her breasts.

She had to groan at the pleasure erupting from the feel of his lips on her breasts and his hand that was between her legs. "You still have your jeans on," she said with yet another sound that was nearly a growl.

"I know."

Nearly desperate, she said, "Take. Them. Off."

"Is that what you want?" he asked.

"Yes. Now."

With a laugh, he gave her a final, long kiss and then crawled off the bed. "I'll be right back. Don't go away."

"I won't." She attempted to use his absence as a reprieve, but was missing him too much for that. It seemed like forever before he returned, climbed on the bed and covered her with his warm, amazing body. She luxuriated in the weight of him, the feel of his skin touching hers, and ran her hands over every part of him that she could reach. Felt the hard muscles beneath his heated flesh as they kissed again, and again.

He lifted his head, stared her right in the eye. "You're sure about this?"

She had never been more sure of anything in her life. "Yes."

He reached between their bodies and guided his way inside her. The pressure, the way her body stretched to accommodate him, was delightful, amazing, until a sharp snap caused her breath to catch.

He went completely still. "Randi?"

The pain was gone, or maybe it had never been there. Maybe it had just been more pleasure than she'd ever known. She wasn't sure, but knew the schoolgirl crush she'd had on him had entered an entirely new dimension.

Grasping the sides of his face, she kissed him, using her tongue, and arched her body into his. She felt the moan that rumbled in his throat as much as she heard it, and following her inner instincts, began to move her hips. He moved with her, kissed her intensely. Who knew what tomorrow might bring? But tonight, here, now, in his bed, she was in a paradise she'd never dreamed about.

When she found something she liked, something she wanted, she never held anything back, and didn't this time, either. She gave all she had, fully joined him in riding the glorious storm they were creating. It was all so new, so wild and pleasurable, she embraced every nuance of feeling him inside her.

When an inner crescendo built to a point where she knew something else had to happen, but didn't know what, she looked at Jason in question.

His mouth covered hers and a moment later, an explosion let loose inside her, washing her with a great gush of pleasure, followed by miniature waves that encompassed her entire being. He continued to kiss her until every last wave faded, leaving her body feeling boneless as it sank deep into the mattress.

She'd known making love with Jason would be magnificent, but when he lifted his head, the glorious feeling of happiness inside her doubled again because of the smile on his face.

It had taken every ounce of control he'd had to bring Randi to completion before he let himself be consumed by the way her hot, slick body was clenching his, causing more intense pleasure than he'd ever known. The smile on her face was the straw that broke his last ounce of reserve. With a final thrust, he closed his eyes as the first wave of bliss washed over him, and then fully surrendered to the best release of his life. The best sex of his life.

He'd thought about kissing her, touching her, making love to her, for so many years, it had been as if he'd already known her body. Knew exactly where to touch, when to kiss and how to bring her to the utmost pleasure. Doing so had been an awakening. He'd put his entire soul into being with her, and it had paid off in ways he'd never imagined.

He was completely drained by the time the final wave dissipated. Bracing himself on his arms, to keep his full weight from crushing her, he opened his eyes. She was still looking at him, still smiling. His lungs were seeking air, and he sucked in a deep breath, held it. He'd never believed this moment, of him and her, making love, would ever come.

Her smile faded, and a slight quiver raced over his shoulders, hoping she wasn't on her way to regretting what had just happened. He could handle anything but that.

She touched his face and then giggled slightly and her eyes shimmered as if she'd just won some sort of contest.

The real world. The one he'd lived in, returned with the strength of a gut punch. Not a contest. Land. That's what she wanted. Not him. His land.

He rolled off her, lay on his back and covered his face with one arm as it all entered his mind. A mind that had been filled with fog since the moment he'd seen her poking her head through his doggie door this afternoon. No, before then. Ever since she'd shown up on his front porch, she'd been the only thing on his mind.

How stupid could he possibly be? He climbed off the bed, headed to the bathroom across the hallway. There he took care of the condom, thanking his lucky stars that he'd had one in the house. He never brought women home. Never. He slapped the sink with one hand and mumbled a curse.

Taking a virgin wasn't his thing, either.

Damn it! The way she'd kissed, rubbed against him, offered herself, he figured she was experienced. That this was…was what? A casual encounter?

No, it was her way of getting to him, thinking he'd give in to her, sell her his land. He didn't have anything else she'd ever want. Didn't have anything else to offer her.

His stomach sank even farther.

Was her plan to use the fact he'd taken her virginity to blackmail him into selling her his land?

The rich were like that. They'd do anything to get richer.

He grabbed a washcloth out of the cabinet, wet it with warm water and carried it back into the bedroom, all the while keeping his temper in check.

She was sitting on the edge of the bed, and without making eye contact, he handed her the washcloth. "The bathroom is across the hall."

"Oh, all right, thank you." She took the washcloth.

Jason kept his gaze averted, but knew the moment she left the room. He got dressed, quickly, and went into the kitchen, where her coat, purse and bag holding her boots were piled on the table. Knowing her car keys were in her coat pocket, he found them, slipped on a pair of shoes from the closet near the front door and went outside to start her car.

The cold air helped tremendously in cooling down his body, but his temper was still smoldering. He'd never learn when it came to her.

She was in the kitchen, fully dressed, when he returned to the house. "I started your car."

"Thank you." She ran a hand over the back of a chair, looked around the room and then back at him. "I'm not sure what to say. Did I upset you?"

"No." He walked to the counter, leaned back against it.

"Then, um…" She shrugged.

Man, he hated how cute she was. How downright beautiful. It was going to take more than six years to forget how perfect her body was, and longer yet to forget making love to her. "There's nothing to say." His anger got the best of him and he added, "My answer is still no."

She frowned. "No to what?"

"Selling you my land."

"Jason, this had nothing to do—"

"Right," he interrupted. "You just wanted to return a fifty-cent pair of socks." The flash of hope inside him shattered as her face fell. "You will do anything for Air America, even sleep with a reform school rebel." As soon as the words were out, he hated himself for saying them. It made it sound like all of it was her fault, and it wasn't.

She spun around and grabbed her coat off the table.

He watched, remained silent. On the outside. On the inside he was berating himself for being so stupid. What the hell was it about her that made him want things he knew he'd never have? Few men would ever be good enough for Randi Osterlund, and he sure as hell wasn't one of those few men.

Coat on, she picked up her purse and bag, then crossed the room, stopped directly in front of him. Eyeball to eyeball, she stood there for a moment, breathing hard and fast. Then she hauled off and slapped his face.

It stung, but he didn't so much as flinch. Let her be mad at him. He sure as hell was pissed. Pissed at himself for forgetting what he'd known for years. He could earn money, succeed in some things, but his past had set his path and that would never change.

He counted to ten after hearing the front door slam shut, then walked into the living room and peered out the window. As soon as she climbed into her car, she put it in gear and backed out of the driveway.

It was cold out, and her car hadn't had time to warm up. She probably couldn't even see out of her windshield. It was snowing again, too. Damn it!

He turned, jogged across the house, grabbed his coat from the laundry room and ran across the backyard, to the garage.

Within a few blocks, he recognized the taillights of her Bel Air, and kept back far enough that she wouldn't realize she was being followed. He followed her all the way to her big, brick home in one of the richest neighborhoods in all of Chicago.

Christmas lights still surrounded the windows of her house and a big evergreen wreath hung on the front door. The shack he grew up in had never been decorated for Christmas. After his mother left, there had been no Christmas presents, no Thanksgiving dinners, Easter eggs or birthday celebrations.

No love had filled his house, either, which was the ultimate stark reality. He'd never be able to love a woman like her the way they deserved to be loved. He didn't know how, and that would never change.

She parked her car in the driveway and ran into the house through a side door.

He should leave. Knowing that she'd made it home safely should be enough, but he couldn't stop himself from continuing to stare at the house, telling himself he'd never see her again and should be happy about that.

A smart man would be.

He definitely wasn't smart. If that was the case, he would never have slept with her.

In her bedroom Randi threw her coat in one direction, her purse in another. She'd given herself a night to remember all right. A nightmare. She had told him she'd do anything, but hadn't meant sleeping with him. His land had been the last thing on her mind, but evidently, the only thing on his.

Why had she thought he was different? Thought he'd see her for herself. No one else did, so why should he?

And why did it hurt so bad that he didn't? She was used to it. Used to being invisible other than her last name.

Knowing the answer, she threw herself on the bed. It hurt because she'd let herself believe in a dream that would never come true. Other than her family, people either hated her, or wanted something from her, all because of her last name.

Jason had more reason than anyone to hate that last name. Hate her.

She curled into a ball, told herself she'd hate him in return. Would hate him for the rest of her life.

She could live with that. Live with being nothing more than an Osterlund.

After a very sleepless night, she set out to prove that when, still filled with anger, she walked in and still didn't have the P&L report.

Her footsteps echoed off the walls as she made her way into Sam Wharton's office. He was sitting behind his desk, his black hair full of beeswax pomade and combed over his ever-growing bald spot. The glower he cast at how she threw open the door had her anger hitting the boiling point. "Where's the P&L report?"

He shrugged.

She stomped over to his desk. "My father will be home tomorrow and expects every department report to be on his desk for review."

"Every department report was couriered over to your father's house last evening. Except for yours. You weren't in your office when I collected them. Your secretary said you'd left early."

"Because I didn't have a P&L report so I couldn't complete mine."

"Everyone else did."

She glared at him.

His green eyes narrowed. "Maybe it's time you realize being your father's daughter doesn't get you everything you want."

After everything that had happened last night, his remark cut to the core. She slapped her hands on his desk and leaned toward him. "Perhaps it's time you learn exactly what it means to go against my father's daughter." With that, she spun around and marched out of his office, purposefully leaving the door of his office open purely out of spite.

She'd get that P&L report, and she'd find another way for Air America to have their own washing bay. One that had nothing, absolutely nothing, to do with Jason's land.

Chapter Six

Three weeks later Randi had more than one new plan in place, and was making good progress on both of them. Setting up a washing bay in California had never crossed her mind before, but nearly all of their planes landed in LA several times each year, and logistically, she could make it work.

The plan of using her status for her instead of against her was also working. She'd requested copies of every report Sam sent down to typing to be delivered to her upon completion. Sam had balked, and had gone to her father, but much to her delight, her father had said he appreciated the initiative she'd always taken to know what was going on in all aspects of the company.

The only plan not working was getting Jason out of her mind. Despite how the night had ended, she couldn't forget the wonderful aspects of their time together. Out of the blue, specific moments would flood her mind and body, and leave her aching.

There was also another issue. She was two weeks late on her monthly.

It had to be something other than *that*.

Had to be.

She couldn't be pregnant.

Absolutely could not.

Jason had used a condom. She'd seen it.

Glancing in the mirror above her bathroom sink, she patted her cheeks, trying to put some color in them. It didn't work. She looked awful.

Sick.

That had to be it. She was sick.

She didn't have time to be sick. Not right now. She was flying out to California next week to look at land for the washing bay—a project that no one but she knew about.

By that afternoon, when the sandwich she'd attempted to eat for lunch threatened to come right back up, she called Dr. Spencer's office. Olivia Spencer had been her doctor since childhood and would be able to give her something to make her feel better.

Being told to come right over to the clinic, Randi left her office, telling Carol that she had an errand to run and would be back within the hour.

However, an hour later she was still in the doctor's office, wearing an ugly green cover-up as she sat on the examination table. Her heart was in her throat and she had her hands clasped together in an attempt to hide how badly they were shaking. "How can that be? We used a condom."

"They aren't one hundred percent effective," Dr. Spencer said. "One tiny pinhole is all it takes."

There were so many thoughts flowing through Randi's mind that it was hard to focus on any particular one. Other than Jason, and how he was sure to believe she'd done this on purpose, too. "You're sure?"

Dr. Spencer closed the folder in her hand. "As I said, we'll know for sure when the test results come back."

"When will that be?"

"A few days. I can call you with the results."

"No!" Randi bit her lips together. She couldn't have the doctor calling either her house or office. "I'll come back in."

"All right, I'll set up an appointment. You can get dressed and I'll be back in with a prescription."

"For what?"

"Vitamins. I want you to take them no matter what the results of the test are. You've lost weight since your last visit. If we aren't careful, you'll soon be nothing but skin and bones."

Randi waited until the doctor left the room before she allowed a sob to escape. Jason would have even more reason to hate her now.

She climbed off the table and got dressed, noting how loose the waistband of her red-and-black skirt was, even with her blouse tucked in. If not for the added decorative belt, that she could tie tight, the skirt would have slipped right off her hips.

After stepping into her shoes, she put on her red cardigan, and then with her coat and purse in her lap, she sat in the chair, waited for Dr. Spencer to return. As much as she wanted to believe that she wanted the test to come back negative, she couldn't deny that the idea of a baby, of Jason's baby, made her heart beat faster. She pressed a hand to her stomach. If things were different, she'd be the happiest woman on earth.

Dr. Spencer returned, but as she held out the slip of paper, another thought hit Randi. "I can't have that filled. Not at my aunt's drugstore, or anywhere else. Every drugstore in Illinois could recognize my name, put two and two together."

"I suspect that is correct." Dr. Spencer wadded up the prescription. "I'll get some vitamins for you before your next visit." Dr. Spencer then handed her a small note card. "Here's when you are to return, but until then, I want you to get some rest. I've been taking care of you for years, and I'm concerned that you aren't taking care of yourself the way you should be."

Randi took the card and tucked it into her purse. "I will. Thank you."

It felt as if the air was locked in her lungs. The tightness wouldn't ease, no matter how deeply she attempted to breathe, even after exiting the clinic, stepping outside in the cold air. Most likely because of her thoughts. If the test came back positive, she couldn't tell Jason about the baby. That was all there was to it. Not ever. It wasn't as if they ran into each other. In the past six years the only time she had seen him was when she'd sought him out, and she would never, ever do that again.

The idea of that made her sick because she wasn't a deceitful person, but what else could she do? He hated her.

She walked the half a block to the lot where she'd parked her car, and was about to climb in when she heard her name.

She froze, could barely swallow, at the sight of the pickup truck with Heim Construction painted on the door. It was black, not red like the one in his garage, and the little arm waving out the window certainly wasn't Jason's, but she couldn't see who was driving the pickup, and that frightened her.

"Randi!" Rachelle repeated as the pickup stopped near the back of her car. "It's me, Rachelle."

"I see that, how are you?" she asked, stepping close enough to see that it wasn't Jason driving, but Stu, Rachelle's father.

"I'm fine! We had to bring some lumber to Jason after Dad picked me up from school. Is that why you're here?

To see him?" Pointing across the parking lot, Rachelle continued. "He's in that building over there. Working. He said Dad doesn't need to work any more today and we are going to Mama's to have a milkshake!"

Randi's glance across the parking lot revealed another pickup. A red one with Heim Construction painted on the side. "That sounds wonderful," she replied, trying her hardest to sound cheerful. "What flavor?"

"Strawberry!" Rachelle giggled. "You should have Jason bring you there for a milkshake, too. He would if you asked him to. I know he would."

Randi knew Jason would never take her anywhere, ever again, which made her eyes sting all over again. "Well, you enjoy your milkshake. It was good seeing you again." She nodded at Stu and then turned, hurried to the driver's door of her car and climbed in before the tears broke loose.

There wasn't time to let them flow, not with Jason's truck on the other side of the parking lot. He was so caring, so loving, toward Rachelle, Randi could only imagine what a wonderful father he'd be to his own child.

Blinking against the blurriness of tears, she started her car and left the parking lot, wondering what she was going to do. How she was going to live through having his baby and never telling him.

Jason flinched at the pain of putting on his coat. Between the swelling and the bandage, his hand was twice its normal size. He was frustrated with himself for not having the injury looked at before now, and at how he'd managed to nearly slice his hand in two in the first place. It had been nearly a week ago. He should never have looked out the apartment house window while using a skill saw.

If he hadn't looked out and if he hadn't seen Randi, he wouldn't have cut himself, and then wouldn't be here now, leaving the doctor's exam room after having the cut cleaned, bandaged and a penicillin shot jabbed into his backside, while a tetanus one had been shot in his arm. He'd thought his hand would get better on its own, but infection had set in, and the doctor had given him a good talking-to about that, about taking better care of himself.

A large part of him wanted to blame Randi. If she hadn't rounded the corner at the exact same moment that he'd looked out the window, he wouldn't have cut himself.

As usual, the mere thought of her set his imagination wild, to the point he heard her voice. Which was impossible.

Growing madder at himself, he twisted the doorknob to leave the room, only to pause from pulling the door all the way open.

It *was* her voice.

"Yes, thank you," she told the receptionist while entering the room directly across the hall from him.

Concern filled him at the idea of her being hurt or sick. He'd thought of little else but her the past four weeks, but that was nothing new. He'd been thinking of her for years. It was just that now he had more memories. Vivid ones.

The receptionist dropped a folder in the metal rack beside the door that Randi had entered and then walked down the hall, toward the waiting room. He checked the hallway for spying eyes, then left the room and pulled out the folder, opened it.

His entire body froze as if his heart had stopped, drained all the blood from his system. Shaking, he returned the folder to the rack, headed down the hall and didn't stop until he was outside, in the icy February air.

There he gulped for air as the words he'd read continued to race through his mind.

Pregnancy Test: positive

She was pregnant.

Randi was pregnant.

It couldn't be his. He'd used a condom.

Had it ripped? Been too old?

"What did they say?"

Jason shook his head, blinked and stared at Stu.

"Your hand," Stu said. "What did they say?"

Jason rubbed his forehead, trying to collect his thoughts.

"Have you been waiting long?" Stu asked. "I went next door, into the café and had a cup of coffee while waiting. Just saw you out the window."

Remembering that he hadn't been able to drive and shift with only one hand, Jason recalled that Stu had given him a ride to the doctor's office, and that Stu would soon need to pick Rachelle up from school. The bus couldn't accommodate her wheelchair, which meant he couldn't stand here and wait for Randi to exit the building, ask her about being pregnant.

He couldn't do that, anyway. Not until he got his head around it all.

"Are you all right?" Stu asked.

"Yeah, I'm fine." He started walking toward the lot where the pickup that Stu drove was parked.

"What did they say about your hand?"

"It's infected. They gave me a shot of penicillin."

"That'll take care of it, but your ass is going to be sore for a few days."

He had deeper worries than his ass or his hand. Pregnant. That had to be why she'd been here last week, at the doctor's office, the day he'd seen her out the window.

"Do you need to stop anywhere else?" Stu asked as they arrived at the truck.

Jason's eyes were on the Bel Air parked in the lot. "No, just take me home." That was where he'd be when she showed up. To tell him that she was pregnant.

He had to have his response ready.

Chapter Seven

Jason waited a week for Randi to stop by his house. When that never happened, he tried to contact her. Called her home and her office. The answers were always the same. She wasn't available, but if he cared to leave a message, she would get back to him.

He hadn't *cared* to leave a message. He wanted to know what kind of game she was playing now. How the hell could she not be available for an entire week? He'd called every day, at different times. She was avoiding him, that was what she was doing.

It was time that stopped.

He glanced into the rearview mirror, smoothed back his hair on both sides. The slice across the top of his hand was still red, the skin puffed and tender, but was healing. He had full use of his fingers again.

Her car wasn't in the driveway of the big house, but that didn't mean it wasn't in the garage. He hadn't seen her car all week. Not here or at the Air America offices and was tired of looking for it. Tired of waiting for her to contact him.

He climbed out of Lottie's car, having borrowed it because he knew if Randi saw his, she'd avoid him. That had to stop. She'd been a virgin. It had to be his baby.

He walked to the door, anxious to know what was going on with Randi, and nervous to see her father again. He'd met Randal Osterlund twice. Once when the man had come to the reform school, told him that he'd discovered the truth and that he'd told the judge to withdraw the charges, and a few years later, at his father's funeral, where Randal had offered his condolences.

His father had been a stubborn man. Hateful at times. Though the money they would have obtained by selling Osterlund a portion of their land would have made a significant difference in their lives, his father had refused to sell. His father had found an odd pleasure in knowing he'd owned something a rich man wanted.

The massive door opened, and an old, gray-haired man, dressed in a black suit, gave a slight nod. "Good evening, sir, may I help you?"

Jason cleared his throat. "I'm looking for Randi—Miss Osterlund."

"I'm sorry, sir," the man said loudly, "she is not available this evening."

Jason's back teeth clamped together. That was the same voice as the one on the phone, the same answer he'd received for a week.

"Who is it, Peter?" a female voice sounded somewhere in the background of the house.

"A young man to see the young miss," the man answered.

A trim woman, wearing a fashionable pale green dress, appeared behind the old man, and though he'd never met her, Jason knew it had to be Randi's mother. She may have gotten her pale blue eyes from her father, but the rest of her beauty was inherited from her mother. "Good evening," he said. "I need to speak to Randi."

"I'm sorry," her mother said. "She's not home right now, but should be shortly. You'd be welcome to wait."

He nodded. "I'd appreciate that."

She nodded toward the old man. "Thank you, Peter."

The man bowed and walked away.

"Do come in, Jason, isn't it?"

He paused in the doorway. "Yes, Jason Heim."

"I'm Jolie, Randi's mother. She's been in California all week, but her plane should have landed about fifteen minutes ago." She waved a hand and repeated, "Do come in."

He stepped into the foyer, where a large stairway on the left swept upward to the second floor. The home held an old-world style that was elegant, without being ostentatious. Many of the older homes had been remodeled, and, appreciative of old craftsmanship, he was impressed to see how well they'd preserved the home rather than making it look more modern.

"This way," she said. "Randal is in the front room. I was on my way to join him when I heard Peter answering the door." Her smile grew. "He's getting hard of hearing, but answering the door has been his job for over forty years."

Jason nodded as he walked beside her to a framed doorway. A butler. One they'd had for over forty years. Jason's stomach sank. He was so out of his league. Yet, he was here, and would stay until he talked to Randi.

"Randal," Jolie said as they entered the room. "You remember Jason Heim."

Tall, with dark hair sporting gray near his temples, Randal Osterlund rose from the chair. "I most certainly do." He held out a hand as he crossed the room. "How have you been, Jason?"

Jason shook his hand. "Fine, thank you. And you?"

"Can't complain." Randal laid a hand on his wife's back. "Come sit down. To what do we owe this pleasure?"

Jason drew in a deep breath. "I'm here to speak to your daughter."

Randal aided his wife in sitting on the sofa, and waved for Jason to sit in an armed chair before he sat down beside his wife. "Randi?"

Jolie laughed slightly. "She is the only daughter we have, dear."

Randal chuckled. "I know that. I'm just surprised."

Jason felt his spine stiffen.

"Surprised only because she doesn't receive many callers," Jolie said.

Jason doubted that was the reason her father was surprised. "Randi had been interested in purchasing, or leasing, some land from me."

Randal frowned. "She had?" He shook his head. "I apologize. I've made it clear that your land isn't for sale and no one was to pursue you about it." He leaned forward, rested an elbow on his knee. "I know there were rumors upon your father's death that our land dispute had something to do with his heart attack. I assure you, that wasn't the case. I hadn't spoken to your father in months."

"I know that, and I know they were rumors brought on by my father," Jason said. He'd tried to quell the rumors back then, but his father had already spread that there was a feud between their families so wide that the lie had become the truth to many. Not so unlike the night he'd gotten arrested for trespassing. The truth was, his father had hated everyone who'd had more than he'd had and that was just about everyone. Very few people were poorer than they'd been.

"Why would Randi be interested in buying land?" Jolie asked.

Randal shook his head. "I don't know."

Jason considered not mentioning more, but changed his mind. "I believe it's due to a man named Sam Wharton."

"Sam?" Randal asked.

"Yes, it appears he's, well, Randi called it sabotaging her."

Both husband and wife sat up straighter, stared at him.

"She claimed Sam refused to give her reports she needed in order to complete her work, and I believe she was interested in buying my land so there would be room to build a place to wash your airplanes, proving she was fully capable of taking over for you when you win the senate seat."

Randal folded his arms across his chest. "It appears that you and Randi have discussed far more than a land deal."

Over the past few weeks he'd gone over every single conversation, every word they'd said to each other. Mainly during times when regret had been eating him alive. "Yes, sir, we have. She's determined to do whatever it takes to gain that position."

"Randal, if Sam is—"

"Don't worry, dear," Randal interrupted his wife. "I will be talking to Sam, and this explains why Randi asked for copies of every report the typing pool creates." He nodded. "You are right, Jason, my daughter is very determined, has always been very determined. She takes after her mother in that sense."

"I believe that is a mutual trait she inherited," Jolie said. "I'm assuming you refused to sell her your property?"

"Yes, I did," Jason replied. "I have plans for it."

Randal was rubbing his chin. "Now we know why she went to California."

Jason frowned. "Why?"

"To build a washing bay facility there," Randal replied. "It's something I've considered, but never pursued for various reasons."

Jolie laid a hand on Randal's arm. "You don't think she's considering moving to California, do you? Is that why she's been so quiet, so sad, lately?"

"I don't know," Randal said. "But she certainly hasn't been herself."

The idea of her moving to California struck Jason deeply. Is that what she was thinking? Moving there, with his child, without ever telling him? For all he knew, she could go out there, marry Gus Albright and pretend the child was Gus's. That wasn't going to happen. He wasn't going to let someone else raise his child, nor would he deny a child the right to know both parents. What he did next was the last thing he'd ever thought he'd do, but it was the only one thing he could do. "Sir—" he moved his gaze to glance at Jolie for a second "—ma'am, I'd like to ask permission to marry your daughter."

Jolie pressed a hand to her chest, while Randal lifted his brows and glanced at his wife before saying, "We could grant our permission, but the answer would need to come from Randi. That's her decision to make."

Jason had a good idea of what her answer and decision would be. He was also fully aware that he would not be living his life without knowing his child. He'd grown up with one parent, having no idea where the other one was, and would not let that happen to his flesh and blood. "I do apologize for being so blunt, and although precautions were taken, I believe that Randi is pregnant with my child."

"Mother, Father." Randi bit her lips together, and forced herself to keep her chin up. She was about to tell her parents something that would cause them to be disappointed in her. Severely disappointed. She wasn't married. Didn't even have any prospects in that direction. Yet, here she was, pregnant. By a man she'd been told to steer clear of for years.

The steam seeped out of her and she slumped her head against the steering wheel. "Oh, Lord, how am I going to do this?"

She'd already put it off for nearly two weeks and couldn't for much longer. Maybe she should have stayed in California. The one plot of land she'd looked at would work for a washing bay, and she could live out there, oversee the project. Which would work into her plan of never telling Jason that she was pregnant.

A plan that would never see fruition because she couldn't see it through. She had to tell him, just like she had to tell her parents. Each day brought the time closer of when her father would announce his bid to run for senate. Having an unmarried, pregnant daughter was sure to cause a scandal. Even if she was in California.

She lifted her head, leaned back against the seat of her car and stared at the airport. Her parents knew when her return flight had been scheduled to land.

She hated the idea of disappointing them. Hated the idea of Jason believing she'd gotten pregnant on purpose. And she hated the idea of having to ask him, trust him, to keep the pregnancy a secret until after her father announced his senate bid.

Leaning forward, she started her car and stared at the sky "Give me strength. Please. Lots and lots of strength."

Far sooner than she was prepared to face him, she arrived at Jason's house. There were no lights on, but that didn't mean he wasn't home. She wasn't going to be caught unaware this time. She backed out of the driveway and drove around to the alley. There, she climbed out and opened one of the garage doors.

The pickup and two motorcycles were there, but his car was gone.

She could wait, but her parents would start to worry if she didn't arrive home soon. Her plane had landed well over an hour ago.

First thing in the morning she'd drive back over here. It would be Saturday. Surely, he'd be home. She'd tell him then. And tell her parents after that.

The idea of waiting a few more hours offered a small amount of relief. Which only caused the guilt inside her to increase.

She closed the garage door, got back in her car and drove home.

There was an unfamiliar car in the driveway, but that wasn't all that unusual. Her parents often had company. She climbed out, got her suitcase out of the backseat and entered through the side door.

Peter met her in the hallway, took her coat. "It's good to have you home, Miss."

She kissed his cheek. He'd been their butler since long before she'd been born. "It's good to be home."

He reached for her suitcase. "I'll carry that up for you. Your parents are in the front room."

She wrapped her hand around the handle of the suitcase that she'd set down while removing her coat. "Thank you, Peter, but I'll take it up myself. I saw a car in the driveway. I know Mom and Dad have company."

"The company is here to see you."

"Me?"

"Yes, Miss. They are in the front room."

Having no idea who it might be, she checked her hair, made sure the scarf holding it in a ponytail was still tight and then smoothed a hand over the front of her printed green-and-white pencil skirt, checking for wrinkles from sitting so long on the plane. There were a few, but there wasn't anything she could do about it, and after making sure her blouse was neatly tucked into the waistband, she walked down the hall, to the front of the house.

Laughter echoed across the foyer. She instantly recognized her mother's and father's, but it was the third one that made her footsteps falter. It sounded like Jason. She closed her eyes, told herself that wasn't possible, that her mind was simply playing tricks on her, and continued onward, into the room, where her footsteps did more than falter.

They stopped dead in their tracks.

The entire world stopped.

The next thing she knew, she was lying on the sofa, afraid to open her eyes. Could things get any worse?

No!

She sat up, swung her feet over the edge of the sofa.

"Whoa." He grasped her shoulders. "Slow down, or you'll faint again."

Pressing a hand to her temple, at the dizziness in her head, she asked, "What are you doing here?"

"Right now I'm making sure you're okay."

"I'm fine." She lifted her head, looked around, testing to make sure the dizziness had truly faded. The dizziness was gone, and the room was empty. "Where are my mom and dad?"

"They left us alone, so we can talk."

She refused to look at him. "I don't want your land."

"Found some in California, did you?"

There was a hefty dose of sarcasm in his voice. She bit her lips together to keep from responding. No one, not even her father, knew that was why she'd gone to California.

"Your father said he'd told you to not attempt to buy or lease my property."

"Then it's a good thing you didn't agree with me, isn't it?"

"He'll also be speaking to Sam, about how he's been sabotaging you."

She twisted, stared at him. All of him. His dress pants, his neatly pressed white shirt, his tie and suit coat. It seemed odd to see him dressed in a suit. He looked as handsome as ever, but she liked the way he looked— She stopped the thought right there. What he was wearing, or not wearing, was of no importance. "You told him?"

He gave a nonchalant shrug that raised her ire even more.

"How dare you! I told you that in full confidence. Trusted—" She leaped to her feet.

He grabbed her arm. "You're not going anywhere."

"Yes, I am. I'm going to talk to my father."

He shook his head.

"They are probably concerned that I—"

"Fainted? Your mother said that's not uncommon in your condition."

Her blood turned to ice right then, making her shiver as it ran through her veins.

He lifted a brow.

She shook her head.

He nodded.

There was no way he could know. No one knew, other than Dr. Spencer, and she didn't know Jason was the father. No one knew that.

"When were you planning on telling me?" he asked. "Or, let me guess. Never."

Her blood was heating up fast, with anger. "I was going to tell you tomorrow. I stopped by your house tonight, but you weren't there."

He laughed. "Likely story."

"I don't care if you believe me or not."

"Good, because I don't believe you."

Her mind snagged on something else he'd said. About her mother. "No. No! You didn't tell my parents—"

"That you're pregnant with my child?" He nodded. "Yes, I did."

"Why? Why would you do that?"

"Because it was apparent that you weren't going to tell anyone." He eyed her, with anger blazing on his face. "You were going to move to California, probably marry Gus Albright and pretend the baby was his."

No one could make her as mad as he could. It was utterly inconceivable for him to know everything! Everything! Other than that stupid mention of Gus. "Gus? Get real!"

"I am. You've lied about everything else, why not that?"

"I haven't lied about anything, you've just got such a big chip on your shoulder, you don't want to know the truth!"

"I'll tell you the truth. Your parents gave me permission to ask you to marry me, but I'm not asking, I'm telling you, we are getting married, because I'll be damned if you are going to keep me from seeing my child."

"I wouldn't marry you if you were the last man on earth!"

"Yes, you will."

"No, I won't." She was so mad she was shaking. "I'll never forgive you for this. Never!"

"I don't care. This isn't about you or me. It's about

the child you're carrying." Glaring at her, he held up one hand, two fingers. "You have two days, until Monday morning, to decide when and where, or I'll decide."

Chapter Eight

Randi was lying on her bed, with one arm over her eyes, wondering how she'd managed to completely screw up her life beyond repair when the knock sounded on her door. She knew it was coming from the moment Jason had stormed out of the house and she'd run up the stairs. There was no sense putting off the inevitable. "Come in."

She sat up, watched her mother walk in and close the door. "Where's Dad?"

Her mother crossed the room. "Downstairs. Pacing the floor. Thinking he should be the one up here talking to you."

Randi glanced away as tears formed. "I don't think I can face him. I never thought I'd disappoint him like this. Or you."

Her mother climbed on the bed, cupped her cheeks with both hands. "You haven't disappointed him or me, not now, not ever."

"I'm pregnant, Mom. Not married. That could hurt Dad's chances at the senate, and—"

"Stop right there. This is about you."

"I don't want it to be about me."

"Well, it is, and about a baby that will arrive before Christmas."

Laying a hand against her stomach, Randi said, "November."

Her mother laid her hand over the top of hers. "And it's about Jason."

The flood hit so fast, there was no stopping it. Randi laid her head on her mother's shoulder and cried until there were no tears left. When she lifted her head, her mother had a tissue in hand. Randi used it and balled it in her hand, while sucking in air. "I don't even know how it happened."

"Yes, you do. We've talked about how babies are created many times." Her mother wiped the residue of tears off Randi's cheek with one hand. "And I know you. I know you've never had sex with anyone else."

Her mother had been open and honest about sex, said when it was with the right person, it was wonderful. It had been wonderful. Jason had made her body come alive and the way he'd looked at her had made her feel so special. "I never wanted to."

"But you did with Jason."

"Yes, so badly."

Hugging her close to her side, her mother said, "I remember the crush you had on him in high school."

"I never told you I had a crush on him."

"You didn't have to tell me. There were all sorts of signs, even before the night that your brother got Jason in all that trouble. You insisted Jason wouldn't have been trying to break into the office building, and didn't give up until you made Joey admit that it had been him and his friends who had been trying to break in to steal the pop."

That had happened right after she'd laughed when Jason had asked her out. "Joey had done that before. Numerous times." She pressed the heavy air out of her lungs. "By the time Joey admitted it, it was too late. Jason had already been sent to reform school." She'd thought she was done, but another sob hit. "He hates me, Mom. Hates me and has a right to."

"How do you feel about him?"

She didn't want to admit it, couldn't admit it. How could she love someone who hated her? Broke her heart. Betrayed her.

Her mother kissed her temple. "Your father and I will never force you to marry someone you don't want to marry."

"I'm pregnant, Mom." That was the reality of it all.

"There are far worse things in this world than being pregnant outside of marriage."

At this moment in time, she couldn't think of anything worse.

Her mother hugged her tight, kissed her temple. "Jason was out of his chair and across the room before your father and I even realized you were fainting. The look on his face, when he caught you, was not that of a man who hates you."

Jason couldn't sit still. Hadn't been able to since he'd left the Osterlund house on Friday night. He'd told her she had until tomorrow morning. What if she left town again? She could get on a plane, go anywhere in the world. He'd never find her.

He reached the kitchen counter, spun around and paced toward the laundry room again. Maybe that would be best. He didn't know anything about being a parent. Other than he didn't want his child to have a repeat of his childhood.

Reaching the laundry room, he walked back toward the counter, and upon arriving, picked up the receiver of the telephone hanging on the wall, just to make sure there was a dial tone, that the phone was working.

She might call.

She might be in Haiti by now, too.

He hung up the phone and leaned his head against the wall. He shouldn't have betrayed her the way he had. Shouldn't have told her she had to marry him. Asking would have been… No, she would have said no if he'd asked.

Tanner barked and Jason ran into the living room, looked out the window. His heart slammed against his rib cage at the Bel Air that was in the driveway. She was alone, wearing her red coat, and left the car running as she climbed out. He could see the exhaust coming out of the tailpipe.

Not sure what that signified, he walked to the door, opened it before she knocked.

She stopped, stared at him until Tanner shot past him.

Giving the dog a pet with one hand, she held out her other hand, handing him a piece of paper.

He took it but didn't look at it.

"That's where and when. I'd like a list of names and addresses for the invitations by Tuesday. There are a few other things. It's all listed there."

His throat was dry. His heart pounding. "Do you want to come in?"

"No." She gave Tanner another pet, then turned, walked to her car.

"Randi." He stepped onto the porch but wasn't sure what he could say in order to make any of this better.

She didn't look his way, just climbed into the car, backed out of the driveway.

"Tanner!" He held the door, waited for the dog to walk into the house with his head down and tail between his legs. Jason followed, feeling as downtrodden as Tanner looked.

That shouldn't be how a man feels when he's about to get married. He glanced at the slip of paper in his hand, read it, then walked into the kitchen to make a few phone calls.

His first call was to Stu, and if the other man was surprised, he didn't let it come through in his voice. Instead, he sounded excited upon agreeing to be his best man.

Jason's second call was to Aunt Marla. She'd have all the addresses that Randi needed. His aunt didn't sound surprised, either, and her excitement came through the phone line so loudly Tanner perked up.

Jason faked it well, even put on a good laugh for his aunt before he hung up. Other things on the list included where he needed to be and when, the location of the church and hotel for the reception, and the size of clothing he wore, with measurements. Actually, the measurements she asked for weren't really necessary. He owned a suit but would buy a new one. After wearing it the other night, he realized the one he owned was too tight through the shoulders.

He taped the note to the front of the refrigerator and went downstairs, hoping to focus on a project rather than her. Rather than marrying her. It went against everything he knew to be true, and that meant one thing. It wouldn't work.

Within an hour he was back upstairs and his house was being bombarded with family members, carrying in platters, kettles and pans full of food.

"You can't call with that kind of news and not expect a celebration!" Aunt Marla said. She had six kids, and they were all there, along with the respective mates of those that were married and their children.

Including Rachelle, who was the first to ask, "Where's Randi?"

"She left a short time ago," he said, making it sound like her visit had been longer and more affable than it had been.

"What's her phone number?" Lottie asked.

Jason shook his head. "She's busy. Has things to do."

"I know! That's why I want to call her, to let her know that I'll help with whatever she needs. We all will. Two weeks isn't much time to get everything done. What's her number? Tell me or I'll call information."

Randi might need help, and if so, he wanted her to have it, so he rattled off her home number. He'd memorized it last week, and her office number.

Later, after everyone had eaten, the women were sitting at the table, making lists from Aunt Marla's address book and the men were in the living room, giving him marriage advice when Tanner ran to the front door, tail wagging.

Upon peering out the window, Jason was out the door in ten seconds flat, meeting Randi on the sidewalk. "Hi."

"Hello," she replied stiffly.

He glanced at the house, at the faces looking out the window. "They—"

"I know. Lottie told me everyone was here. When I asked if Rachelle could be the flower girl, Lottie suggested that I drive over and ask Rachelle myself." She sighed. "So here I am."

He hated how stiff, how prickly and strained, things were between them. Letting out a sigh, he said, "I'm sorry."

She averted his gaze for a moment, and then looked at him. "For what? Did you tell them about the baby, too?"

Stung, he rocked on his heels. "No."

"Thank you for that."

His jaw muscles tightened. "Don't thank me too soon. They all think we're happy about this. About getting married."

"I assumed as much." With a smile that only he knew was fake, she waved at those still gawking out the window. "Don't worry, unlike some, I know how to keep secrets."

She was working hard at getting his goat. It was working, too. "Secrets or lies?"

Leveling her fake smile on him, she shrugged. "I'm sure that difference ranks right up there with nosy and curious in your world."

It appeared that she, too, remembered every conversation they'd had. Not about to remember certain ones right now, he stepped aside so she could step onto the porch. "Might as well go in, get this over with."

"Might as well."

He crossed the porch at her side and opened the door, let her step over the threshold first, and into the room that erupted with clapping and cheering.

"I have to see your engagement ring," Lottie said, rushing forward.

Jason draped an arm around Randi's shoulders. "She just agreed to marrying me. Give me a little time, will you?"

"You asked her without a ring?" Lottie laughed. "You're slipping, Cuz. Either that or head over heels."

Randi laid a hand on his chest and looked up at him. If he didn't know better, he'd think the shine in her eyes was real.

"He wants me to help pick it out," she said. "I told him any ring would be fine, but you know how stubborn he can be."

"Don't we all," Lottie said.

Someone in the background agreed, and others soon joined in with laughter and jokes. Jason returned the teasing with his own jokes and kept his arm around Randi as if all was right in the world.

Lottie broke into the noise by saying, "Rachelle is in the kitchen, Randi."

"No, I'm not, Mommy, I'm right here, behind you."

The room quieted more as Lottie stepped aside and Rachelle rolled forward.

"Mommy says you and Jason are getting married!"

Randi knelt down in front of the chair. "We are, and that's why I drove over here, to see you."

"Me? What for?"

"To ask if you'd like to be in our wedding," Randi said. "Be the flower girl."

The room went completely silent, and Jason's heart swelled as he saw Rachelle's face light up.

"You mean it?" Rachelle asked, eyes wide. "Me, in a wedding?"

"Yes, I mean it." Randi reached into her coat pocket and held up a tape measure. "I need to get your measurements so my mother can sew you a new dress to wear."

Rachelle's little face scrunched up, and she rubbed one eye with a fist. "But, Randi, I can't walk."

Jason stepped forward, ready to say that was just fine, but Randi had already taken a hold of Rachelle's hand.

"That makes it even more special," she told Rachelle. "We can decorate your wheelchair with flowers. All sorts of them." She touched the tip of Rachelle's nose. "You are going to be the most beautiful flower girl ever."

Lottie grasped a hold of his arm, squeezed it tight and whispered, "No wonder you fell in love so hard and fast. She's an earth angel."

Jason's stomach sank. He wasn't going to be able to pull this off. Neither was Randi, not with the way she hated him. She probably thought he got her pregnant on purpose, just to have access to her money.

She said something about measurements, and soon all the women were in the kitchen again, and the men in the living room. Including him. And holding the smile on his face was growing harder by the minute.

He had to put a stop to this, before it went any further, but what could he do? She was pregnant. There was nothing else that could be done, other than getting married, and being miserable for the rest of their lives.

It wasn't long before Randi walked into the living room, took a hold of his arm. "Your turn."

"My turn for what?"

"Measurements. My mother is sewing you a suit for the wedding."

"I already have a suit."

She tugged on his arm. "Now you'll have two."

With cheers and jeers from his male cousins, he let her pull him into the kitchen, where he had to remove his shirt, hold his arms out and be exposed to all sorts of giggling as Randi proceeded to measure his arms, neck, chest and waist.

"Are we done now?" he asked after she measured his biceps.

Aunt Marla, who had written down the measurements as Randi had taken them, said, "No, she has to measure you for the pants now."

His insides quivered. "No, she doesn't."

"Yes, I do," Randi said with a challenge in her eyes.

He'd been measured before, and didn't want her hands in the vicinity of his inseam. His body had a hard enough time behaving when she was near; having her touching him would put flame to fire.

"It won't hurt," she cooed.

She was enjoying this too much. He caught her by the waist, whispered in her ear, "It's not me I'm worried about."

"Then who?" she whispered in return.

"You."

"Me?"

"Yes, you might find something you want."

She laid a hand on his bare chest, making the skin tingle. "I've already found that and wasn't impressed."

He could tell by how her breath caught that she was far more affected than she was willing to admit. That made him grin, outside and inside. "All right, go ahead. Measure away."

She did, and he had to tighten every muscle in his body, especially when she measured his inner thighs, one at a time, more than once.

Standing up, she pressed a finger to the tip of his chin. "All done. You can put your shirt back on now."

Her smile said she'd thought she'd won. She hadn't, and she would pay for this. His jeans were now a full size too small and walking wasn't going to be pain-free.

It took time, but he found his moment of payback while everyone was preparing to leave. She was in the laundry room, collecting her coat. He walked up behind her, reached around and cupped both of her breasts while nuzzling the side of her neck.

She flattened her coat against her front, pushed at his hands. "Jason, stop it. Someone might see."

He nibbled on her ear. "I'll shut the door."

"No, you won't." She spun around. "You'll—"

He covered her mouth with his and kissed her until he felt her melt against him. Then he deepened the kiss, used his tongue, growing more and more satisfied as she returned the kiss, twist for twist.

Then he broke the kiss, turned around and left her, standing there, breathing hard and holding on to the counter.

She was steaming mad when she exited the room. Her eyes told him so. He laughed, took a hold of her arm, walked her to her car. It was parked behind others, who were waiting to leave.

"That will not happen again," she hissed while climbing into her car.

"You started it."

She glared at him and slammed her door shut.

He laughed.

Chapter Nine

He wasn't laughing now, a week and a half later. The contest that had ensued was killing him. Anytime they were together, they tried to make the other one as hot and bothered as possible, as if that would make them the winner. Jason knew the truth. He wasn't winning. Neither was she. They were doing little more than making each other miserable.

Life itself was miserable.

More than that, he was worried about her. He hadn't seen her every day, but often enough and for someone who was pregnant, she was losing weight rather than gaining it. He could tell each time he touched her.

It was not quite noon when he pulled up next to her car in the Air America office parking lot. He'd driven by the place thousands of times but hadn't pulled into the lot since that night years ago, after Randi had turned him down for a date.

He'd been mad at the world and had been driving like a bat out of hell on his motorcycle. After almost laying the bike down on the last corner, he'd slowed down, and his teenage mind had been questioning his life. How nothing had ever gone right, when he saw four people jump out of a car and run to the building. He'd slowed his bike, watched them check the doors and then run around to the back of the building. Randi had still been on his mind, and still wanting to impress her, he'd sped around to the back of the building, climbed off his motorcycle and yelled at the kids.

They'd been young, he could tell that, and one of them had smashed a window with a tire iron. He'd run over, taken away the tire iron. The night watchman had shown up right then. The other four ran, got in their car and sped away, and he'd been the one left holding the tire iron.

The one the police hauled off.

The one the judge sentenced to reform school, because his bad-boy reputation had preceded him. A teenager with no mother, a drunken father and a list of drag-racing tickets.

He'd been a month away from his eighteenth birthday, and that had set his sentencing. Thirty days of reform school.

If he'd been smart, he'd have gotten over Randi that very night.

But he hadn't.

Now he was about to be married to her.

He climbed out of the car.

A receptionist on the ground floor told him where Randi's office was located on the second floor. He chose the stairs over the elevator. Halfway down the long hall on the second floor, someone yelled.

"You there! What are you doing up here? What do you want?"

Jason looked over his shoulder at the man behind him in the hallway.

Tall, yet pudgy, with greased-back black hair and

squinting eyes, the guy said, "Yes, you. What do you want?"

Jason would bet dollar to dime that this was Sam Wharton, and deep loathing rose up inside him. Randi was going through enough and the idea of this guy making her life worse had his hands balling into fists with wanting to smack Wharton's smug face. He let his feelings show on his face, in his glare. "I'm not here to see you." Jason gave the guy a final glare before adding, "Not today."

He turned, continued down the hall and entered the room with Randi's name on a plaque by the door.

An older woman with short, dark hair was behind a desk. "Is Miss Osterlund available?" Jason asked.

With a smile, the woman stood. "Yes, she is. One moment please." She walked over to a door, knocked and opened it. "Mr. Heim is here to see you."

It seemed even here, his reputation preceded him, because he hadn't said his name. He walked forward, entered the room. His steps faltered slightly when he saw her sitting behind a large desk, wearing a dark purple-and-white blouse, or maybe it was a dress, he couldn't tell. She was a beautiful woman. The very one he went to bed thinking about and woke up thinking about. This morning it had been different, though, and right now he was seeing what he'd seen become prominent the past few days. An unnatural paleness, darkness under her eyes, even her face was growing thinner.

"Hello, Jason."

He tugged his gaze off her, and saw her father sitting in another chair.

Jason stepped into the room. "Sorry to disturb you," he addressed both of them before looking at Randi again. "I stopped by to see if you had time for lunch."

She shook her head. "I—"

"That is a splendid idea," Randal said. "I was just telling her she needed more time off."

"I'll be taking several days off," she told her father. "And have things to finish before then."

While she'd been talking, a ruckus was coming through the door the secretary had closed moments ago.

The door flew open and Sam Wharton barreled his way through the doorway, followed by two other men. "Right there! That's him!" Wharton said.

"What the hell is going on?" Randal asked.

"This hoodlum's casing the joint," Sam said.

Randi slapped her desk as she stood. "He's not casing the joint!" She marched around her desk. "Get out of my office! Now!"

Jason hooked her by the arm when she would have marched past him.

Randal stepped up on Jason's other side. "I'm assuming you haven't met Randi's fiancé, Sam," Randal said. "Jason Heim, my soon-to-be son-in-law."

Jason didn't need either Randi or Randal fighting his battles and met Wharton's glare with one of his own. The other man was taking note of his jeans, boots and leather jacket, and was definitely finding them lacking. With Randi filling his mind all morning, he hadn't given his clothes a second thought. He was dressed for work, and after checking on the crews at his different building sites, he'd gone back home, made lunch for her and then drove here to pick her up.

Wharton mumbled something under his breath.

Jason ignored the insult. The guy wasn't worth his time. However, he couldn't ignore the way Randi stiffened. He stepped forward, putting himself between her and Wharton.

The man took a step back.

"Jason." Randal slapped his shoulder. "You and Randi enjoy your lunch. You men go back to work, and Sam, I'll see you in my office in five minutes."

The two other men flew out the door like birds espying a cat, and Wharton's face turned red as he pivoted on one heel and left.

"Collect your coat, honey," Randal said.

She huffed out a breath, but spun around, walked to the coat hanger behind her desk.

Randal gave his shoulder another slap. "She has always jumped to your defense."

By the time Randi was in the front seat of Jason's car, the boost of energy the anger at Sam had given her was waning. It wouldn't be if Wharton was still in front of her, accusing Jason of casing the joint! At that moment she'd wanted… She wasn't sure what she'd wanted, other than to blister Sam within an inch of his life. Jason was ten times the man Sam would ever be, in every way. If only she was bigger, stronger, she would have taken Sam out.

She wasn't bigger, though, or stronger, and pinched her lips together, not sure there was enough energy left inside her to go another round with Jason. Since the day she'd agreed to marry him, they'd gotten caught up in some kind of game to see who could drive the other one crazy first.

She was on the losing end.

He didn't even have to touch her to make her body beg for more. A single look from him was capable of doing that, and it was exhausting. To the point it kept her awake at night. When she did manage to sleep, dreams of him woke her.

Going to work had become the only time she could escape him, but it was also exhausting because Sam had increased his antics. He was twisting everything she did to make it look wrong. She didn't want her father involved, nor did she want Jason involved.

Add all the wedding preparations, and she was nearly worn out. Her mother, grandmother and Lottie were taking on the brunt of the planning, thankfully. She wouldn't have been able to get everything done without them.

When she'd told her parents that she wanted to marry Jason, they'd said the wedding could be whatever she wanted. Large. Small. Here in Chicago or on some exotic beach.

She hadn't been able to tell them that all she really wanted was for Jason to want her as his wife. Really want her. Not because she was pregnant, but because he loved her. Loved her for herself. Loved her like her parents loved each other.

That would never be, and because others would expect it, she'd said the wedding should be here, in Chicago.

"I have to get back as soon as possible," she said. "I have a lot to get done at work and I have to pick up Rachelle to try on her dress this evening."

"It won't take long to eat," Jason said. "I have it staying warm in the oven."

"You made lunch?"

"Yes. You sound surprised."

"I didn't know you cooked."

"How do you think I eat?"

That had never been a part of all of her thoughts about him.

"I've cooked since I was eleven," he said.

That had been something she'd thought about. Marla was his mother's sister, but no one spoke of his mother. "What happened to your mother?"

"I don't know."

"How can you not know?"

He shrugged and sent her a quick glance. "She was there one morning when I went to school and gone when I came home that afternoon."

"What do you mean *gone*?" Compassion filled her. "Dead?"

"No, just gone. Some of her clothes were gone, a few other things. My father said she went to Florida. I don't know if that was true or not."

He sounded nonchalant, noncaring, but he couldn't be. "How old were you?"

"Eleven." He kept his eyes on the road as he continued. "My father wasn't an easy man to get along with, he was very stuck in his ways. She couldn't take it any longer and left, and I figured out that if I wanted to eat, have clean clothes, clean sheets, I had to do it myself."

She'd had no idea his childhood was so...sad. It made her heart ache and she wished she could touch him, hug him, even just hold his hand, but that could only happen when they were around others, playing their game of intense attraction that was nothing more than a superficial facade. His admission wasn't a facade. She could feel the honesty in his words. "You never heard from her again? From the time you were eleven?"

"No, but I've heard she's doing fine."

"Heard? From who?"

"My aunt." He turned the corner that led to his street, and had to slow down, stop for someone backing out of their driveway.

A plethora of questions filled her mind, along with empathy. "Jason, I—"

"I'd like to call a truce," he said, interrupting her.

She stared at his profile, wondering where his comment had come from. "A truce?"

"Yes, between us. We are getting married in two days, and…" He drove forward, following the car that had backed out. "I don't think marriage is easy even for people who are in love, who love each other. I think we should try to get along, make things as easy as possible, for the baby's sake if no one else's."

His honesty wasn't brutal, but its effect on her heart wasn't tender. A loveless marriage hadn't been her goal. Getting pregnant hadn't been, either. Yet, that was what had happened and she had to make the best of it. "I agree."

He turned into the alley and drove to his garage. Stopping there, he looked at her. "I know the position this has put you in, and know there will be times, at the wedding for instance, that we'll have to pretend…"

That we're in love, she finished silently.

"But we don't have to do that all the time. We can just—" He shrugged. "Be who we are when we're alone. No pressure. No faking."

No pressure? No faking? She wished that were possible. Wished so many things were possible.

"Is that okay with you?" he asked.

She nodded, more to herself than to him. "Yes, that sounds fine."

He shut the car off. "I'll give you a ride back to work when you're done eating."

She nodded again, and opened her car door, climbed out.

Tanner met them in the backyard and she was grateful that there was nothing fake about the dog. He was happy to see her, and she didn't have to pretend that she adored him.

"Oh, you poor dog," she told Tanner once in the house.

"Poor dog?" Jason carried her coat into the laundry room. "He has a pretty easy life."

"Easy? It smells delicious in here. He's probably been drooling for hours. What are you cooking?"

"Stick-to-your-ribs stew. Sit down and I'll get you a bowl." With a grin, Jason winked at her. "I'll even give him a bowl if you eat all of yours."

"Is that called bribery?"

He chuckled. "Possibly."

"More like probably." She rubbed Tanner's ears one last time. "Don't worry, I'll make sure you get a bowl." On her way to the sink, she asked, "What is stick-to-your-ribs stew?"

"The only stew I know how to make," he replied, carrying additional plates to the table. "It fills you up. Sticks to your ribs."

Her laughter came easy. His truce idea must be making her feel at ease, because she did. After washing her hands, she sat down at the table, and pressed a hand on her stomach as it growled. Besides the meaty stew, there was bread, milk, cheese and a plate of cookies. "You've been busy."

He sat down across from her. "Aunt Marla made the cookies." Nodding at her bowl, he said, "Eat up."

She took a bite of stew and nearly moaned over how delicious it tasted. "This is scrumptious."

"I'm glad you like it. You've lost some weight."

Not wanting him to think that was on purpose, she quickly chewed and swallowed. "Dr. Spencer says it's not unusual for women to lose weight at first. That it'll all come back sooner than not."

"What else does she say? Is there anything that you should be doing or not doing?"

It was the first time they'd discussed the baby, her pregnancy. "No, not really. Other than I shouldn't reach my hands over my head because that could make the umbilical cord wrap around the baby."

"It could?"

"Yes, that's what she said." Dr. Spencer had said a few other things, about hemorrhoids and breast soreness, but those weren't subjects she wanted to share with him. Not when she was more curious about something else. "How did you find out? Dr. Spencer was the only person who knew."

"By chance. Being in the right place at the right time."

His secretive grin made her smile. "What place?"

"The clinic. I'd heard your voice when the receptionist put you in the exam room across the hall from me. Your folder was in the holder on the wall. I took a peek. It said the rabbit died."

She shook her head at him. "It did not say the rabbit died." Then, truly curious, she asked, "Did it?"

He chuckled. "No. It said positive, but that is how they test. Rabbits."

"I know, isn't that crazy?"

"Actually, I recently read that they are using frogs for the testing more and more, because it doesn't kill the frog."

"Really? Where did you read that?"

"In a magazine I bought."

"What sort of magazine?"

His face slightly pinkened. "A women's magazine about pregnancy. It's in the bedroom, on the nightstand. You can read it if you want."

Her insides warmed that he was interested enough to buy a magazine. However, something else did concern her. "Why were you at the clinic?"

"I'd cut my hand."

He didn't point to it, didn't need to. She'd already noticed it and had been watching it, without letting on, to make sure the redness and puffiness were going away. It looked far better now than the first time she'd noticed it. "How had you cut it?"

"Bumped it with the skill saw."

Her heart leaped in her throat. "Skill saw! Good Lord, Jason, you could have cut your hand off!"

"It wasn't that bad and it's fine now."

She could see the scar, how it went all the way across the back of his hand. "It had to have hurt."

"The tetanus and penicillin shots hurt worse."

"I hate shots," she admitted.

"The needle isn't so bad, it's when they shoot the serum in that burns, and hurts for days." He nodded at her bowl. "Ready for seconds?"

She glanced down, unaware that she'd eaten the entire bowl, and the bread and the cheese. Her stomach felt fine. Full. But fine. No queasiness. There was still some milk in her glass, and she picked a cookie off the plate holding several. "No, thank you, but I am going to eat this with the rest of my milk."

He took a cookie off the plate and held it toward her. Laughing, she clicked her cookie against his as they both said, "Cheers."

A short time later she was helping him clean the kitchen when the phone rang. He answered it, and his question a moment later—about what supplies were missing—let her know it was about one of his building sites. She finished cleaning and putting away everything, including rinsing out Tanner's dish that Jason had filled with stew as promised.

"I have to make a couple of phone calls real quick, then I will give you a ride back to your office," he said.

"That's fine." She had a lot to do, but was no longer in a hurry to do it. While he dialed the phone, she walked down the hall and used the bathroom. When she exited, she could hear that he was still on the phone. Curious, she glanced in his bedroom and saw a magazine on the bedside table.

She entered the room, picked it up and grinned at the title of an article claiming everything a woman needs to know about pregnancy on the cover. Flipping through to the page indicated, she sat down and started to read.

When Tanner jumped up next to her, she swung her legs onto the bed and leaned against the headboard, petting the dog as she continued to read.

Chapter Ten

Jason hung up the phone, feeling guilty that it had taken him so long to find out where the materials that Stu was missing had been delivered. They were now on the way to the right site. The lumberyard was usually spot-on, but a new driver had put a wrench in the morning deliveries. All was in order now, and he went looking for Randi.

He found her in the bedroom, snuggled up against Tanner, sound asleep, with the magazine lying on the bed beside her. He'd bought it at the drugstore, while picking up bandages for his hand shortly after seeing her chart at the clinic. The article had said weight loss in the beginning wasn't unusual, but whoever had authored that article hadn't seen her. She'd lost too much weight. In his mind, anyway, and he was glad she'd eaten as much as she had at lunch.

Tanner lifted his head. Jason pointed at the dog, silently telling him to stay put. Tanner didn't seem to mind that command and laid his head even closer to Randi.

Jason collected a blanket from the linen closet in the hallway, removed her shoes and carefully draped the blanket over her. After watching to make sure she was still sound asleep, he left the room, closing the door behind him. A nap would do her good. The article had said rest was also needed for expecting mothers.

He checked on her regularly, and when she was still sleeping by four in the afternoon, he called Air America and spoke to her father, explaining how she'd fallen asleep and was still sleeping.

"Thank you, Jason, her mother and I have been worried that she hasn't been sleeping enough. There's nothing here that she needs to worry about. Would you like me to have her car delivered to your house?"

"No," Jason replied. "You can have it delivered to yours. I'll give her a ride home when she wakes up. I just wanted you to know so you weren't worried about why she hadn't returned to the office."

"I appreciate that very much."

He bid Randal farewell and then placed a call to Lottie. Once again explaining how Randi had fallen asleep and was still sleeping. Lottie assured him that she'd drive Rachelle to the dress fitting.

When he checked on Randi again, Tanner was sitting near the door, but she was still sleeping. After making a trip outside, the dog lay down in the hallway, outside the bedroom door.

"Sorry, boy, I don't want you to wake her by jumping on the bed."

Tanner covered his eyes with both paws.

"Nice try, but I don't feel sorry for you," he told the dog and went back into the living room, where he was using the coffee table to draw up plans for a cradle and a crib. Normally, he'd use the table in the basement, but wanted to hear when she woke up.

As a builder, he knew the sturdiest buildings would fall if the foundation hadn't been properly set, and so far, he wasn't creating much of a foundation for him and Randi to build upon.

He'd failed before. Not in building, but in life, and didn't want that again. He had to find a way to make this work. To make her not regret marrying him. Not regret having his child. He'd do whatever he had to in order to make sure his child knew they were loved, by both parents. Even if those parents were from two different worlds.

The part that was hard to swallow was knowing what it was like to live with parents who didn't love each other. He knew what that was like, and had to find a way to make sure that didn't show. Not to anyone. He didn't want Randi to be embarrassed, to be hurt.

Around seven the phone rang and he ran to catch it on the first ring.

"Hey, Cuz," Lottie said. "Rachelle and I are getting ready to leave Randi's house and want her to know the dress fits to a T. Rachelle is ecstatic over it, and it looks absolutely adorable on her."

"I bet it does." He was happy to have Rachelle in the wedding. "I'll let Randi know when she wakes up."

"She's still sleeping? She must have been exhausted."

He started to answer, but heard Lottie speaking to someone else.

"Hey, Cuz, Jolie wants to speak to you," Lottie said. "Talk to you later."

Jason shifted his stance, not sure why Jolie would want to speak to him.

"Hello, Jason. I just want to say thank you. I don't know how you did it, but I'm so thankful you managed to get her to take a nap."

She sounded so sincere he was comfortable admitting the same. "I am, too." Then he added a joke. "I'm just hoping it wasn't food poisoning from my cooking. She fell asleep right after eating."

"You got her to eat, too? You are a miracle worker." She laughed. "And don't worry. If it was food poisoning, she'd be throwing up not sleeping."

He chuckled. "Good to know."

"All right, dear, I'll see you tomorrow."

"Tomorrow?"

"Yes, I need you to try on your suit. Maybe you can do that when you bring her home?"

"Tomorrow," he repeated, not sure what her mother was suggesting.

"Yes, tomorrow. If she wakes up this evening, you tell her to go right back to sleep."

"Okay," he said hesitantly.

She let out another soft laugh. "Jason, the two of you will be married in a couple of days. I think it's okay if she spends the night."

Stunned that he was having this conversation with his soon-to-be mother-in-law, he couldn't help but wonder how his mother would have reacted to the situation. He knew how his father would have reacted, and it wouldn't have been good. "Okay, I'll tell her that, but—"

Jolie laughed louder. "But she may argue. You do know my daughter so well. Goodbye, now, see you tomorrow."

"Bye," he got in, just as she was hanging up. Replacing the receiver on the metal hook, he shook his head. The Osterlunds were proving to be nothing like he'd expected. He wasn't sure why, but had thought they'd be standoffish, rude, prude. Especially to him. There was no justification for why he'd thought that, other than the bias he'd grown up with about the differences in the rich and the poor. The haves and the have-nots. His father had

had plenty to say about that. About how the two worlds can't mix. Can't get along. And how he'd better stop mooning over *that rich girl*.

He'd tried more than once to discuss the property Randal had wanted to buy with his father, but that topic had been volatile, and he'd given up.

It had been his short stint in reform school that had given him the kick in the butt he'd needed to put himself on a different track. He'd accomplished a lot in the past six years, things he could be proud of. Was proud of. But he'd never be in the same category as the Osterlunds. Which was exactly what his father had always said. Right up until the day he'd died.

That may have been because of his mother. His father claimed that she'd run away with a rich man because money had meant more to her than her husband and son.

Rubbing the back of his neck, he walked back into the living room. He couldn't believe he'd told Randi all about his mother. That was a subject no one brought up. Not even Aunt Marla. Yet, he'd told Randi.

Tanner sat up, looked at the bedroom door. Jason walked to the door and carefully opened it to peer inside. The light was off, but the one in the hallway gave enough light for him to see that she'd moved, rolled from her side to her back.

"I think I fell asleep," she said groggily.

"Yes, you did."

She let out a tiny groan. "Why is it so dark? What time is it?"

"About seven thirty."

She shot upright. "Seven thirty!" Kicking her feet, she tried to get the blanket off her legs.

He sat down on the bed beside her, laid a hand on her

legs. "Slow down. You don't have anywhere you need to be."

"Yes, I do. I have work to do and Rachelle! I was supposed to pick her up at six o'clock. Oh, why didn't you wake me?"

"Lottie took Rachelle to your mother's, and the dress fits perfectly. Rachelle loves it and Lottie said she looks adorable in it." He smoothed the blanket over her stomach now that she had lain back down and was no longer trying to get out from under it. "Your father said there is nothing that you need to worry about at the office, and he had your car delivered to your house. Your mother said when you wake up, I'm supposed to tell you to go back to sleep."

She looked at him. "Is there anyone you haven't spoken to?"

"Is there someone you want me to call?"

"No." She sighed. "I can't believe I slept so long. So hard."

"You were tired."

"But I have so much to do."

"Not tonight. Are you hungry? There's plenty of stew left over." He searched his mind for quick meals. "Or I could make you some scrambled eggs or oatmeal and toast."

"Oatmeal?"

He chuckled silently at the way she said it.

"That sounds good, doesn't it?" she asked. "With cinnamon and sugar."

"I have cinnamon and sugar. I'll go make you some."

She laid a hand on his arm before he stood. "No, that's okay. I just need a ride home."

"That is the one thing I can't give you."

"Why not?"

"Your mother."

"My mother?"

"Yes, she told me you are to spend the night."

Smiling, she closed her eyes. "She would." She stretched her arms over her head and sat up again. "Don't worry. Her bark is worse than her bite. She won't be mad if you give me a ride home."

He couldn't quite imagine her mother angry. Nor could he imagine Randi looking more adorable. The desire to kiss her was so strong he had to get off the bed. "I'm not worried. I'm going to make you some oatmeal." At the door, he added, "With cinnamon and sugar."

A few moments later, while he was in the kitchen, waiting for water to boil, he heard her talking to Tanner.

"You're the reason I fell asleep, silly old dog," she said. "You were so warm and snuggly it was impossible not to."

Tanner let out a bark. She laughed, and then told him, "No, you don't, I don't need your help in the bathroom."

As smart as he was, Tanner still hadn't mastered privacy.

The old saying *a watched pot never boils* was coming true, because Jason was still waiting for the water to boil when she walked into the kitchen.

"May I use the telephone?"

"Of course." He nodded toward the wall. "There's that one, or the one in the living room, on the table by the window."

"Thanks." She nodded toward the stove. "The water's boiling."

"Hi, Mom." Randi leaned against the wall and watched Jason pour oatmeal into the pot on the stove.

"Hello, honey. Did you have a good nap?"

"Yes, I just woke up. I'm blaming it on Tanner."

"Tanner?"

"Yes, he has yellow hair, big brown eyes and his snuggles put me to sleep."

Her mother laughed. "I'm assuming this Tanner has four legs."

"Yes, he does, and he's about as big as a small horse."

"You sound happy, dear."

She was happy, a content happy. "I feel so much better. You were right, I needed to eat and sleep."

"Yes, you did, and you need to do that again."

Smiling at him, she said, "Jason is making oatmeal right now."

"One of your favorites."

"I just wanted to call, ask about Rachelle's dress."

"Oh, honey, she is so adorable! Your father didn't want to let her go home. He was prepared to play checkers with her all night. Right now he's attaching wire to the silk flowers I had the girls at the shop make so they can be attached to Rachelle's wheelchair. He was adamant that if we just tied them on, they might fall off."

That was her father. Both the checkers and finding a way to make sure the flowers wouldn't fall off. "He'll have them twisted on her chair so tight that they'll never fall off."

Her mother laughed. "That could be his plan."

"And the dress? She liked it? It fit?"

"She loved it, and it fit perfectly. The rosy pink of the silk was perfect for her complexion. Just like you said. It had been so long since I'd sewn a little girl's dress, I'd forgotten how fun it was to work with all that lace and ribbons. I'm making her a little veil as a surprise. I'm sewing the pearls on it right now."

And that was her mother. They truly were really, really good people. "Thank you, Mom. She'll like that."

She heard background noise before her mother said,

"You're welcome, dear. Your father says hello and that he needs my help with something, so I need to go. We'll see you in the morning. I told Jason he can try on his suit when he brings you home. We love you."

"Love you, too." Randi hung up the phone. Her mother was fully convinced that everything would work out fine between her and Jason. Randi didn't want her mother to be disappointed, but she wasn't convinced her mother was right this time.

"Everything okay?" Jason asked.

"Yes. Mom is sewing a veil for Rachelle, and Dad is putting wire on the silk flowers for her wheelchair."

"That was really special of you to ask her to be the flower girl."

"She is a very special girl." Randi pushed off the wall and walked toward the fridge to get the milk. "I wish she'd been able to receive the vaccination."

"She wasn't in school yet, and that's the only place they are inoculating children."

"That's just where they can inoculate the most children at one time, it's expanding to clinics and other facilities, but it takes time."

"How do you know that?"

"I've served on the fundraising committee for several years and collect a lot more than dimes." Fundraising was one time her last name was a blessing, and she appreciated that.

"Thank you for doing that."

"You're welcome." As she opened the door of the refrigerator, she saw the note taped there and frowned. It was his wedding, too. "Was there anything specific about the wedding that you wanted?"

"No. Whatever you want is fine."

She lifted the milk off the shelf and turned around. He was spooning the oatmeal into bowls. "You're sure?"

"Yes." He looked at her. "Just that you're there."

Her insides nearly melted. She'd never forget what it felt like to be kissed by him. Touched by him. She had to take a deep breath and hold it in order to carry the milk to the table. "You said no faking while we're alone."

"I'm not faking. You will be there, won't you?"

Her face grew flush. "Yes, I'll be there."

He set the bowls on the table. "So will I. Nothing fake about that."

That was true. They talked about different people who would be at the wedding, and a variety of other things while eating the oatmeal and washing the few dishes they'd used. Tanner got the last of the oatmeal, as well as a good portion of dog food, before they all went into the living room.

She debated asking him to take her home. There was a lot to be done before Saturday, but she didn't want to go out in the cold. Truthfully, she didn't want to leave. Now that her stomach was full again, she was trying not to yawn.

"Want to watch the television set?" he asked. "I think *I Love Lucy* is on tonight."

She sat down on the sofa. It was dark brown and soft. Tucking her legs beneath her, she eyed him closely. "You like that show?"

"I figured you did."

"My mother and I love it, my father, not so much. He says it's too silly."

"I'd probably be on his side, but we can watch it if you want to," he answered while gathering several papers on the coffee table into a pile and setting a ruler and pencil on top of the stack.

"How about we watch whatever you want?" Gesturing to the pile, she said, "Or you can work on that if you need to."

"No, they are just some plans I'm drawing."

"For a new job?"

"No." He filtered through the papers, handed her one and then walked to the television on a table near the far wall and turned it on.

Her heart thudded as she recognized the drawings. "It's a crib and a cradle."

"I figure we could stain them, or paint them, whichever you'd like. Whatever color you'd like. I thought I'd make a rocking chair, too. And a high chair later on."

"Jason..." Her heart was thudding at his thoughtfulness. "I don't even know what to say."

"We could buy furniture instead, the—"

"No. This is so thoughtful. You making it for the baby is wonderful. Truly."

He nodded, then shrugged. "The furniture store has mattresses that will fit both the cradle and crib."

She had to pull her eyes off him before her mind went to other things. "What's this down in the corner?" She pointed at the bottom of the drawing.

He sat down beside her. "That's the pattern of the spindles for the legs."

"They are going to be beautiful."

"I thought I'd use maple, it's a good hard wood. Won't nick or scratch."

She continued to ask questions, and listened intently to each of his answers, using her imagination and the drawings to see each piece in her mind. "I'm looking forward to watching you build them."

"You'll be building the important thing."

She laid the drawing on the table and flatted both

hands on her stomach. A deep warmth filled her. Leaning her head against the back of the sofa, she asked, "This truce between us, what does it entail?"

"What do you want it to entail?"

"I don't know, I've never called a truce before."

"I haven't, either." He leaned back.

Everything felt so complicated, and it was, but there was also this baby growing inside her and she couldn't believe that was anything short of wonderful. Her greatest hope was that he thought that, too. "I did stop here, at your house after my plane landed that night, so I could tell you that I was expecting. Your car wasn't in the garage, so I left and planned on coming back the next morning."

He laid a hand over the top of one of hers. "I believe you, and I'm sorry. I should have handled things differently. I should have been more patient and waited for you to contact me."

Though it was hard to admit, she had to. "No, you shouldn't have. I was afraid to tell you and petrified about telling my parents. You saved me from having to tell any of you."

She huffed out a breath in preparation of telling him that she hadn't gotten pregnant on purpose, but didn't want to disrupt things more than they already were. Therefore, she stuck to the topic of her parents. It was hard for people to understand what it means to be the daughter of such a successful couple. "My parents are wonderful people, the best, and the idea of disappointing them—" She pinched her lips together.

"Scared you."

"Yes." Her breath grew heavy again. "I shouldn't have been, but couldn't help it, and now they are so excited about the wedding and everything, I don't want to disappoint them again."

He released her hand. "You won't. That'll be part of our truce. We'll get through the wedding just fine, and no one else needs to know about the baby until we decide to tell them. I think that shouldn't be until after your father announces his senate bid."

It was all so complicated and weighed so heavily inside her, she was grateful for his truce, even if it was only for a short time. Hopefully, it would be enough time for her to figure out how to make all of this work out. That was what needed to happen, for the baby's sake. "Thank you."

"You're welcome." He nodded toward the television. "Your program is coming on."

Chapter Eleven

"Hey, sleepyhead, it's time for bed."

She didn't want to move, didn't want to open her eyes, and snuggled closer to the warmth at her side.

"You're going to end up with a crook in your neck if you sleep like that much longer."

Letting out a sigh, she opened one eye, realized it was Jason's shoulder that she was using for a pillow and it was his warmth that she was snuggled against. "Hmm?" she asked, still not wanting to move.

He rubbed her shoulder. "Come on, Miss Rip Van Winkle. It's time for bed."

Sighing, she opened her eyes, sat up. "Is Lucy over?"

"About two hours ago."

She stretched, rubbed the back of her neck with both hands. "I remember seeing the beginning."

"You made it through the first five minutes." He helped her stand and kept an arm around her as he escorted her down the hallway. "I don't have a nightgown to loan you, but I have a pair of long johns and a T-shirt."

At this point she didn't care what she wore, she just wanted to sleep. All of her sleepless nights seemed to have caught up with her. "That'll work."

"Do you need to go to the bathroom?"

"Yes." She stumbled slightly.

He chuckled softly. "Are you going to be okay by yourself? Or are you going to fall in?"

She wasn't totally sure and forced her eyes to open wide. "I'll be fine. But I'll take those clothes so I can change in there."

"Okay." He walked her into the bathroom and set her down on the toilet seat. "I'll be right back."

She rubbed her eyes, trying to force herself to wake up enough to get undressed.

He was back in no time and set clothes on the edge of the sink. "Do you need help getting undressed?"

She was tired, but could still remember how dangerous his help might be. "The last time you helped me undress, I got pregnant."

"Well, that won't happen again."

Her heart thudded. "Ever?"

He lifted her chin with one hand. "Are you half-asleep or half-drunk?"

What had made her ask that? And why wasn't she embarrassed to have asked it? "I don't need any help."

He released her chin. "I'll be in the hallway. Yell if you do."

She didn't need help in undressing. The help she needed was in making sense of all this, but she was too tired to think. Too tired to think about anything but going to bed. To sleep.

Yawning, she removed everything except her panties, draped it all over the rod holding the curtain that hid the bathtub and put on his long johns and T-shirt. Then she used the toilet and washed her hands before opening the door.

He was in the hallway and looped an arm around her

waist, walked her into the bedroom, where the covers were folded back. She crawled in, rolled onto her side and sighed at the comfort. Then, feeling chilled, asked, "Can Tanner sleep on the bed again?"

"No."

"Why not?"

"Because then there wouldn't be room for me."

"I hope you snuggle as good as he does."

A moment later the bed shifted as he climbed into it. One arm went under her neck, the other around her waist and his body aligned itself against her back. "Will this do?" he asked.

His warmth surrounded her. "Yes. That's nice. Very nice."

"Good night, Randi."

She covered his hand that was resting on her stomach with hers. "Good night, Jason."

Jason counted sheep, estimated how many boxes of nails were in his basement and tried to recall how many episodes of the *Red Skelton* show he'd seen, but none of it helped. Every part of him was still responding to holding her. Not just his body and mind, but his emotions. He felt things for her. Deeply. Should he have told her that the reason he'd gone to her parents' house was because he'd been worried about her? He had been. She'd been the only thing he'd thought about for days, weeks, and not being able to get a hold of her had driven him crazy. He hadn't planned on telling her parents she was pregnant, but the idea of her leaving town had struck him like a bullet and he'd responded out of fear.

He wasn't proud of that, or of forcing her to marry him. All he'd been able to think about was her, and what she'd go through being unwed and pregnant. What that would do to her reputation. He was to blame, not her. If he'd have had more self-control, he would have stopped before making love to her. He hadn't, and not taking responsibility for that had never been an option.

The baby, their baby, would be his responsibility for the rest of his life. He'd be responsible for Randi the rest of his life, too. He accepted that completely, but what about her? That wasn't what she wanted. Had never wanted, and he didn't know what to do about that. Other than to make it as easy upon her as possible. That was all he could do.

If he could love, could learn to love, he'd do it, for her, but that could never happen. He was his father's son and everyone knows that the apple doesn't fall far from the tree.

The trouble was, desire and love were two different things, and he desired her. More every day.

However, what he desired, what he wanted, wasn't as important as what she needed.

He repeated that over and over, until he fell asleep and then repeated it when he woke up. His body was definitely reacting to how she was snuggled up against his side and had one leg thrown over the top of his thighs.

In the midst of repeating it one more time, he felt her shift, and then watched her eyes open. There were no dark circles under her eyes and her cheeks were flushed pink.

He was happy to see that. "Morning."

Her lips curled into a smile. "Good morning."

"How do you feel?"

"Wonderful." She rolled onto her back and stretched. "Completely refreshed."

The white T-shirt she was wearing didn't hide things

very well. He should climb out of bed, but if she glanced at him, she'd see something he couldn't hide very well.

Flipping onto her side so quickly the bed shook, she kissed his cheek. "I'll go make coffee, and then I'll make you breakfast." She tossed aside the covers. "It's only fair, you did all the cooking yesterday."

She bounded out of the bed, and he had to swallow a groan at how cute her butt looked wearing his long johns. No truce on earth was going to make this easy. Not with the way his desires had his blood pounding stronger than ever.

As soon as she disappeared into the hallway, he leaped out of bed and pulled on a pair of jeans. He couldn't wake up like this every morning for the rest of his life. He'd have to buy a bed for one of the spare bedrooms and sleep there.

She already had the percolator filled and plugged in when he arrived in the kitchen. Once again, it struck him at how perfectly she completed the space.

"I'm going to get dressed before I start cooking," she said, patting his chest as she brushed past him.

He grasped her hand, held it. She was so pretty, so… above him. She raised money for the organization that had helped Rachelle while she'd been in the hospital. Her father was running for the senate. The only thing his father ever ran for was town drunk. He wanted to apologize for who he was, but it wouldn't do any good. It wouldn't change anything.

She smiled up at him.

It wouldn't make him not want to kiss her, either. Nothing would do that. He gave her hand a squeeze and released it.

"Don't touch anything," she said while walking toward the doorway. "I'm cooking breakfast."

"I won't," he answered while walking to the refrigerator to get the cream she'd need for her coffee.

She returned to the kitchen, once again wearing the purple-and-white dress and looking not only refreshed, but also gorgeous. There was a shine in her eyes and on her face, and her energy was boundless as she fluttered around the kitchen.

"My cousins are arriving today," she said while they were eating eggs, bacon and toast. "You might remember Wendy. We were in the same grade and she's my very best friend. Was the entire time we were growing up. Her dad is a photographer. His company takes all the school pictures. He'll be taking pictures at the wedding."

The name didn't ring a bell. Not surprisingly. The only girl he truly remembered from school was her. "What does she look like?"

"My height. Short blond hair. She looks like Doris Day, and she laughs all the time. Makes everyone else laugh, too. She's my maid of honor. Both her and her sister Sandy are going to school out east. Wendy is going to be a doctor and Sandy a veterinarian. Sandy is younger by a few years. They were home for Christmas but only for a couple of days and I'm excited to see them both."

By the time she was done talking, he could no longer hold back a grin. "I can see you're excited, and I hope you don't wear yourself out within the first hour of the day."

Her plate was empty and she jumped up to carry it to the sink. "There's no chance of that. I feel amazing. Better than I've felt in weeks. I guess I really was tired."

He stood, stacked and carried the rest of the empty plates from the table to the sink, where she was running water to wash them. "That was delicious, thank you."

"You're welcome." She glanced up at him and scrunched up her face.

"What's wrong? It really was good."

"I'm glad you like it, but um…" She glanced around the room. "My bridal shower is at noon today."

He knew that. It was on the note she'd given him and he'd taped to the front of the refrigerator. A hint of nervousness struck. "Do I have to be there?"

She giggled. "No, but it's at my aunt's house, and I'm wondering if I could bring the gifts here, rather than to my parents' house after the shower. That way we don't have to move them twice."

He grabbed the towel to dry the dishes she was stacking in the rack. "Sure. What time?"

"I'm not sure. It could be around three or four, I really don't know."

After opening a drawer, he pulled out the spare key to the front door and laid it on the counter. "Here's a key so you can come and go as you please." He winked at her. "And not have to use the doggie door."

She punched him in the arm with a soap-covered fist. "Very funny, but thank you for the key."

The urge to kiss her just wouldn't go away. He grabbed another plate to dry. "You're welcome. I'll try to be here to help carry things."

"You don't have to. I'm sorry I kept you from your work yesterday."

"You didn't."

"I think I did, and I thank you. I really do feel much, much better."

"I'm glad."

They finished washing, drying and putting away the dishes, and she picked up her engagement ring from where she'd set it on the windowsill in front of the sink. She turned, looked at him. "Thank you for the truce, too."

The day after she'd agreed to marry him, he'd gone to

the jewelry store and had been at a loss as to which ring to buy. He'd settled on one with a diamond in the center, and two sapphires on each side. None of the stones were overly large, but that had been why he'd liked it. Its delicateness reminded him of her. At the time he hadn't been sure how to give it to her, so had had it sent to her office.

He stopped her from sliding the ring on her finger. Took it. Held it between his thumb and forefinger. "We could go to the jewelry store this morning and you could pick out whatever ring you want."

"Why? I like this ring."

"You could pick out a bigger one."

"This one fits perfectly."

"I mean a bigger diamond. Or a different-shaped one, different stones, or—"

"Jason, I like this ring exactly as it is. Don't you?"

"Yes, I do. It reminded me of you the moment I saw it." He wanted to ask her to marry him. Really ask her, not tell her, but it was a moot point. Their wedding was the day after tomorrow, and it wasn't like her answer would mean she wanted to marry him.

"It reminds me of you every time I look at it," she said.

He took her hand, slid the ring on her finger. Then, because he wanted to kiss her, have her kiss him in return, he released her hand. Neither of them moved, just stood there, staring at each other. The air, the energy between them, was shifting, growing electrifying, and he stepped back. "I'll go start the car so it can warm up."

Randi stared at the door to her father's den, waiting for Jason to exit. He'd looked so handsome in his suit her heart was still pounding. Just as it had been doing since she woke up next to him in his bed.

She felt so much better today. It could have been because she'd finally eaten and slept, but those things had happened because of him. Therefore, he was the reason she felt better. Him and his truce. She didn't know exactly what that all entailed, but it felt as if she wasn't alone. That they were in this together, which they were, but it felt different now.

The sound of the front door opening had her turning about, and she squealed upon recognizing a familiar voice. She ran down the hallway to the front foyer, where she and Wendy met, and hugged and squealed at the happiness of seeing each other.

"I couldn't wait!" Wendy pointed to the suitcases on the floor. "My plane just landed. I haven't even been home yet. Sing! Now! Asking me to be your maid of honor, but not telling me who you are marrying has been driving me crazy!"

"I couldn't tell you," Randi said, giving Wendy another hug. If she'd told her cousin who she was marrying, she'd have had to tell her everything, and she didn't want even Wendy to know why Jason was marrying her, or that he didn't love her.

Wendy's blond hair was brushed back in waves, making it look like Doris Day as always, and her blue eyes narrowed slightly as she asked, "Why?"

Just then, as if he'd known the exact moment to appear, Jason stepped into the hallway. He'd used her father's den to try on his new suit, and was wearing his jeans again now, cuffed, and his leather coat was hooked on a finger and flung over his shoulder as he walked down the hall, toward the foyer where she and Wendy stood.

"DDT!" Wendy hissed. "Drop dead twice! Again and again! You're marrying—"

"Yes!" Randi hurried to meet Jason as he reached the foyer.

"I left the suit in the den," he said.

"That's perfect." She wrapped a hand around his arm and nodded toward Wendy. "This is my cousin Wendy."

He gave Wendy a nod. "Hello."

"Hel—lo," Wendy replied, elongating the word in a way only she could do.

Randi laughed at the way he looked down at her, one brow risen.

"Jason Heim," Wendy said, nodding. "Jason Heim. How have you been?"

"Fine, thank you," he replied. "You?"

"Fine. Just fine." Wendy crossed her arms and tapped a toe on the floor as her eyes widened to look at Randi. "Meanwhile, back at the ranch."

Jason glanced from Wendy to her and asked, "Do you need anything else from me right now?"

"No," Randi said.

He swung his coat off his shoulder. "Then I'm off to work."

Wendy had moved to the other side of the foyer, where Peter was waiting to take her coat, and Randi walked with Jason to the door.

"You go slow today," he said while putting on his coat. "Don't wear yourself out again."

"I will, and I won't." She giggled at her own nervousness. "You know what I mean. I'll be fine."

He stopped at the door, zipped up his coat and gently touched her side. "I hope so."

She was fine in many ways, but in others, not at all. If she hadn't agreed to his truce, she could kiss him right now, in front of Wendy. She'd been able to do that when they'd been playing their game, but now, with the truce, she couldn't. Why didn't anything seem to work out in her favor?

"What's the matter?" he asked.

She reached up, flipped his collar up around his neck and leaned close, so no one could hear. "Can I ask a favor?"

"Yes," he whispered in return.

She bit down on her bottom lip, hard, not wanting to break the truce because yesterday, last night, this morning, had all been wonderful, in a comfortable, easy way. She'd eaten, slept and felt better than she had in a long time.

"What is it?" he asked.

"Will you kiss me goodbye?" she whispered quickly, before she lost her nerve, and then attempted to explain, "It's just that Wendy—"

"I get it," he said. "Big or little?"

The bigger the better, but she wanted it to look real. "Medium?"

"Medium?"

She nodded. "Is that okay? Little would—"

"Medium is fine," he said while cupping her face with both hands.

The next moment his lips met hers with such tenderness, it sucked the air right out of her lungs. She buried her hands in his collar and arched against him as his lips moved across hers, giving her several small, tender kisses that accumulated into a very special feeling that settled deep inside her.

When the kiss ended, she was floating on cloud nine.

He gently bumped his forehead against hers. "I'll see you later."

"Okay." She knew she had to release his collar, but couldn't quite make her fingers uncurl.

He kissed the tip of her nose, then gave her lips another single, quick kiss.

She forced herself to release his coat and patted his chest. "Bye."

As he opened the door, he winked at her. "Bye."

She barely had time to shut the door behind him, when Wendy let out another squeal and ran across the foyer.

"I can't believe you didn't tell me! I didn't even dare ask my mother, because I knew if it was anyone except him, I'd have to object to the wedding! DDT! He's even better-looking now! I knew it! I knew it, knew it, knew it. Knew that you'd find a way to make him marry you! You said you would, and you did!"

Randi's stomach fell. She had said she would find a way to make him marry her, years and years ago.

"Sing! Girl! Sing!" Wendy continued. "I need to know everything!"

"Um, well, let's go up to my room. I have to get ready for the bridal shower, and I'll tell you everything."

"You better believe you will."

No, she wouldn't. Not everything.

Chapter Twelve

Randi hadn't told Wendy about being pregnant, but had told her about going to his house to ask about buying his land, and about how she'd left, mad, wearing only his socks, and how she'd returned and dropped her glove, along with his socks through the doggie door.

Standing in his kitchen, she was in the midst of telling her other cousins that same story, when Jason opened the back door. She sidestepped closer to him. "I was just telling them about when I accidently lost my glove in the doggie door."

"I heard the laughing from the garage." Glancing at the others, he asked, "Did she tell you she lost her glove, or dropped it on purpose?"

She slapped his shoulder. "It was not on purpose!"

Her cousins, however, found his question hilarious, and because not a one of them was shy, they instantly started asking him questions about the event, which he answered with such humor and charm that every woman in the room was swooning. Including her.

She finally ended the storytelling by shooing everyone out to the cars to carry in another load of gifts she'd received at the bridal shower.

Once the room was empty, she told Jason, "I'm sorry, I was hoping we'd have everything put away before you got home."

"And I was hoping you'd wait for me to carry things in for you. I'll go help."

"No, none of it is heavy." She lowered her voice. "I wanted to mention that I moved your drawings off the coffee table. I put them in the laundry room."

"Sorry. I forgot I'd left them there."

"No, don't be sorry. I just—"

"I know, and it's okay."

She pressed a hand to her stomach. In a way, she had done exactly as she'd vowed—found a way to make Jason marry her. She hadn't gotten pregnant on purpose, but she had come to his house. He would have never searched her out. He would never have searched her out if he hadn't been at the clinic that day, either. Knowing all that made her feel awful. She had vowed to marry him, but she also wanted him to love her.

"What's wrong?" he asked.

"Nothing."

He rubbed her upper arms. "Are you not feeling well?"

"No, I'm fine."

"No, you're not."

The front door opened, filling the house with chatter and giggling. She glanced that way and swallowed against the burning in her throat. "Yes, I am. I'm fine."

In the next instant his arms were around her and he was kissing her, in the same, wonderful way he had this morning. It was so different from their kisses before they'd become engaged. Those ones had been hot, full of unrefined passion. His kiss now, and this morning, were affectionate, caring. Loving. Which made her feel better and worse at the same time.

By the time the kiss ended, feeling better won out, and increased when he held her in a long hug.

"What are your plans now?" he asked.

Her arms were around him, inside his unzipped coat, and she kept them there as she leaned her head back, looked up at him. "We are going back to my house, to paint our fingernails and toenails and practice how we want our hair to look for the wedding. Want to join us?"

He brushed the hair away from the side of her face. "No."

"It'll be fun," she teased.

"For some."

"We are also going to be packing up my bedroom, and will drive it over here tomorrow, and then we have to be at the church at five for rehearsal."

Clearing her throat before she spoke, Wendy said, "Sorry to interrupt, but we put everything in the spare room down the hall, and are just sort of standing around, twiddling our thumbs, trying not to stare. You know, in a sort of, take-a-picture-it'll-last-longer kind of way."

"I do remember her," Jason said.

Randi gave him a quick hug. "I thought you would." Wendy had always made everyone laugh, and she needed that to get through the next few days. When Wendy was near, it was easy to pretend that Jason loved her and was marrying her because he wanted to, not because he had to.

Jason closed the front door as Randi and the other women drove away in two cars. He did remember the cousin, because he remembered her telling him to take a picture once when he'd driven past her and Randi walking across the school parking lot. He'd been embarrassed at being caught staring.

He'd gone out with dozens of women since then, but none of them had left the lasting effect that Randi had on him. Still did.

The air in his chest seeped out slowly. This truce idea was backfiring on him. Kissing her before had been a challenge, and though it had left him heated, wanting more, his heart hadn't been in them, not like it was today. It made something deep inside him ache.

Tanner let out a bark.

Jason turned, looked out the window on the door, disappointed to not see Randi's car. "No one's out there."

The dog barked again.

"She's not coming back tonight."

Tanner lay down on the floor with a solid thud and sighed.

Jason shook his head at the dog, but admitted aloud, "I know the feeling." The house felt empty. She'd never been here for a full twenty-four hours, yet had left her mark. Just like she had on him.

"Come on, bud. It's leftover stew and *Red Skelton* for us."

Tanner didn't lift his head. Jason figured he wasn't hungry, either, and sat down on the sofa. With his feet on the coffee table and his hands clasped behind his head, he stared at the television set that he hadn't turned on. Last night, when she'd told him about being afraid to disappoint her parents, he'd been surprised. Had never thought about how hard it must be for her. To have such successful parents.

He knew the exact opposite. For years he'd been determined not to become his father and had hit the workforce. Hard.

He'd done well so far, and the future looked good, but he was still the boy who'd grown up in a shack on the edge of town. Still the boy whose mother had left because... Well, because not even love lasted forever.

Money won out. His mother had left because she was tired of being poor.

The phone rang and his thoughts instantly went to Randi. He leaped to his feet, answered it before the first ring completed.

"Hey," Stu said. "Since we are both home alone to-night, do you want to hit a burger joint and then hit a tav-ern for a couple of beers?"

"Why are you home alone? Where's Lottie and Ra-chelle?"

"Heading over to Randi's. Rachelle is in her glory. Lottie let her miss school this afternoon so she could at-tend the bridal shower and now they are on their way to get their finger- and toenails painted. It's really great how she's being included in everything. That doesn't happen a lot for her. So what do you say to the burgers and beers?"

"I say yes," he replied, even as his thoughts contin-ued to remain on Randi, and how special it was that she was including Rachelle in everything. Too many people, who didn't understand polio, thought Rachelle was con-tagious and shunned her.

"Meet you at Rolly's in twenty?" Stu asked.

"I'll be there."

Stu was there as promised, along with nearly every male member of his family. They ate burgers and then headed across the street, where they had more than a couple of beers.

There were plenty of stories told, some good old-fashioned ribbing and a few serious conversations be-fore the night ended well past midnight.

Then he spent a sleepless night feeling alone in his own bed.

* * *

Shortly after noon the following day Randi appeared, and rather than two carloads of women, it was two cars and a pickup.

"I brought help," she said, giving him one of her adorable grins as she stepped onto the porch. "I didn't want to take up all your dresser space, so I brought my own. And a dressing table, and a few other things."

The back of the pickup was heaped full and tied down with heavy ropes. "I see that."

"Is there any particular place you want it?" she asked.

It was still February and cold. "You can decide that while staying inside where it's warm."

"I won't argue. It's freezing out." She grasped his arm. "Just let me introduce you to everyone first."

Her cousin Wendy was with her again, along with a couple other women who had been with her yesterday, and the men were two other cousins and her brother, Joe.

They unloaded the cars first, so the women could stay inside, and then attacked the load in the truck with gusto in order to get it all inside before anyone ended up with frostbite.

The women were busy, finding places for everything with only a small amount of rearranging, and soon the men's work was done.

Joe approached him. "Hey, Jason, could we talk—alone—for a moment?"

Joe had returned home from college for the wedding, and assuming he wanted to put in his own two cents concerning his sister's choice of marriage, Jason nodded. "Sure."

His house was one of the top-selling models on the market, with three bedrooms, living room, kitchen and other necessary rooms, but there were women in every room, reorganizing and putting things away.

"We can go downstairs." The doorway was off the kitchen. Jason opened it, turned on the light and led the way down the stairs.

"Man," Joe said, stepping off the last stair. "This is quite the workshop."

"Thanks." The basement was the entire size of the house above, and unfinished other than a workbench that ran the length of one wall. He'd carried the plans for the crib and cradle down here this morning, and slid them out of the way while clearing a spot near a stool. "Have a seat."

"Thanks." Joe looked a lot like his dad, tall with dark hair, but had his mother's brown eyes.

Jason sat down on another stool.

"I want to apologize for what happened that night years ago," Joe said. "Young and dumb, that is what it was, and I've felt bad about it for years. I hadn't known that you had gotten caught and blamed for everything until the next week, when Randi almost killed me."

Jason had figured the topic would come up. "It's in the past, forgotten." However, he was curious as to why Randi would have been so mad. Other than thinking he'd been vandalizing her family's business. That would have been enough. She loved Air America.

"The night watchman always left a door unlocked," Joe said, "and I'd take people there to get free soda pop, which was stupid, I know, but kids, you know, they always want something to make them stand out. Free sodas got me rides when all I had was a bicycle."

Jason nodded, though he couldn't figure out why a rich kid would want to steal sodas, especially from his own father.

"Sam Wharton had figured out it was me and wanted me to get caught. He hired a different watchman, ordered the doors locked. I thought that I'd show him and break a window." Joe shook his head. "You know how that worked out."

"Sam Wharton has worked for your father for a long time," Jason said, thinking aloud. After meeting Wharton, he didn't want the man anywhere around Randi.

"Yes, he's an ass, but he knows numbers inside and out. Most people wouldn't have missed a few bottles of soda, but Sam could tell you how much each ounce was worth. Like I said, I hadn't known you got caught until Randi nearly cut my life short, and then I fessed up to Dad. I think that was the only time I was truly afraid of my father. He was furious. I went to the judge with him, explained everything. My dad insisted that you be released, but—"

Jason held a hand up to cut him off. "There wasn't any more your father could have done. My father wouldn't let them release me." His father had wanted him to hate the Osterlunds as badly as he had. "I was a minor, with a notebook full of drag racing tickets, which was enough to keep me there until I turned eighteen."

"Aw, man, I'm sorry. I didn't know that." Frowning, Joe asked, "Why didn't you return to school when you got out?"

"I couldn't. Westward High wouldn't allow it. There was only a month left, so I went to night school."

Joe let out a low whistle. "Man, I know it's a lot to ask, but I'm hoping you can forgive me for what I did."

Jason wasn't sure what he'd expected from Randi's family; Joe's sincere apology, her parents' full acceptance of him, their wedding, along with the rest of her family's friendliness was proof of one thing. They loved Randi and would do anything for her. Even accept him into their family. "Like I said, it's forgotten, with no hard feelings."

Joe's cheeks puffed as he let out a breath. "You have no idea how much that means to me. Just between us, I love my sister, but she can be brutal."

"She told you to apologize to me?"

"No, the subject hasn't come up for years. I apologized for me. So there wouldn't be bad blood between us." He chuckled. "And because if the two of us couldn't get along, she'd disown me."

"Jason? Are you and Joey down there?" Randi's voice echoed down the steps.

"Yes, I'm showing him my workshop," Jason replied.

"Do you have a hammer?" she asked.

Jason picked a hammer off the table. "Yes."

"May I borrow it, please? The leg came loose on my dressing table."

Joe shook his head. "Don't let her borrow it," he whispered. "She and tools are a dangerous combination."

Having carried in the dressing table, and the attachable mirror earlier, Jason also picked up a screwdriver, knowing the legs had screws, not nails. "I'll remember that warning," he told Joe before shouting up to Randi, "We're bringing it up!"

"Thank you!" she responded.

Joe slapped his shoulder as they stood. "Welcome to the family, man. It's a little bit crazy, awkward at times, but we all get along and know how to have fun."

Jason laughed as they walked toward the stairway. "Sounds like mine." Ironically, it did sound like his family. Now, at least. After his mother had left, his father had refused to let him see his aunt or cousins.

Randi was waiting for them at the top of the stairs. "I

didn't mean to interrupt, but the leg needs to be nailed tight before we can put the mirror on."

He held up the hammer. "Will it also need a screwdriver?"

Her face scrunched up. "Oh, maybe."

He held up the screwdriver in his other hand. "I got you covered."

She laughed, then whispered, "I had them put it in your bedroom."

"Okay," he whispered.

Chuckling, he headed toward the bedroom. Halfway there, his thoughts shifted to something that wasn't humorous. Her whisper must mean she wanted separate bedrooms.

Chapter Thirteen

"How are you doing, sugarplum?"

Randi pressed the side of her face against her father's shoulder as he tugged her closer to his side. "Good. How are you doing?"

"I can't lie. I need a drink." He kissed the top of her head. "I don't like the sound of giving away my daughter."

The two of them were waiting for their turn to practice walking down the aisle to the altar, while anyone not in the wedding was decorating the church with flowers and big bows made of white netting. "You can have a drink when we get home after the rehearsal. And I'll just be a few miles away. We'll see each other all the time."

He looked down at her, seriously. "You know you can always come to me for anything."

"I know that, Dad."

He nodded. Sighed. "Marriage isn't an easy thing, darling. It takes work. Hard work. On both sides. Give and take. But there is nothing more rewarding than living life with someone who loves you completely. For who you are and who you become. Everyone changes over time. Grows older. Wiser. More handsome." He winked at her. "Love changes over time, too. It grows and becomes wiser, as long as you let it. That's the hard part. You have to let go of what you expect it to be and let it become what it is."

If there was anyone who truly knew what love was, it was her parents. Randi's gaze went to Jason. From what he'd said about his parents, he hadn't grown up with the kind of love that she had.

He was capable of it. She saw it in his eyes as he watched Rachelle roll her wheelchair along the aisle, pretending to throw flower petals. But would he ever love her? *Could* he? There was so much between them that they'd had to call a truce to get through their wedding. She'd said she wouldn't settle for anything less than the kind of love her parents had, yet she was. She had to.

"You two are next," the pastor's wife said.

Randi looked up at her father. If she said she couldn't do this, he'd accept her decision, and call the wedding off, whether she was pregnant or not. She was certain of that, because he loved her. Without love, could she ever be certain of Jason?

"Ready?" her father asked.

She nodded. There was no other option. As Jason had told her, this wasn't about him or her, it was about the baby.

They started down the aisle, one slow step at a time.

By the time they arrived at the altar and her father handed her off to Jason to practice the words they'd vow to each other tomorrow, her entire being was trembling from the inside out.

Jason smiled as he took her hand.

She tried smiling in return, but her lips were trembling too hard. They were sealing their fate, putting themselves into a loveless marriage because of one night. It didn't seem right, didn't seem fair, but it was to the baby inside her. It would need both of them.

* * *

The rehearsal went off without a hitch, even the part where Pastor Williams told Jason he could practice kissing his bride, and before long, everyone, his family and hers, was gathered at her parents' house for dinner and drinks.

She'd lived here her entire life, and loved the big, old house, but as she and Jason roamed from room to room, saying hello to everyone in attendance and making introductions, she couldn't help but wish they were at his house, sitting on the sofa watching television.

Her younger crowd of cousins, and Jason's, were gathered in the dining room near the food and drink tables, and as they arrived in that room, Jason asked, "Why didn't you go out east to college? Joe and all of your cousins have."

Before Randi could answer, Wendy laughed.

"Because all she ever wanted was here," Wendy said.

Although she wanted to give her cousin a glare to shut her up, Randi couldn't. Wendy thought this all was on the up and up, therefore, she had little choice but to shrug at Jason.

The conversation quickly changed to another topic, and another and another.

The entire group was in the midst of laughing, when someone shouted, "Late but still great!"

Randi instantly recognized the voice, and so did half of the others in the room because shouts of "Gus!" echoed off the ceiling.

The big blond buffoon that he was, Gus made a bee-line for her and lifted her off the floor into one of his big bear hugs. "My flight had a layover in Minneapolis and was delayed because of snow."

She returned his hug. "You should have flown Air America."

He laughed and put her down. "I did!" He then shook Jason's hand. "Hey, man, still agitating the gravel?" Slapping Jason's shoulder, Gus continued. "Do you still have that souped-up red Chevy with the V-8?"

"Yes," Jason answered.

"Dig it! That car's cherry! Still drag racing?"

"When I have time," Jason replied.

"Me, too. You should bring that Chevy out to California. We got some screaming drag racing out there, and we can ride motorcycles along the coast year-round." Gus looked at her again. "I can't believe you didn't tell me about this when you were in California."

"Because you can't keep secrets," she lied.

"I kept your secret for years." He chucked her under the chin. "Congratulations, kid. I'm happy for you." Turning to Jason, he said, "Good luck, man." Winking at her, he added, "You'll need it." Laughing at his own joke, Gus moved on, saying hello to others by shaking the men's hands and giving every girl a big bear hug, whether he knew them or not.

"He always makes an entrance," she told Jason, who was looking at her quizzically. She'd never told Gus she'd had a crush on Jason, but had the gut feeling that Gus had known. Just like her mother had. Perhaps she hadn't been as discreet about that as she'd thought.

Jason's gaze followed Gus, with a somewhat contrite expression. "He's a likable guy."

"If you like someone who doesn't have a serious bone in his body," she replied. "He'll never grow up."

His gaze shifted back to her. "Is all this getting to you?"

"No—" The air left her lungs. "Yes. I've never liked parties, not even when I was little."

"Where did you hide out then?"

She had no idea how he knew she'd done that, but he was right. "Why?"

"We can't cut out, but no one will notice if we're gone for a few minutes."

A short break would be wonderful. She took a hold of his hand, led him out of the dining room and to the very end of the hallway. "This is my mother's office now." She opened the door and clicked on the light to reveal the large desk near the windows that overlooked the backyard as well as walls of bookcases and file cabinets. "But it was my great-grandfather's bedroom when I was little. He and I used to sneak in here and play checkers when the house was full."

Jason closed the door behind them. "Why didn't you go to your bedroom?"

She plopped down on the powder-blue sofa across from the desk. "Because it was more fun to play checkers."

He sat down next to her. "I'm sure it was."

Checkers or not, it had been the escape she'd liked. "He died when I was eight, but I still snuck in here, even after it became Mother's office."

"Didn't you want to play with your cousins?"

"Family gatherings were fine. It was dinner parties and other events when people would make their requests that made me want to escape."

"Requests? What sort of requests?"

A knot had formed in her chest, like she'd swallowed something hard and it burned while going down. She'd never told anyone about how those requests had made her feel, but it was pressing to get out now. She knew the benefits of being who she was, had lived with those benefits every day, but those benefits also had their downfalls. "From money to band uniforms and everything in between."

"People asked you for—" He shook his head, staring at her as if he didn't believe her.

"All the time, everywhere I went. My parents are very generous, but the expectations…" It was hard to explain. Hard to understand. "It's always been like that. Even kids. I never knew if they wanted to be friends with me, or my parents' daughter." She looked at him. "You were the only one who acted as if my last name didn't mean anything."

"Really?"

"Yes." She sighed. "I should be used to it by now, but parties always give me a hard knot in my stomach because I know before the night is over, someone will expect something from me."

He touched her chin with one knuckle so softly, was looking at her so tenderly, her heart flipped. Her mouth went dry, too, because she was sure he was going to kiss her. Not because others were nearby, but because he wanted to.

Disappointment flooded her when a knock sounded on the door. She huffed out a sigh. "Come in."

Joe opened the door just wide enough to stick his head inside. "I thought I'd find you here. Uncle James wants to take some family pictures."

"Okay. We're coming."

Jason tugged at the tie around his neck. It wasn't tight—the suit, shirt, all of it fit him perfectly and was comfortable. As comfortable as anything could be for a man who couldn't breathe.

It was here.

His wedding.

To Randi Osterlund.

He was standing at the altar, watching Rachelle roll down the aisle in her flower-coated wheelchair, looking happier than he'd ever seen.

He should be that happy.

Would be if he belonged here.

He didn't.

The reasons went beyond the pomp and circumstance surrounding him. The few minutes he'd spent alone with Randi in her mother's office last night had been an eye-opener that he hadn't expected. He'd always assumed growing up wealthy would have been a walk in the park, but it hadn't been for her. What she'd said had him understanding why Joe had stolen pop from Air America. As payment for rides, to friends who hadn't been friends except for what they could get.

He'd thought of little else after going home last night and wished he could have told her that her last name hadn't mattered to him. But it had. It still did. It had been the reason he'd been afraid to ask her out and the reason he shouldn't be standing here, about to marry her. He hadn't wanted anything in exchange for her friendship back then. It was the opposite. He hadn't had anything to give her. Still didn't. Not in comparison to what she'd always known.

Jason sucked in another breath, held it. He wasn't the poor kid he'd been growing up. In all rights, he had plenty of money, but he wasn't wealthy. Not like the Osterlunds and Albrights and most of the other people in the pews. There was more wealth in this church than rocks on the shores of Lake Michigan. Hell, just the gifts she'd received for her bridal shower filled one of the bedrooms at his house. Her clothes, shoes and other personal items filled the other bedroom and half of his.

There was nothing that he could ever give her that she didn't already have. Ever.

But not even all that made his stomach sink as much as the other thing she'd said last night. People always expected something from her. He hadn't expected anything from her after Rachelle's party, but he'd taken it.

And now, because of that one act, he was taking even more from her.

The music changed, the crowd stood and his heart crawled its way into his throat, completely blocking off his airway as his gaze settled on the couple walking down the aisle. She had a hold of her father's arm, and a long veil covered her face, but he knew how beautiful her face was underneath the lace. The long white dress with lacy sleeves fit her like a glove, and all he could think was that he was going to disappoint her. He didn't want to, but he would.

He already had. In one selfish act. He should have stopped as soon as he'd realized she was a virgin.

He'd stayed away from her for six years, knowing that he wasn't good enough for her and should have continued to stay away from her. This was her wedding, and because of him, she was having to pretend to be happy. Pretend this was what she wanted.

She and her father arrived at the altar, her father handed her off to him, shook his hand and all Jason could think was that being married to him was going to ruin her life. She could have done anything, become whatever she wanted to be, but now she was stuck with him for a husband, and a house that was a fourth of the size of what she was used to, with a child on the way. The pregnancy was an accident. An accident that was his fault.

What if this pregnancy was too much for her? Too much for her delicate frame? What had he done?

The preacher talked, people chuckled and prayed for them.

It wasn't going to help.

He repeated the vows, because there was nothing else that he could do; he put the wedding band on her finger that he'd bought along with the engagement ring, and when told, he kissed her. However, when she melted against him, he held back, didn't let himself get lost in the touch of her lips, because this shouldn't be, and he had no idea how to make this right for her.

As they left the church, he tucked her close to his side in order to shield her from the rice pelted on them while they ran from the church to the limo waiting to give them a ride to the hotel.

It was black. A Cadillac, with tin cans tied to the bumper and Just Married painted on the windows with shoe polish. The seats were leather. Soft. Warm, because the car had been running so they wouldn't need coats.

Horns started honking as the driver pulled the car away from the curb and continued honking as cars pulled in line behind them to follow them all the way to the hotel.

"I guess we did it."

The tone of her voice, the way it cracked, struck him hard. This wasn't her fault and he had to make her life as easy as possible.

"We did." He kissed her forehead. "You look beautiful." That wasn't pretend. There was no one more beautiful. "Really beautiful."

Color tinged her cheeks. "You look very handsome." She laid her head on his shoulder. "And Rachelle was so adorable. It was hard not to cry as I watched her roll down the aisle."

The blaring of a horn filled the car.

"Oh, shirts! Look!" She pointed out the window. "It's Gus and Joey!"

The two guys had pulled their car up next to them and were gesturing for him to roll down the window. Jason did.

"Here! We bought you a present." Joe tossed a box through the window. "Don't use them all before you get to the hotel!" he shouted as Gus hit the gas and swerved in front of the limo just in time to get out of the way of an oncoming car.

"What is it?" Randi asked.

Jason had caught the box, and held it out, showing it to her.

Frowning, she read the label. "It's a box of—"

"Condoms," Jason supplied.

"Those two will never grow up! Buffoons! That's what they are."

He was trying hard not to, but it had been a funny gesture and his smile broke loose.

"I told you it was like I had two brothers," she said. "When one wasn't trying to embarrass me, the other one was."

"Are you embarrassed?" he asked.

"No. It just irritates me that I can't get them back."

He opened the box, took out a package and opened it.

"What are you doing?"

Removing the condom from the packet, he stuffed the condom back in the box and held up the empty packet. "I'm going to give this to them and say thank you."

She giggled. "Good idea."

"Unless you want to give it to them."

Her eyes lit up. "Oh, I do!" She pulled the bottom of her dress over her knee and slid a lacy blue garter down her leg. Kicking off a shoe, she completely removed the garter and handed it to him. "And you can show them this."

He laughed. If this was real—could ever be real—he'd be the happiest man on earth. She was not only the most beautiful woman on earth, she was also fun, charming and had gumption. "You sure?" he asked.

She slipped her shoe back on and took the empty condom packet. "Very."

They arrived at the plush hotel downtown a few minutes later, where Joe and Gus were standing just inside the door, grinning from ear to ear.

With her arm hooked through his, she walked straight to the two of them. Holding up the packet, she said, "Thank you both. That was so thoughtful." She slid the packet in front of the pocket square on Joe's suit, making sure the packet was visible. "A little backseat bingo is exactly what we needed."

With an astonished look, Joe lifted the packet out of his pocket. "It's empty."

"Of course it is," she said.

As Gus and Joe looked at each other, Jason twirled the garter around his index finger. "Bingo."

She giggled and leaned her head against his biceps as they walked toward the ballroom door. "Thank you, I've never seen them speechless before."

He read her eyes, the way she was looking up at him, and knew what she wanted. A kiss. Like she had in front of her cousin the other day. He had to oblige, and told himself once again that it was only for show, and that he was a very good actor.

He kept telling himself that over and over again

throughout the evening. The massive room was decorated as brilliantly as the church had been. Flowers and bows made of netting were everywhere, as were bottles of champagne that were soon filling long-stemmed glasses. The sky was the limit when it came to what her parents were spending on the event, including the impressive meal that was served before the dancing started with music performed by a live band.

Kissing her on demand when someone shouted, "Kiss!" or when she turned her face up toward him, became second nature for the next several hours; so did acting like they were truly in love and the happiest couple in the world.

He kept up the act, all the way to the end, when it was time to leave. In front of the excited crowd bidding them farewell, he scooped Randi into his arms, and carried her out the door, to the once again awaiting limo.

Chapter Fourteen

Randi stood in the bedroom, staring at the door, wondering what she should do. Nothing about the wedding could have been more perfect. It had been glamorous, beautiful and fun. The way he'd carried her out of the hotel, to the car, had been like a fairy tale.

The end of a fairy tale.

That was how they all ended, with the prince carrying his princess into happily-ever-after. That part wasn't true for her and Jason.

The ride to his house had been completely silent.

When she and her mother had started planning, her mother had suggested renting the wedding suite at the hotel for their wedding night, but Randi had declined. She hadn't wanted Tanner to be home alone all night.

She patted the dog's head, who was sitting near her feet, and glanced down at her dress.

It was gorgeous. Her mother had paid seamstresses to help with the sewing of dresses and suits the past two weeks, but not this dress. Although people often begged, her mother always refused to sew wedding gowns. She'd sewn only her own, and now this one.

The dress had long lace sleeves, a fitted bodice with

scalloped neckline, and a layered skirt that was puckered and adorned with dozens of miniature pearls. And it buttoned up the back. There was no way she could get out of it by herself.

Barefoot, because she'd removed as much as she could by herself, she left the room and headed to the basement, where Jason had disappeared upon their arrival home over half an hour ago.

He'd removed his jacket and tie, had the sleeves of his white shirt rolled to the elbows and was sitting on a stool at a large wooden workbench. He was still wearing the golden-brown silk vest and looked as handsome as he had all day.

She stepped off the bottom stair. "What are you working on?"

"Just some plans."

"For the crib and cradle?"

"No. A house. It's work."

His quick, clipped answers stung. "Is our truce over?"

"The truce included no pretending while we're alone."

It had. She pinched her lips together to prevent any sound from emitting.

"It's late," he said. "You should be in bed."

A fair amount of pity washed over her. Pity for herself. Caused in part by pretending all day. There was no one to blame but herself. "I can't unbutton my dress."

He set down the pencil and spun on the stool. "Turn around."

She turned her back to him and grasped a hold of the scalloped neckline as he started unbuttoning the row of silk-covered buttons near her waist.

Her heart was pounding by the time he undid the last button between her shoulder blades. Not only that, her body was throbbing with desire. Wedding night desires.

He didn't say a word, but she heard the stool creak as it spun back around. Silently, she walked back up the stairs, to the bedroom, and got ready for bed. It was foolish to want love when there wasn't any there. No hope for it.

Hours later, and surprised that she'd slept, Randi rolled over, checked the other side of the bed. Empty. The covers, the pillow, untouched.

She rolled onto her back and stared at the ceiling until a thud sounded in the hallway, then she threw back the covers. This was her life. She might as well start living it.

Tanner was lying outside the bedroom door, in the hallway. She gave him a quick pet and, wearing a housecoat over her nightgown and a pair of house slippers, she entered the kitchen to find Jason making coffee. He had on jeans, a white T-shirt and socks, and the mere sight of him made heat swirl deep inside her.

Hero-worship, that was what Wendy called it. Her cousin thought that hero-worship had turned into real love. Trouble was, hero-worship was always one-sided.

"Good morning," she said, walking to the refrigerator to collect the cream.

"Morning," he replied. "Coffee will be done shortly."

She closed the fridge door, and the note stuck on the front made her stomach sink. She'd nearly forgotten.

"What is brunch?" he asked.

He hadn't forgotten that they had to be at her parents' house by ten for brunch and the gift opening. "A meal between breakfast and lunch."

The look on his face was classic, and she couldn't stop a tiny laugh from escaping.

"Why would anyone need a meal between breakfast and lunch?"

"It's for those days when you don't eat breakfast or

lunch, and for special occasions," she replied while carrying the cream to the counter.

He lifted down two cups. "Like gift openings."

"Yes."

He poured coffee into both cups, handed her one and then a spoon. "You already have a room full of presents."

While adding cream and sugar to her coffee, she explained, "Those were from the bridal shower. These are wedding gifts, for both of us. After we eat brunch, we'll open them."

He was leaning against the counter and his cup paused before his face. "We?"

She nodded.

"Before or after we haul them home?"

She took a sip of coffee. "Before."

He grimaced. "I knew you were going to say that."

Giggling, she asked, "Then why did you ask?"

He emptied his cup in little more than one swallow. "Because I was hoping I was wrong."

As she watched him set the cup on the counter, she wondered when he'd been in the bedroom to get the clothes he was wearing. While she'd been sleeping, obviously, but why hadn't it awoken her? He had to have been in the closet and the dresser, and had to have let Tanner out of the room. "Look at the bright side."

He lifted a brow.

"We'll never have to buy a set of glasses, or dishes, or pots or pans, or towels or sheets, ever." She'd already received a large supply of those things for her shower. "I'm going to go get dressed. Do you need to use the bathroom first?"

He shook his head.

If there were other people here, all she'd have to do was lift her face to him and he'd kiss her. Even knowing all she did, she wanted that to happen. Then again, there was nothing different about that. She'd wanted to be kissed by him for years.

She'd vowed to marry him, too. Guess she'd proven that she couldn't have her cake and eat it, too. Carrying her coffee, she left the kitchen and after using the bathroom, returned to the bedroom to get dressed.

Hoping to look bright and cheery, she chose a shimmering pink dress with red ribbing, and red shoes. After brushing her hair, she added a wide red headband and put on a set of string pearls and earrings that her father had given her one year for Christmas.

Before they left the house, Jason changed into black pants and a white shirt under a V-neck black-and-red sweater. He looked so handsome she bit her lip to cover up a tiny moan that rumbled in her throat.

The ride across town didn't take long, and the house was already full of people. Jason's hand cupped her side as they greeted everyone, and though she knew they'd both gone into acting mode again, she found solace in the closeness they portrayed throughout the event.

"Man, I don't know how you sat through that," Joe said while lifting a box out of the trunk. "All that gushing over towels and sheets. I had to cut out, went and talked to Peter."

"Randi enjoyed it," Jason replied, trying to sound diplomatic as he grabbed a box. Truth was, he'd have sat there all day, just for the chance to have her look at him the way she did at times. With her eyes all bright and glowing.

"Good answer, Jason," Randal said, as he, too, took a box out of the trunk. "Take note, Joe, once you get married it's no longer all about you."

Joe guffawed.

"Your mother wrote thank-you notes for the entire first week we were married," Randal told Joe as they walked toward the house.

"It's going to take Randi two weeks to write notes for all this crap," Joe muttered.

Randal shot Joe a look before asking, "Do you have a certain place you want us to put all this stuff, Jason?"

"One of the spare bedrooms for now," he replied. "I'll build some shelves in the basement to store some of it. I have no idea what we'll do with five coffeepots."

Randal laughed. "Are you sure it was only five?"

"No." Jason shifted the box in his hand to unlock the front door. "I lost count after the third one."

"This is a nice house," Randal said. "I understand that you built it."

"Yes." Jason opened the door, and instantly told Tanner, "Stay."

The dog sat, tail thumping as Jason held the door open for the others to enter.

"Nice job, nice craftsmanship," Randal said, walking inside. "I like it. Good-looking dog, too."

"Thanks. That's Tanner. His bark is far worse than his bite."

"You have to see the workshop in the basement, Dad," Joe said. "It's impressive. And I warned him not to let Randi borrow tools." As he walked past, Joe added, "I didn't mention why—that she once flooded our house with only a hammer."

"Down the hall, second door on the right," Jason directed as he stepped into the house behind them.

"In her defense," Randal said, "our house is old. The plumbing had been very old."

"She took a hammer to the sink, Dad," Joe said.

Randal chuckled. "She couldn't get the water to turn off, the handle was stuck, and she thought she could just tap it with a hammer. Suffice to say, she hit it a little too hard."

"Suffice to say you had to have the entire house re-plumbed," Joe said.

"Jason won't have to worry about that happening here, everything is new." In the bedroom, which was already half full of gifts, Randal set down his box and looked around the room. "Did you hand-make all this trim work? The molding?"

Jason set down his box. "Yes." The small amount of work that it took to put up ceiling moldings was well worth it when it came to selling houses. People were willing to pay for the little extras that made his houses unique.

"It looks sharp," Randal said, "really sharp."

If the other man hadn't sounded so sincere, so truly impressed, Jason might have wondered if Randal was only saying that because he was now his father-in-law and this was the house his daughter would now be living in. "Thanks."

Randal continued to point out things he liked about the house as the three of them carried in box after box out of the car. Randal and Joe had ridden with him in his car, and Randi and her mother arrived in another car, also full, before the first one was empty.

"We packed up some of the leftover food," Randi explained as he opened the car door for her. "There was too much for them to eat, and we didn't want it to go to waste. We will carry that in first and then be back to help."

"No, stay inside where it's warm," he told her. "It won't take long for us to get everything hauled in."

After about another dozen trips, both cars were empty,

and he, Randal and Joe were shivering and blowing into their hands as they set down the last of the boxes in the bedroom.

"Come into the kitchen and have some hot coffee," Jolie said, stepping up beside her husband.

Randal put his arm around her shoulders, and Jason noted how Jolie looked up at Randal, and how Randal bent down and kissed her.

That was how Randi had perfected that look, that silent request for a kiss. She must have seen that between her parents her entire life. He'd never seen anything like that growing up. His mother and father had done little more than fight. Day in and day out.

When it came to his children, his child, he knew which one he wished they'd see, and which one they wouldn't.

Randi sidled up next to him, and shivered. "Brrr. Your coat is cold. Take it off."

Laughing and shaking his head, Joe said, "That makes sense, Sis, take off your coat because it's cold."

"It does make sense," she said. "His coat is cold on the outside."

"It's cold outside," Joe said, tossing her a sneer over his shoulder as he walked out of the room.

"Brat!" she hissed.

"Coffee sounds good," Randal said.

As her parents walked out of the room, Randi turned to follow them, and on impulse, Jason wrapped both of his arms around her from behind and pulled her back up against his chest.

She giggled and lifted her shoulder as he nuzzled the side of her neck. "Your face is cold, too."

"I know," he said. "I'm hoping you can warm me up."

She turned around, slowly, cupped his cheeks and whispered, "I'll try."

The kiss she started, and he completely gave in to, raised the temperature of his blood by a good ten degrees. Or more.

"Better?" she asked.

"Much." Questioning if he should have done that, he released her and shrugged out of his coat. "This sure is a lot of stuff."

"It is." Her face scrunched up. "I'm not sure where we are going to put it all." Her hands were on her stomach. "Eventually, we are going to need this room."

"I'll build shelves in the basement," he said, laying a hand on her back to escort her out of the room.

"But that's where your workbench is."

"That's only half of the basement. The other side is empty. I already have the wood down there. It won't take long."

"That would be wonderful! Thank you!"

Her face was alight with excitement. He was amazed that such a little thing could delight her so much. That excitement continued as they entered the kitchen.

"Mother," she said, "Jason has figured out the dilemma. He's going to build shelves in the basement. I won't even have to unbox things. Just store them down there until we need them."

"That is the perfect solution," Jolie replied.

Jason wasn't sure that Randal and Joe had been prepared to build shelves, but by the time they were done drinking their coffee, it had been decided the three of them would work on the shelves while Randi and her mother decided what should be stored on them.

He'd planned on putting shelves in that area. Had the lumber stacked in the basement, cut and ready to be assembled, but had never completed the project because he'd needed someone to hold the long boards in place while he nailed them.

It turned out to be an enjoyable project, and the stories that Randal and Joe told him about Randi during her growing-up years had them all laughing.

"You men have been laughing the entire time you've been down there," her mother shouted down the steps while they were putting away the tools. "Come upstairs and eat and tell us what's so funny!"

"Not on your life," Joe whispered. "Randi will kill me if she knows I told you about how awful her cooking was."

Randal slapped Jason's shoulder. "Don't worry. It's gotten much better."

Supper continued to be a fun family affair. Jason had known those, but only after his father had died and he'd started spending more time with his cousins. The differences between his father and Randal were stark, and embarrassing. He'd been ashamed of who he was for years, of who his father was and how his mother had left them. The humiliation of that had been tough for a kid. He'd thought he'd gotten over it but knew he hadn't. Some things were just too embedded in a person to ever go away.

After the meal the men helped him carry the boxes that Randi designated downstairs, and then the others prepared to leave.

While giving him a hug goodbye, Jolie whispered, "Thank you for making my daughter so happy."

Jason nodded, but wasn't convinced he would be able to make Randi happy. Not completely. Not ever. The time would come when she would regret marrying him. Living in his small house instead of the huge one she was used to. How could she not? There was nothing that he could ever give her that she hadn't already had.

"I'm sorry that took all day," Randi said as he closed the door. "But the good news is that the bedroom is cleared out except for a stack of towels that I want to wash before putting away."

Last night when they'd arrived home, he'd headed straight to the basement, because the want to carry her into the bedroom had been overwhelming, and was feeling much the same right now. Taking her to bed again would only make him want her more, want it to happen again and again.

"Jason?"

Giving his head a clearing shake, he said, "That sounds good, about the room, the towels." Then, needing an excuse, and escape, he walked past her. "There's a shelf in the basement that I need to reinforce. There are some heavy things on it."

"Do you need any help?"

"No. None."

Chapter Fifteen

Randi forced herself not to follow Jason as he disappeared into the kitchen. Every time they were alone, he didn't even want to be in the same room as her. If this was a work issue, she'd walk up to him and lay down how things are going to be, period. She'd had to learn to fight her own battles and wasn't afraid to do so, but this was so different. She didn't want to fight with him.

Feeling the frustration clear to her bones, she walked down the hall into the bedroom to collect items to take a bath before going to bed.

Reclined in the tub, with her eyes closed and fully submerged in warm water, she could hear the pounding of a hammer below her, in the basement. If only…

What? If only she wasn't pregnant?

She didn't wish that.

She laid her hands on her stomach, thinking about exactly how that had happened. Every aspect, and a groan rumbled in her throat as heat swirled inside her and specific parts tingled with their own memories, creating desires she couldn't control.

The ringing of the phone shot her upright. She'd forgotten to call Wendy, set up a time to meet her cousin before she flew out tomorrow.

Leaping out of the tub, she grabbed a towel to wrap around her torso as she hurried to answer the phone.

She pulled open the door, rushed into the hallway and collided with something hard. It took a brief second to realize it was Jason she'd run into, who'd caught her by her arms.

Jason without a shirt on.

Her palms were plastered against his bare flesh, and her mind instantly returned to where it had been in the bathtub. So did her body. She had to swallow against how certain muscles contracted.

She could feel the rise and fall of his chest, of how his breathing quickened.

"Are you okay?" he asked.

She wasn't, but nodded.

He released his hold on her. "The phone—" He stopped because the ringing had stopped.

Not sure what to do, she pressed her hands harder against his chest, pushing herself backward as she took a step back, separating them. The action wasn't thought out. Without her holding it up, her towel fell, exposing her breasts. Exposing all of her.

They both acted at the same time, bending down to retrieve the towel, and smacked heads so hard it sent them both stumbling backward, against the walls of the hallway, with the towel on the floor between them.

He bent down, picked up the towel and as he straightened, mumbled something.

Randi wasn't sure what, but didn't care, either, because then his lips were on hers. His hands cupping her face, holding it as his tongue entered her mouth, igniting the flames that had been smoldering inside her for weeks.

A storm erupted, one of passion, of unmet desires, needs that had been building every time they'd kissed, touched, the past several days. It was mutual, his hands were as frantic as hers, touching, feeling, caressing.

He was the only man she'd ever craved, ever wanted, but had never known something could overtake a person so fully. Nor had she ever known such desperation. Nothing else mattered. Just this. Him and her, coming together. She found the waistband of his pants, unfastened them.

"Randi—"

She stopped him from saying more by covering his mouth with hers. It would be impossible to live with him and never kiss him, never— She pulled her mouth off his, took a step back. Her breathing was coming hard and fast, so were her thoughts. "I know you don't love me, Jason. I don't expect you to, but we are married, and married people have sex."

Silent, he stared at her.

She couldn't read his face, didn't know what he was thinking, but kept her chin up, even as her insides began to tremble. Their marriage had to have something or it would never last. "We both have needs and there's no reason for us not to satisfy them."

He let out a low growl, picked her up and carried her into the bedroom. They landed on the bed together, arms locked around one another and kissing wildly.

A crinkling sound reminded her that she still had on her shower cap. Any other time, that might have embarrassed her, at how she must look, but Jason didn't seem to care. Therefore, neither did she.

His hand was between her legs, teasing her, pleasing her, making her body feel fully alive, but it wasn't enough. She knew the full pleasure of having him inside her and nothing except that would ever be enough. "Now, Jason. Please."

He separated them long enough to remove his pants.

During that time, because even the cap felt like a restraint keeping them apart, she tore off her shower cap.

"You are so beautiful," he whispered as he lowered himself on top of her, entering her at the same time.

Overwhelmed with the pleasure, she couldn't speak. Memories and instinct had already taken over. She met his hips with hers, thrust for thrust. Met his lips kiss for kiss. The perfect connection and friction of their bodies made tension grow inside her like a balloon getting bigger and bigger. Every stroke of him moving inside her thrilled her more and more, knowing she would soon reach her limit.

She bit down on her lip, trying to hold off, because she didn't want this to stop. Not yet. It was too wonderful. He smelled so good, felt so good. It was enough to make her believe there could be hope for their marriage. But that wasn't what this was about. This was just him and her, and what they had right now.

The tension reached its peak inside her, she arched into him, held on to him and welcomed the burst of pleasure that consumed her.

During that moment she comprehended it wasn't the pleasure, the act of making love, that thrilled her, it was the fact that neither of them was pretending. At this moment everything between them was real.

Jason refused to let anything else in while losing himself in bringing Randi to full pleasure. She'd wanted him, needed him, and despite knowing it wasn't going to change anything, he couldn't deny giving her exactly what she'd wanted.

He'd wanted it, too, and the pleasure of being inside her, of having her warm wetness cloaking him, the smell of her surrounding him, was beyond bliss. It was out of this world like nothing he'd ever known.

Her body tightened, clenched onto him and then shuddered as she gasped, moaned his name.

It was his undoing and he succumbed to the waves of pleasure that washed over him as his release hit, and lingered, sucking all of the strength out of his body until he felt completely spent. Completely satisfied. Completely content.

She made him feel like that. Content. She made him feel other things, too. Things he'd never felt before. At times that made him feel helpless, like he was sinking into an abyss, and if he went too deep, he'd never be able to climb out.

It was a struggle, because he wasn't sure that he wanted to climb out.

Still breathing hard, he rolled off her, knowing that any moment now regret would strike. For her sake, he wished he were someone else. Someone who could love her, provide for her, in the way she deserved.

She snuggled up to his side, kissed his shoulder blade, laid a hand on his chest. "Don't leave. Please. Stay here next to me."

He covered her hand with his, squeezed it.

She kissed his shoulder blade again, then rested her cheek there and sighed sweetly.

Jason lay there, half wishing he'd stayed in the basement, and half-glad that he hadn't. He'd figured she was in the bathroom when he saw the door had been closed.

He'd decided to take advantage of the empty bedroom and change out of his shirt and sweater, and put on a T-shirt, fully prepared to sleep on the couch again tonight. That was where he'd be right now, if the phone hadn't rung, and if she hadn't barreled out of the bathroom like the house was on fire at the same time that he'd left the bedroom.

She'd looked so adorable with that bright pink-and-white polka-dotted plastic cap covering her hair, wearing nothing but a towel. He'd gone hard instantly, and when her towel had fallen to the floor, he'd started throbbing like nobody's business.

The rest had been inevitable. The past few days of kissing and hugging had left them both with unmet needs. He hadn't wanted to complicate things more than they already were, but that was impossible. And they were married, going to have a baby together. A little tiny life, a child, who would deserve to grow up happy, being loved and not wanting for anything.

Like she had.

He could make that happen for their baby. He would make that happen. The baby would have everything that he'd never had. That included a mother. For the baby's sake, for Randi's sake, he had to do everything he could for them.

Lifting her hand, he kissed her fingers that were curled around his.

She let out a soft, sweet-sounding little moan, and then rolled so that portion of her upper body was lying across a section of his chest. Running her fingers through his hair, she looked him in the eye. "I didn't plan a honeymoon because I didn't know what we'd do with Tanner."

Blood rushed to his groin so fast air hitched in his lungs. "He could stay with Lottie and Stu." Her hair was flowing over the front of her shoulders, hiding her breasts from his sight. But he could feel them. One against his upper arm, the other against his chest. Sucking in a breath of air, he asked, "Where had you wanted to go?"

"Nowhere in particular." She hooked a leg over his thigh. "Where would you have wanted to go?"

"Nowhere in particular."

Still combing her fingers through his hair, she asked, "Could you have taken the time off work?"

Parts of him were starting to throb, jolt. "Yes, I could spare a few days. What about you?"

"I already took this week off work, I thought there would be things I'd need to do."

"Like what?"

She wiggled her hips closer to his. "Putting things away, writing thank-you notes, little things like that."

"Do you want to go somewhere?"

She kissed the side of his jaw. "Packing, traveling, would take time."

He was following her thoughts completely, and her actions. "And we'd have to drop off Tanner."

"He might get lonely for you."

Jason ran his hand down her back. "And you."

She giggled, and slid a bit more of her body on top of his. "We could have a honeymoon here."

He was more than ready for round two. Grasping her hips, he lifted her, settled her body on top of his. "Starting when?"

She tapped her chin. "I'm not sure. When do you think we should start?"

He ran his hands down her sides, across her lower back. Their game of questions was intensifying every touch. "Probably not now."

She wiggled against him, kissed the side of his neck. "Probably not."

"And probably not like this." He reached between them, guided himself into her and wasn't sure which was more gratifying, entering her slick heat, or watching the way her eyelids fluttered.

Arching upward slowly, she lowered onto him fully. "Probably not."

He began to move. "Or like this."

"Or like this." Rising and lowering, she matched his every movement.

Her face glowed with the pleasure she was receiving and giving. He took it slow, taking time to fully experience every nuance, but before long they were both breathing hard, working together to reach their completion.

Knowing she was as close as he was he covered her mouth with his, kissed her deeply as completion struck, shrouding them in intense pleasure.

First thing the following morning he called Stu, told him to let the crews know that he was taking the week off, and that they could call him if needed, but he hoped they wouldn't. Other than later that day, when her cousins and brother stopped by to say goodbye before flying back to school, he and Randi were in full honeymoon mode.

The entire week was one that Jason figured would have fulfilled every man's dream. The closeness and familiarity that grew between them enhanced all aspects of living together. Including in the bedroom. Randi was not only receptive, she was also adventurous and demanding in a way that not only suited him, it thrilled him as well.

She was spontaneous, too. Showed it by joining him in the shower, sitting down next to him on the sofa wearing nothing but a robe and bringing him breakfast in bed stark naked.

More than once, the thank-you cards that he helped

her complete by licking stamps and envelopes had been left on the table as other needs overtook them.

He enjoyed listening to her sing along to the radio as she cooked, her body swaying to the rock-and-roll songs, and how when a particular favorite song of hers would come on she'd make him dance with her. He'd soon learned that many songs were particular favorites of hers.

They left the house a few times, to go out and eat and buy groceries, but for the most part, they stayed home, ate, slept and made love.

He couldn't say he was pretending, and neither was she, yet it felt that way, as if they were playing house with adult actions.

Lots of real adult actions.

So real that when the following Monday rolled around, they were both so used to staying up late, enjoying each other, they overslept.

It was a mad dash of dressing, brushing teeth and eating toast while drinking coffee. The only time they slowed was for a long, leisurely kiss in the garage before they climbed into separate vehicles and left for work.

At the parking lot of the apartment complex he was remodeling, Jason climbed out of his truck, tossed his keys in the air and caught them while closing the door.

Then the location hit him, and it was like being hit with a bucket of cold water. He remembered the day he'd watched Randi walk to her car. A week later he'd found out she was pregnant with his child.

A shiver rippled his spine. She'd become a part of his life since then. A major part of his life, but nothing else had changed. Nothing about him.

The passion between them was electrifying, but that wouldn't always be enough.

Chapter Sixteen

Randi was on cloud nine. An entire week of living with Jason had been exactly as she'd dreamed it would be for years. She even smiled at and said good morning to Sam—after she'd dropped off a stack of thank-you notes in the mail room—which made her laugh, because he'd done little more than scowl at her.

She was still going through phone messages when her father entered her office. Jumping to her feet, she met him in the center of the room, returned his hug and kissed his cheek.

"You're looking more radiant than ever," he said.

"Just happy."

"Then I'm happy, too." He lifted a brow. "Other than the fact that, since seeing your house, your mother is talking about having Jason build us a new house."

"I might be able to pull some strings." Pride filled her as she walked around her desk and sat in her chair. "But it will be a long wait. He's juggling several job sites at the moment. Besides building a couple of houses, he's remodeling an apartment building downtown."

"He told me about that while putting up the shelves in your basement." Her father sat down across from her desk.

"Thank you for that, Dad. Thank you for everything."

"You're welcome. It was my pleasure and your mother's." He leaned back, glanced around the room. "Were you surprised to see this place still standing after being gone over a week?"

"No, I knew it would be fine. You were here."

"And others."

She'd expected this to be coming when she'd returned from California. Other things had taken precedence.

"I know you and Sam haven't always seen eye to eye," her father continued. "And I've talked to him about a few issues lately, but if you're interested in running this place someday—"

"Of course I am," she interrupted. "Why wouldn't I be?"

"You're married now, with a husband to consider and a baby on the way."

"That's not going to change anything. Jason doesn't expect me to quit my job. Mom worked while Joey and I were growing up."

"I know. That was a decision that she and I came to together, as all of our decisions have been."

"Jason and I will—"

"That," he said, cutting her off, "will be between you and Jason. What I want to talk about is you. If you do end up overseeing things here, you need to realize what an asset Sam will be to you. He's been here a long time. He can be brash and opinionated, but he knows what he's doing. There's not a dime that rolls in or out of this place that he can't account for, and I rely on that. Whoever is overseeing things will need to rely on that, too."

She'd had talking-tos from her father before, and a part of her knew she needed to hear this. Yet, at the same time, she wanted her father to understand her frustration. "I know he's great at accounting, and I'll try harder to appreciate that. But I believe we can do other things that if done right, will not only cut costs in some areas, but could increase overall revenue."

"A washing bay?"

"Yes."

"On Jason's land."

"No. I admit, I considered that, but then did more research. That's why I went to California. Not just to visit our ticket sales office there, but to look at land. If we were to build a bay there, we could not only wash our planes at a significant savings, we could wash planes for other airlines."

Elbows on the arms of the chairs, he tapped his fingers together, an action he was known to do. "Land costs? Construction costs?"

"I've put estimates together. It'll be an investment, but one we should be able to recoup in three years." She'd heard numerous times about how, when he'd bought the original plane company from Carl Jansen, he'd expected it to take five years to recoup and start generating income. It hadn't taken him that long, and it wouldn't take her three years to recoup the costs of the bay, either. "The preliminary numbers could shift slightly once we actually buy the land and contract the construction, but not by much."

"What about the companies that wash our planes now? And those of other airlines?"

Frowning, she asked, "What about them?"

"Have you spoken to any of them? Remaining competitive is important, but while doing so, it's imperative that you think of the overall industry. We've worked with some of the companies a washing bay would affect for years. They depend on our business to meet their goals, just like we depend on them to make ours. Receiving without giving never works out in the long run. Not in business, or life. It has to balance out, honey, everything does."

She understood what he was saying, and hadn't looked as deeply into things as she should have, but she would. "You're right. I'll look into that. Put some more planning in place before going any further."

"Take your time." He gestured toward her desk as he stood. "You have a lot of work to catch up on, so I'll let you be."

Although she was disappointed, she'd rather have learned mistakes now than later. "Thanks, Dad. I was getting ahead of myself."

With a nod, he winked at her and walked to the door. Before opening it, he said, "Your mother will be calling you later, wants to know if you and Jason could join us for dinner one night this week."

"Okay." She picked up her messages again, to start reading through them. "Any night will work."

"She's going to ask you to check with Jason, and I suggest you do."

"I will, but I know any night will be fine."

He acted as if he was going to say something more, but didn't.

She stared at the door for a moment, wondering what he hadn't said, until she figured the dinner date was to let them know he'd chosen the date to announce his bid for senate. That had to be it.

As she turned back to her messages, she thought of one thing her father had said. That everything had to balance. Give and take. Jason had given her everything, but she hadn't given him anything. She didn't have anything to give. Didn't own anything.

She stood, moved to the window and stared out it. The

only thing she could give him would be proof that she didn't want his land.

Her phone rang, she answered it, listened to the fire brewing over the backlog in licenses being renewed and promised to see to it right away.

The good thing about all the work that had piled up was it made the day fly by, and as if they'd timed each other, she and Jason arrived at the turn onto his street, each from a different direction, at the same time. He waved for her to go first, and when they arrived at his garage, he jumped out of his truck, told her to stay put as he opened the garage door.

A mutual welcome-home kiss was shared before they left the garage, and Tanner greeted them as soon as they entered the backyard. Jason asked about her day as they walked to the house. She told him about a few things, but not the washing bay or talking with her father, and then asked about his day.

He told her that a representative for an investment company had stopped by the apartment building, interested in buying the property once it was completed.

"That's wonderful," she said.

"Maybe, but we'd make more money in the long run by renting out the apartments."

"That's true, but you'd have the expense of managing the renters."

He said he was aware of that and they continued to discuss the options, along with a few other subjects while preparing supper. She also told him that her parents would like them to come over for dinner one night this week.

"I can make any night work," he said. "Whatever is good for you."

She kissed him. "I knew you'd say that. Should I tell them Friday?"

He kept his arms around her. "Friday will be fine." He kissed her again. And again. Until supper was forgotten and she was too happy to care.

The bliss filling her remained all week, and well into the month of March, until Sam walked into her office one morning and tossed an old expense report on her desk. "All flight tickets need to be approved by the immediate supervisor. Your ticket to California wasn't. Without approval, the ticket price will be deducted from your next paycheck."

Her immediate supervisor was her father, and she had never needed to get a ticket approved before. A single ticket was not the issue he was making it out to be, and she wasn't going to make it be, either. "All right. Take it out of my pay."

He stared blankly for a moment, then sneered. "Your father gave up on the Heim land years ago. The cost of keeping a washing bay heated during our winters would be counterproductive."

Her spine quivered. "Exactly what is your point?"

He shrugged, turned, but stopped at the door. "Does your father know you married Heim just for his land? Or is it the other way around? He married you for what he can get?"

Anger filled her and she jumped to her feet, but he was already gone. Grabbing the expense report, she balled it up and threw it at the door, then her knees gave out. Sam was an ass, knew how to strike a nerve, but that was too close to home.

That afternoon Sam's comment was still twisting her mind in knots. Jason was also in those knots. She'd thought she could deal with him not loving her. That what they had was enough, but was it? Would everyone think like Sam did? That the only reason Jason had married her... No, they'd soon learn it was because she'd been pregnant.

Her door opened and her father stepped in. "Got a minute to talk?"

She tried to clear her mind. "Sure."

"Are you okay?"

"Yes." She tapped the stack of papers on her desk. "Just have a lot going on."

"I want to discuss a couple of decisions I've made," her father said.

"Okay." Hands clasped, she set them on her desk. She'd been in contact with several other airlines about her California washing bay, and was proud of the collaborative efforts that were now in place. Her father would be impressed when it all came together. There was still a lot to do, but she was feeling even better about it than before. Especially after Sam's comment. Once she was his supervisor, she'd put Sam in his place. But that wouldn't help the issue between her and Jason.

"Your mother and I started this business shortly after we got married," her father said while sitting down in front of her desk. "It would never have been this successful without her. We started her clothing business at the same time, and found out she was pregnant with you in the midst of it all. Every decision we made, we made together, and after we found out you were on the way, we agreed on the importance of hiring people to help us with both companies, because dedicating time to each other and to you and Joe was always at the top of our list. My bid for senate is a decision we both made, too. Win or lose, we are in it together."

"I know you'll win, Dad, and that you'll do good things for our country."

"I hope to." He leaned forward, set his hands on the top of her desk. "You are a great asset to this company, and I'll be extremely proud to see you at the helm of it."

Her heart skipped a beat.

"Someday."

A hint of shiver tickled her spine.

"I want you to know that on Saturday, when I announce my run for senate, Wayne Klein will be in attendance." He paused for a moment. "I'll be announcing that he'll be the interim president until I make a more final decision after the election in November."

Her heart sank and she forced herself to sit straight, to breathe. Wayne Klein oversaw flight acquisitions and sales and was not someone she would have considered for the position.

"I know that's a disappointment to you, and I'm afraid this next one is going to be, too."

She lifted her chin.

"I want you to put off the washing bay project. Wait until next year. You have a lot happening in your life, and should be enjoying this time, not making extra work for yourself."

Put off the washing bay? She couldn't do that. She had to open that bay in California to prove to Jason that she doesn't want or need his land. Prove to others, too.

"As long as I'm here," Jason said to the banker, Adam Freeman, "I wanted to let you know that I've added a name on the title of my land." He'd borrowed against the land in order to buy the apartment building downtown, and while at the courthouse, paying taxes on the building, he had them add Randi's name to all of his properties.

"Always good to have things in order. We appreciate you letting us know. Let me get your file." Freeman pushed a button on the phone, requested the file through an intercom system and clicked off the button. "How is the remodeling of the apartment building going?"

"Ahead of schedule, planning on having tenants in the building by June instead of August," Jason replied. "I just stopped by to make a payment on my loan, but like I said, thought I'd go ahead and have you note the name change." He only had a few payments left, but if anything were to happen to him, he wanted things in Randi's name. His worth wasn't close to her father's, and he certainly wasn't planning on anything happening to him, but when his father had died, he'd had to jump through hoops to hold on to the property and get it changed into his name. That had been due to owed back taxes, which he'd kept current ever since.

"I was down near that building a couple of weeks ago. Prime location. With the shortage of housing right now, that could be a real moneymaker."

"I'm counting on that," Jason replied. He'd declined the offer to sell the building to the investment group. He'd bought it with the long-term plan of it generating a regular income. That had been his plan when he built his first house, to rent it out, but the first people to look at it wanted to buy it instead. He'd sold it to them, and invested that money in the next one and so on and so on. He didn't need that quick turnaround of cash now. His company had a solid, comfortable base and the only reason he didn't pay off the loan on the land was because it kept an open line of credit if he needed it. That had taken years to build up. Though the land was worth it, the banker had been cautious of loaning him more than a portion of the value.

A woman entered the office and laid a file on Freeman's desk and left as quietly as she'd entered.

Freeman, a middle-aged man with salt-and-pepper hair and thick, black-rimmed glasses, flipped open the folder and shuffled through the papers. "Here it is. What name have you added?"

"Randi, spelled R-A-N-D-I. Last name Heim."

Freeman's frown grew as he wrote the name. "Randi, that's a unique name. I've only heard it once before. A local girl."

"Randi Osterlund."

"You've heard of her?" Freeman asked.

Jason had to hold back his grin. "I married her." Married life had suited him well the past few weeks. Coming home to her every night and waking up next to her was paradise. One he didn't want to disrupt.

Freeman's brows were raised. "I heard she got married. Congratulations."

"Thank you." Jason stood. "And thanks for adding her name to that."

"Wait a minute." Freeman held up a hand. "Looking at your loan here…"

"Is there a problem?"

"No, other than we certainly can increase the amount, and I'm sure we can do something about the interest rate as well."

Jason gritted his teeth together at the quiver that raced over his neck. Three years ago he'd practically had to beg to get the loan. "No, I'll have it paid off shortly."

"Well, perhaps there's another project you're looking at? Another apartment complex? We could write up the loan today, deposit it into your account, so it's there when you need it."

Jason would bet the Osterlunds didn't bank here, and

Freeman would love to have them as customers. Them. Not him. "No, that's not necessary."

Freeman closed the file. "I understand your financial situation has changed since your wedding, but our bank has enjoyed doing business with you, and hope you will continue utilizing our service."

Jason had to pull his jaw apart to say, "Have a good day."

He left Freeman's office, left the bank, and once in his truck, pushed the hot air out of his lungs. Freeman had merely been doing his job of drumming up business for the bank. That didn't surprise him, nor had Freeman's comment.

He'd spent years digging himself out of the poor house he'd been born in, and before that he'd spent years hardening his heart. He'd had to. Watching his parents verbally tear each other apart day after day, night after night, had been hell. The two, the lack of money and the fighting, had merged into one, making him into who he'd become. It had also provided him with the ability to build an armor around himself, one strong enough that everything bounced off him. Except for one thing.

Randi had put a kink in that armor years ago. Even from afar, she'd touched something deep inside him. Made him want things, dream of a different life, to the point he'd given in, and had failed. Ended up in reform school.

He'd rebuilt that armor, swore he'd never be that weak again, never give someone that much control over him again, but once again, she'd put a kink in his defenses the day she'd shown up at his house asking to buy his land.

Since then she'd completely penetrated the armor he'd built around himself. He could feel her inside him, all the time. Her smile, her touch, her sighs of pleasure, were like sledgehammers battering that armor until she'd gotten inside him.

That scared him. If he couldn't protect himself, how could he protect her? Not from him, but from his reputation, his past. Which were one and the same.

Jason started the truck.

He'd already failed to protect her by getting her pregnant.

With his gut churning, Jason shifted the truck into gear and headed toward his accountant's office to give her the receipts for the taxes and loan payment. He'd hired Brenda Owens to do all of his book work three years ago, and it had been the best move he'd made.

For his business.

If only he could get his personal life in order.

It had been in order, had been rowing along just fine. Until Randi had shown up out of the blue. Is that how she'd leave, too? He'd come home to an empty house one day. Have to learn how to live without her like he'd had to learn to live without his mother. Randi didn't need to leave him for a rich man. She had more wealth at her fingertips than he'd ever have.

At some point she'd get tired of him.

Of all the pretending.

Living with her was amazing. All parts of it. But it was pretend.

Her car wasn't in the garage or the driveway when he arrived home, but the phone was ringing. Concerned, he rushed inside to answer it.

"Hey, Jason, it's Gus, how are you doing?"

Jason was relieved and frustrated at the same time. It

was past the normal time she usually got home. "Fine. You?"

"Can't complain. I got Randi's message, is she there?"

"No." He glanced at the back door. "She's not home from work yet."

"I just called her office, there was no answer." Gus paused before asking, "Will you be coming to California with her?"

Jason's entire body went stiff. "No."

"That's a drag. Maybe next time. Tell Randi I'll call her tomorrow."

Knots were forming in Jason's stomach. "I will."

"Thanks! Later, gator."

"Later." Jason hung up the phone and stilled himself, trying to keep his thoughts at bay. Her father had said a washing bay, here or in California, wasn't on the agenda right now, yet she must be pursuing it. There was no other reason for her to go to California. If she'd defy her father, she'd defy anyone. Especially him. And what did Gus have to do with it?

He'd been jealous of Gus for years. Not because of Albright's money, but because of the fact that Randi had always been with Gus. She claimed it was because of their families' friendship, but friends could become more a whole lot easier than enemies could.

He didn't want to jump to conclusions and wouldn't. They were married. There had to be a modicum of trust between them. Trust. Not love. Their marriage wasn't based on love.

It wasn't based on trust, either.

It was based on sex. The outcome of sex. No matter how amazing that was, it wasn't a solid foundation. Or enough to keep her happy.

Tanner barked and shot out the doggie door.

Jason walked to the door, held it open as she walked toward the house. His body reacted to seeing her, filled with a familiar warmth that he had no control over.

"Hi." She held up a bag. "I stopped at the meat market. How do pork chops sound for supper?"

"Fine."

She arrived at the door. Kissed him before walking inside. "How long have you been home?"

"Just a few minutes." He closed the door.

"That's why you still have your coat on." She set the bag on the table and unbuttoned her coat.

He removed his coat and took hers, hung them both up in the laundry room. "Gus called for you."

She stiffened and paused in emptying the bag.

He leaned against the wall, crossed his arms. "He tried your office first."

"Okay. Thanks." She lifted out a package of wrapped meat. "Baked or fried?"

Any other day, he'd be helping her, but today he forced himself to stay put. "Doesn't matter."

She lifted out a few other items, carried them to the refrigerator. "How was your day?"

"Fine. Yours?"

"It was fine. I think I'll bake the pork chops and some potatoes."

He pushed off the wall to cross the room and help her. "Gus mentioned you going back out to California."

She stood with the fridge door open for a few seconds before closing it. "Possibly. I won't know for a while. Maybe you could go with me. See a drag race or ride Gus's motorcycle along the coast."

She'd just come up with that. He could tell by the way she was fidgeting.

The phone rang and the way she nearly ran across the room to answer it, confirmed there was something going on. Something she didn't want him to know about.

Chapter Seventeen

Randi's relief at hearing Lottie's voice was massive. After listening, she said, "Just a minute, I'll ask Jason." Covering the mouthpiece, she told him, "It's Lottie. Everyone is meeting at Mama's for hamburgers in an hour. She wants to know if we can join them."

He shrugged. "I don't care."

"We'll be there," she told Lottie, and hung up the phone. "I'm going to change my clothes."

He nodded while putting the package of pork chops in the fridge.

She questioned telling him about her day, about her plans to continue with the washing bay project, but despite how wonderful things were going between them, they were pretending. The only time they weren't was when they were making love. There were no barriers between them then.

But there was something missing. She could feel it. Knew what it was.

Love.

He didn't love her, and he didn't want her to love him. Therefore, she wouldn't. She'd save all of her love for their baby. But she'd still prove that she didn't want his land.

No matter what her father said, she wasn't going to give up on that project. He could appoint anyone he wanted to oversee the company. In a way, he was right. She wasn't ready for that commitment. Didn't have time. She had to get this washing bay built, in California.

After quickly changing into a pair of hem-cuffed blue jeans and blue paisley-print blouse, she brushed her hair into a ponytail, secured it with a white scarf and put on a pair of black-and-white saddle shoes.

As the radio filled the car with rock-and-roll music while they drove to the café, her thoughts continued to twist and turn. Everything from wondering if their baby would have Jason's amazing brown eyes to estimating how quickly she could find a construction company in California to build the washing bay. Gus had connections out there, and she was counting on him helping her.

The moment they walked into the café, all of her other thoughts vanished and she grabbed a hold of Jason's arm. "Look at her!"

Jason nodded and swallowed, as if he couldn't speak. Together, they rushed to where Rachelle, fitted with leg braces and using crutches, stood near a booth.

"The doctor said it's time I can start walking again," Rachelle exclaimed. As if further explanation was needed about her wearing her flower girl dress, she added, "Mom said I could wear my wedding dress to celebrate."

Kneeling down in front of her, Jason gave Rachelle a hug. "This certainly requires a celebration."

Randi hugged Rachelle as soon as he released the girl. "Yes, it does, and you look so beautiful!"

The party became a real celebration with food and dancing—that included Rachelle, albeit for only a short time because just standing with the braces tired her out after not being able to use her legs for so many months.

That didn't stop the little girl from making the most of the evening, though, nor anyone else, and the party was still on Randi's mind the following day as she drove home from work.

Jason's entire family accepted her, treated her like family, but they had to know her family was the reason why he'd been sent to reform school. Had they forgiven her because they thought he loved her? Would that all change when the truth came out? It would eventually. Once the baby was born, anyone who could count would figure out why they'd gotten married.

That thought hung on, stuck in her head. Left her unable to think of anything else.

Later that night, after they'd climbed into bed, she couldn't remain silent and flipped on her side, stared at the moonlit shape of his back as he lay on his side, facing away from her. "Jason?"

"Hmm?"

"Did you ever think of getting married? Before I became pregnant," she quickly added.

He lay there, silent for a moment, and then flipped onto his back, looked at her and then at the ceiling. "I never thought I would get married."

Her heart sank a bit more. "Why?"

"Probably because of my mother."

"Because of how she left?"

He nodded. "I guess a lot of people get tired of who they are at some point in their life. What they'd once wanted changes and they get stuck. Trapped. Feel they have to get out."

She swallowed and the lump in her throat nearly choked her. Trapped. That was what their marriage had done to him. Trapped him.

Tears pressed hard and knowing she couldn't keep

them at bay, she kicked the covers off, flung her legs off the bed.

"Where are you going?" he asked.

"The bathroom," she managed to say on her way to the door.

Once inside the bathroom, she leaned the back of her head against the door, closed her eyes and kept them closed until the burning eased. Until she could swallow. Until she could breathe.

"Randi? Are you all right in there?"

She shot across the room and flushed the toilet even though she hadn't used it. "I'm fine."

"You didn't even turn on the light."

After crossing the room again, she opened the door. "Didn't need to. There's a window."

"It's dark outside."

She entered the bedroom and crawled back into bed. "Not that dark." It was far darker inside her.

He got under the covers, curled an arm around her waist. "Are you okay?"

Her body reacted to his touch. That wasn't pretend. Her body craved him. Worse yet, so did her heart. Could she go on pretending that wasn't the case? Forever? That thought hurt. Badly.

The following evening, at a dinner party where her father announced he was running for senate to the wider group of the Osterlunds' friends and family, Randi realized just how big the trap was that she'd put Jason in. She'd been in it her entire life.

She'd been trying to escape it her entire life, too. Though her parents were amazing people and her home life wonderful, she had always felt trapped, confined. That that was the way she had to live. Not dictated by her parents, but from outside forces because of their social standing. Everyone always expected something from them.

She loved her parents and was proud of them, proud to be their daughter. Her family were the only people who loved her for who she was, and all this pretending that Jason was now having to do, too, was eating away at her.

Beneath the table, he grasped a hold of her hand, bringing her attention back to what was happening just in time to hear her father announce that Wayne Klein would be filling in for him at Air America for the time being.

But not even that held her attention. As his fingers threaded through hers, her mind went completely to him. This was all so unfair to him.

So very unfair.

"I'm sorry things didn't turn out like you wanted," Jason said while backing out of the driveway. He'd tried to get her out of there as soon as possible after her father had mentioned she wouldn't be taking over the helm of Air America. He knew it had to be a great disappointment.

"It was my father's choice."

She hadn't seemed to be surprised, or overly upset by the announcement, and he could guess why. "I take it he told you about his decision in advance."

She stared out the side window. "Yes, he did."

"When?"

"Earlier this week." She sighed. "Wayne will do a good job."

Taking over at Air America was her dream. If he'd have leased her his land, that might have happened tonight.

The rest of the ride home was completed in silence, as was the walk into the house. He took off his coat and reached to help her, but wrapped his arms around her instead. "I know you're disappointed—"

"Stop." She pushed his hands aside and stepped out of his reach. "We're alone. You don't have to pretend to—" She shook her head. "We don't have to pretend."

He took a step back, held his hands up at his sides. "Okay."

She kept her back to him. "I'm not as good at it as you."

He thought of the past few weeks, of their lovemaking. "You're wrong about that."

She turned, faced him. "This isn't going to work, Jason. It's just not."

"We don't have a choice of it not working. You're pregnant. Or have you forgotten that?"

"Of course I haven't forgotten that! How could I? It's the reason you married me."

That may be true, but there was far more that she wasn't saying. "Just because you didn't get the job you wanted right now doesn't mean—"

"Air America has nothing to do with this."

He was still mad at himself for what he'd said in bed last night, about being trapped. Her question about getting married had caught him off guard, and he hadn't been able to tell her the truth. That she'd been the reason he'd thought he'd never get married. Every woman he'd ever dated he'd compared to her, and they'd come up lacking. Therefore, he'd never thought he would get married.

But he was married and he hated arguing. Didn't want to argue with her, but was growing more frustrated by the minute. "It has everything to do with it. It's the reason you showed up on my doorstep in the first place."

She threw her hands in the air. "And ended up pregnant and trapped you into marrying me!"

"I didn't say you trapped me." No one on earth would

believe that. "It's the other way around. The richest girl in high school marrying the poorest boy."

"You aren't poor! And I'm not rich."

He may no longer be poor, but she was still rich. "Yeah, right."

"I'm not. My parents are rich, but I'm not. It's no different than your father was poor, but you're not."

Tired of that subject, of the entire argument, he said, "It doesn't matter. The fact is we are married and we are going to have a baby. So what are we going to do about it?"

She ran her hand through her hair. "I don't know. I just know I can't go on pretending we're in love when we aren't. Pretending everything is fine, when it's not."

Bingo. It was only a matter of time before she left. "Okay, then we don't pretend."

She stared at him for a long, somber moment. "Including when we are alone."

A sudden need for air struck and he pulled off the tie around his neck. He'd worn a suit and tie more in the past two months than he had his entire prior life. That was as fake as everything else. "Fine."

She spun around and marched out of the room.

Tanner got up off the floor, where he'd been lying, and followed her out of the room.

Jason squeezed his temples with one hand, wishing there was something he could say, something he could do, but there wasn't. It would all be for naught. He'd expected this. Her to get tired of it all.

He slept on the sofa that night, and the next night because no stores were open on Sunday, but first thing Monday morning, he went to the furniture store, bought a bed and hauled it home, set it up in one of the spare bedrooms.

Their marriage became another masquerade. This time

of not speaking, not even seeing each other, except for bumping into each other on mornings when she'd venture into the kitchen before he'd left for work. He tried to leave prior to her waking each morning, and each evening he stayed late, long after sending the crews home at the apartment building or the houses. There was always something that he could do by himself.

People noticed, and questioned him working every night and weekends, especially Stu, but he was the boss, therefore, no one pressed him for more of an explanation than he was willing to give. Not wanting Randi to be blamed for his shortcomings, the reasons he gave often related to her father's campaign. That she was doing something for it. Which she did on a regular basis.

So did he, and oddly enough he found solace in spending time with Randal. He accompanied his father-in-law to union meetings and job sites, listening to questions about laws and regulations that workers felt would benefit them and their families. Randal was serious about helping people and committed to making changes nationwide that would do just that. Jason had learned how down-to-earth and sincere Randal was, and knew if anyone could make a difference, it would be his father-in-law.

It all gave him food for thought, and the ability to look at things differently than he had in the past. Money wasn't the root of all evil. It was the love of money that was. When used in the right ways, everyone benefited.

Being with Randal also helped Jason with what he was missing most.

Randi.

Randal had all sorts of tales about her, when she'd been young, and it seemed like that was the only connection Jason had to her right now.

Living, yet not living with her, was complex, and

every week that passed their separation grew wider, deeper, darker.

She didn't seem to mind, so he kept his wish of trying to fix it to himself.

It had been almost a month, when one Sunday late in April, he found himself with nothing to do. The sun was out, had been for a few days straight. The grass was getting greener and the puddles left by the melting snow in March and the rainy days of April were drying up. He considered taking Tanner with him, but not wanting Randi home alone, he left the dog at home and pulled one of his motorcycles out of the garage, drove out to his property.

He stopped the bike as he pulled off the highway and got off to check the mailbox. No one had lived here since his father had died, but there was still mail in the box every so often. Catalogs, advertisements and the occasional letter from a Realtor interested in the property.

The dirt road needed to be graded. He had to dodge a few deep puddles before reaching the turnoff to the old homestead. He'd rebuilt the barn a couple of years ago, turned it into a functioning garage for his cars. Three of them. Souped-up to run a quarter-mile drag race in record time. He was going to take the red Chevy out today. Run the strip. Hoping that might make him feel better.

His plan had been to start working on an official drag race strip this summer, complete with bleachers for spectators and electric timers. It would be the first in the state and a draw for drivers. Real drivers. Not just teenagers.

That was who used the strip he had now. He'd had gravel hauled in, with a clay base to keep it from getting rutted, and ran his cars on it during the summer months regularly. But it was his cousin Wally and Wally's friends who used it more often.

Wally was Lottie's younger brother, and like him in his younger days, Wally had ended up with a couple of tickets for drag racing. Knowing what could come of that, and knowing that simply telling Wally to stop wouldn't work, Jason had told him to use his track. Drag racers were going to race, and without someplace to do it, they'd end up with tickets or worse, cause accidents that could get people hurt and killed.

So far Wally had kept his part of the agreement. Nothing had been trashed or damaged, and because it was private property, the cops had left the drag racers alone.

Jason stopped the bike near the garage. His plan was to build the strip on the piece of land Randi had wanted for her washing bay. He could give her that chunk, build his drag strip on another section.

However, the other section was low land. He'd have to haul in a lot of fill and have a culvert put in for the creek. That would more than double his costs, and the work would put him back at least a year, but it would work. He'd thought about it a lot lately, and the fact that he didn't want to go against Randal by supporting her washing bay project.

Yet, she was his wife, and far more important to him than anyone else. Anything else.

He huffed out a sigh. Things couldn't keep going as they were. That was for sure.

With nowhere to stash the junk mail on his motorcycle, he pulled up next to the house. It was looking worse for wear every year. Hardly any paint left, the roof of the porch sagging. He'd only been inside a half a dozen or so times since his father had died.

The key was on top of the door frame, he used it to unlock the front door. Dust, cobwebs and more than one sign that mice had moved in, greeted him. The house wasn't large. Kitchen, living room area, two small bedrooms and a bathroom you could barely turn around in. He'd cleaned out anything worth keeping long ago, and should just set a match to what was left, including the house, but for whatever reason, he hadn't.

He was thankful for a lot of things in his life, and right now one of them was that this hadn't been the house Randi had shown up at. She was right in the fact that he wasn't as poor as his father had been, but it might have been better if this had been where she'd first found him. She'd never have returned to give him back his socks or for any other reason.

There were times when he'd arrive home, late, after she was already in bed, and open the bedroom door to let Tanner out, when he'd just stand there. Staring at her, wanting to crawl into bed beside her so bad every part of his body and soul ached. The want to hold her, feel her in his arms again, was torture.

There were times when he wondered if he should just give up. Being half Osterlund, his baby wouldn't ever want for anything, especially not love.

But he couldn't stomach the idea of not being there, of not knowing his child.

Pushing the dead air out of his lungs, he looked around, wondering if instead of burning the shack down, he should remodel it. Give the house in town to Randi and he could live out here. Bring his child out here, give him or her rides in his hot rods and motorcycles, then take them back home to their mother.

He crossed the small living room area to the kitchen table, where years of junk mail had piled up, and figured this place would be more work than it was worth. He could build a new house, on the other side of the barn. A big one. Nice one. That, too, would take time.

His crews had just broken ground on three more houses that already had buyers lined up. Too bad he'd already rented out all of the apartments in his building, or he could have moved there.

That would really fit his reputation. Cutting out on a pregnant wife. That was something a reform school guy would do.

He glanced around the house. Selling this place, all of it, was what he should do. His cars, too. Drag racing wasn't for married men. Neither was a drag race strip. He could give Randi the acreage she wanted and sell the rest. Be done. Completely done with his past.

Tossing the mail from his hand onto the table stirred up dust, and as he pivoted to get away from it, the toe of his boot caught the table leg, jostled it enough that a pile of mail slid onto the floor.

Prepared to leave it, because it really didn't matter, he turned away, but a gut instinct had him twisting back around to look at a catalog that had landed on the floor. It was flipped open, and between the open pages there was an envelope. With his name on it.

There was something familiar about the handwriting. He wasn't sure what and picked it up. No return address, but the postmark was from four years ago.

He slid a finger under the flap and pulled out a card.

A sympathy card from when his father had died.

He almost tossed it on the table unread, but folded it open instead.

There was a check, and a folded-up letter. His heart stopped for a fraction of a moment at the signature on the card.

Your mother,
Scarlet (Heim) Crosby

Chapter Eighteen

Randi buried her face in the pillow on the bed Jason slept in, breathing in the scent of his aftershave, of him. How a person could live with someone and miss them as much as she missed Jason was unfathomable. She tried to stay busy, working and helping on her father's campaign, but Jason was on her mind no matter what she was doing.

All she had ever wanted was Jason Heim and now that she had him, they were both absolutely miserable.

Letting out a groan, she flipped onto her back, stared at the ceiling.

She missed his grin. That bad-boyish hooded grin that made her heart skip. She missed the butterflies in her stomach when he'd wink at her, but mostly, she missed the way he'd looked at her when they'd made love.

The number of nights that she'd heard him come home, and lay there, wishing instead of just opening the bedroom door to let Tanner out that he'd come in, lie down beside her.

That hadn't happened and it was stupid to keep wishing.

It was just that wishing was all she'd known to do when it came to him. She'd wished he'd noticed her. She'd wished she'd run into him somewhere. She'd wished. Wished. Wished.

The phone rang and she considered not answering it. Her mother knew things weren't going well, and was probably calling, going to try and talk to her again, even though she and her father were in Springfield this weekend. Randi didn't want to talk to anyone, but as the ringing continued, and not knowing where Jason had gone on his motorcycle hours ago, she leaped off the bed and ran into the living room to answer it.

"Hey, girl!" Wendy exclaimed. "I haven't talked to you in ages. I hope I'm not interrupting anything. Like you and your husband having a moment."

There hadn't been any type of *moment* in over a month. As she did at work, Randi put a smile on her face and attempted to sound as normal as possible. "You aren't interrupting anything. I'm home alone." She patted Tanner's head as the dog sat down beside her chair. "What are you doing?"

"Studying. I'll be so glad when this quarter is over. Why are you home alone? Where's Jason?"

Forcing the smile to remain on her face, Randi said, "It's nice out today. He took his motorcycle out for a ride."

"Why didn't you go with him? That sounds like fun."

It did sound fun, but she hadn't been invited. "I had things to do. What about you? What have you been up to?"

"Studying. Going to class. Studying. Going to class. I did go to a movie two weeks ago, fell asleep. The usher woke me up and told me I needed to leave because they were closing."

Flinching for her cousin, Randi said, "Uh-oh."

"Yeah, worse yet, I'd gone to the five o'clock show. They close at midnight."

"Oh, Wendy!"

"Yeah, so meanwhile, back at the ranch, how about you? Any news?"

"No."

"No? Like no…baby on the way?"

Randi rubbed a temple. She'd have to tell people soon.

"DDT!" Wendy exclaimed. "I hit it, didn't I?"

Why had she answered the phone?

"Randi!"

"I don't know, Wendy," she said for lack of anything else.

"What do you mean, you don't know?"

"It's…it's too soon."

"No, it's not! You go to the doctor, get a test. If the rabbit dies…"

"They use frogs now."

"Oh, my God! You did have a test!"

Randi smacked herself in the forehead. "I read that in a magazine."

"Have you missed a period? Experienced morning sickness? Tired? Emotional? Fuzzy headed? Dizzy?"

Wendy continued listing off symptoms until Randi interrupted her. "Do you have a medical journal in front of you?"

"Several," Wendy answered. "When was your last period? I'll calculate your due date."

"No!" Randi drew in a deep breath. "Can we just change the subject?" Knowing that wasn't likely, she added, "When the time is right, telling people is something Jason and I will do together." She and Jason hadn't done anything together lately. Not even drink coffee.

"All right, I can respect that." Wendy gasped. "But I have to know as soon as possible! I have a baby shower to plan! Oh, this is so exciting! How fun is that going to be?"

Randi had to swallow at the burning in her throat. "I— It's going to be fun." She squeezed her eyes shut at how her voice broke.

"Oh, Randi, I'm sorry. I didn't mean to make you cry. It's just emotions. That's very normal, your body is producing a baby."

"I know."

"Tell me about Jason," Wendy said in her happiest voice. "I bet he's excited."

Her cousin was attempting to cheer her up, but Randi was slipping further into sadness, regret, despair. "He's drawn up plans." The tears hit and a full sob emitted. "To build a crib and cradle."

"Oh, I'm sorry, now you're really crying," Wendy said. "When will Jason be home?"

"I don't know," Randi sobbed.

"Do you want me to call your mom?"

"No."

"Do you want me to shut up, and still be on the line when you're done crying?"

"I wish you were here, Wendy."

"I wish I was there, too, but Jason will be home soon, and he loves you so much."

"No, he doesn't."

"Yes, he does."

"No, he doesn't."

"I don't believe that," Wendy said. "But I'm not going to argue, because I know how much you love him."

She couldn't love him. He didn't want her to. The tears flowed faster. Harder. She couldn't talk, sobs were all that came out. Wendy talked, reminded her of how beautiful and fun the wedding had been. How Jason had carried her out of the hotel.

Tanner barked, stood and ran into the kitchen.

Knowing what that meant, Randi's head snapped up. "I—I have to go."

"Why?" Wendy asked. "Is Jason home?"

"Yes. Bye."

"No! Wait! Let me talk to him."

"No! And don't tell anyone anything! Nothing!"

"Ran—"

"I mean it! No one!" Randi hung up, and swiping the tears from her face, jumped up to run to the bathroom.

Jason walked into the living room, blocking her way to the hallway. "What's wrong? Why are you crying?"

If she looked at him, the tears would increase. She kept her eyes downcast. "Nothing."

He didn't move, repeated, "Why are you crying?"

"I was talking to Wendy on the phone." She wiped her cheeks again.

"Is something wrong with her? Did something happen?"

"No. She's fine. It…it's just me. It's just—" A sob escaped.

His arms folded around her, and she had no control over her response. Her body melted against him; she wrapped her arms around him and held on.

He rocked her back and forth, kissed the top of her head, rubbed her back and whispered that everything would be okay in her ear.

She cried harder because nothing would be okay.

He continued holding her, whispering, and she tried hard to make them stop, but the tears wouldn't stop. Not until after several minutes of being in his arms.

Her breathing was still shaky when he framed her face with both hands, forced her to look up at him.

"We can't keep living like this," he said.

He looked so sad, so glum. It was her fault and she

didn't know how to fix it. To make anything better. All she could do was agree. "No, we can't."

"What do you want to do?"

She had no idea and shrugged. "What do you want to do?"

"Right now?"

She nodded.

"This."

Air locked in her lungs as his lips met hers. Warm and soft and perfect, the kiss made everything inside her become more complicated because this was the last thing she'd expected. While also being what she'd wanted the most. She told herself to be cautious, to proceed slowly, but that was impossible. She'd missed him so much. Missed being with him.

Arching into him, she parted her lips and took the kiss to the next level. Within seconds pent-up desires exploded between them. They practically tore off each other's clothes while stumbling toward the bedroom, sharing openmouthed kisses and feasting on any inch of exposed skin while sucking in enough air before another mating of their lips.

There was no time for a moment of thought to form, other than how much she needed him.

They made it to the bed, ripping off any last bits of clothing, and came together with the same frenzy that had struck in the living room. There was no holding back, not on either of their parts. Her body knew the pleasure he provided. Her heart knew neither of them was pretending. And that was what it was all about.

Emotions exposed. Bare flesh upon bare flesh. Hands touching, feeling. Lips meeting. The indescribable pleasure incited by their joined bodies.

The velocity never slowed, even as the tension inside

grew to the point they were both gasping so hard for air that kissing was impossible. Randi couldn't pull her eyes off him, reveling at how he was watching her with just as much intensity.

When the commotion inside her broke loose, she clung to him, holding on to him as his body stiffened and she knew his time had come, too. They collapsed into the mattress as one, still gasping, still holding on to one another, still kissing whatever skin their lips touched.

His lips were touching hers, and as they parted, he chuckled.

All she could do was smile as he lifted his head.

"The phone's ringing again."

"Again?" she asked.

"Yes, again." He planted his hands on the mattress near her shoulders and straightened his arms, pressing upward.

She grasped his shoulders. "It's probably just Wendy again."

"It must be important. That's the fourth, maybe fifth time it's rung."

"It is?" She had no recollection of hearing the phone ring.

He kissed her nose. "I'll be right back."

Reluctantly, she let him go, but as he disappeared into the hallway, she remembered her conversation with Wendy and leaped off the bed.

He already had the phone to his ear when she arrived at his side. Giving her a wink, he wrapped an arm around her waist and held her against his side as he said hello to the caller.

"Fine, how are you today?"

She could tell it was a man's voice, not Wendy's, and let out a sigh that was a mixture of relief and delight as she laid her head on his shoulder.

"That's good," he said into the phone.

His hand caressed her side as he listened to the speaker. "Okay. When?"

She glanced at him as his hand stilled and his frame stiffened.

"Okay. Thanks for calling," he said, followed by, "Good day to you, too."

"Who was it?" she asked as he hung up the phone.

With his arm still around her waist, he tugged her across the room at a quick pace. "Your parents are on their way over."

"My parents are in Springfield this weekend."

"Their plane arrived half an hour ago." He started picking up their discarded clothes. "They called. When we didn't answer, they called Peter and asked him to keep trying, to let us know that they were stopping by."

She started grabbing clothes, too. "They could be here any minute!"

Their underclothes were in the bedroom, and they ran into the room, dashed around, finding pieces and tossing them to each other, getting dressed as fast as possible.

Having already pulled on his jeans, Jason had just put on his white T-shirt when Tanner barked.

She only had on her panties and jeans. "They're here."

He handed her the bra he'd tossed on the bed moments ago. "I'll go meet them outside."

Hopping on one foot while putting a sock on the other, he left the room, taking the time to close the door behind him.

She would have liked to relish the moment with a laugh, but there wasn't time. Once dressed, she tightened her ponytail by separating her hair and pulling it tight, then quickly straightened the pillows and bedspread.

Jason's coat was on the floor. As she picked it up,

tossed it on the chair near the closet, an envelope fell out. She picked it up, carried it to the chair. It appeared to be a card, mailed to Jason, but not at this address. She slid it under the coat and hurried to the kitchen, where she quickly filled the coffeepot, giving herself an excuse to not have met her parents outside with Jason.

When she heard the front door open, she said, "I'm in the kitchen, putting on coffee."

"It's just me," her mother replied. "Your father and Jason went to the garage to see his motorcycles."

Randi plugged in the percolator and spun around just as her mother entered the kitchen. "How was Springfield?"

"Fine." Her mother crossed the room and kissed her cheek. "You must have been outside with Jason when we called. Your face is glowing, as if kissed by the sun."

Her face had been kissed, but not by the sun.

"I'm happy to see that," her mother said. "I've been worried about you."

"I told you that I'm fine."

"I know, but just because you'll soon be a mother, doesn't mean I stop being yours." Her mother's lace-trimmed blue blouse was tucked into her black slacks, and her long hair was pulled back on both sides, held in place by a barrette.

When she'd been little, she'd thought her mother was the most beautiful woman on earth. Still did. "You don't look old enough to be a grandmother," Randi said.

"That's what your father says, but I am, and I'm happy about it." Hooking their arms, she said, "It is a beautiful day. Let's sit outside on the patio while the coffee perks."

Randi curled her bare toes against the linoleum. There hadn't been time to put on her socks or shoes, and she wondered about Jason wearing only his socks until she remembered he had shoes in the closet near the front door. "Let me just slip on a pair of shoes."

She collected a pair of white canvas shoes that didn't need socks from the closet near the front door, glad to notice that Jason's brown-and-white penny loafers were missing.

Once seated in the outdoor chairs on the patio, her mother said, "Your father and I have been worried about both you and Jason."

Randi sucked in a breath. Nothing had changed between her and Jason, other than satisfying one particular need. If only they were as good at other things as they were at that.

"I've never told you, but your father and I only knew each other for two weeks before we got married."

Stupefied, Randi said, "What?"

Her mother nodded. "Your grandmother arranged it because we were about to lose our house. Your father thought a wife would give him a better chance at buying Dad's airplane company, and I agreed, because besides my family needing money, I wanted to be a clothing designer. I thought everyone would see the wedding dress I sewed for myself and want one. That didn't happen. I became a designer because Jane was pregnant with Gus and needed a bra that fit."

Randi knew about Jane's needing a bra, but not the rest. She'd always assumed her parents had been as in love as they are now when they got married.

"It didn't take long before I realized what an amazing man I'd married and was completely in love with him." Her mother reached over and took a hold of her hand. "What did take a little bit of time, was figuring that together we could do anything, as long as we put our love for each other first."

Despite what had just taken place between her and Jason, Randi knew she and Jason didn't have love to put first. "I'm afraid, Mom."

"Of what?"

Her throat thickened. "That he feels trapped. We had to get married because I'm pregnant."

"People get married for a lot of reasons. That's the easy part."

That was true. "I don't know what to do," she said, desperate.

"I can't tell you what to do, honey, but I do know that you've never given up on something you've wanted."

"Except a pony," she said, just to lighten the mood.

Smiling, her mother replied. "Riding lessons was a compromise on both sides."

"Dad only won because he's a better negotiator than I am." Those negotiations had resulted in her agreeing to clean her father's office once a week to pay for a portion of the lessons. She sighed. "Once I started working at Air America, everyone assumed I'd take over someday."

"Yes, people did, but it's your choice, always has been. Your father and I have told you that."

"I know you have."

"And I know being our daughter hasn't always been easy for you. We've been fortunate, very fortunate, and along with that comes expectations. Large and small ones."

Randy huffed out a breath. "Like free band uniforms."

"For your brother, it was free soda pop."

Randi's gaze went to the garage.

"Your father has always been a generous, caring man. During the Depression, when others were unable to give to the soup kitchen, he increased his donation. We've been blessed and have found joy in helping others. Look at Rachelle. All the work you've dedicated to raising money for polio research helped her when she needed it. The iron lung she needed was there because of the work you'd put in."

Randi understood that, but it had nothing to do with her and Jason.

"What I'm trying to point out is that there is balance in everything, honey. Even in being our daughter. I know the expectations have weighed heavy on you. You've always taken everything to heart. But there are good things about being our daughter that I hope outweigh the others."

"Yes, there are, Mom." Once again, she thought about how different her and Jason's lives had been growing up.

"It's that way in other things, too. I didn't know anything about airplanes when I met your father, but his dream was to own an airplane company and I wanted that for him, more than I wanted to become a designer."

"You did both."

"No, *we* did both, your father and I, because he wanted my dream to come true more than he wanted his." Her mother touched her hand. "I sense there is something bothering you, and Jason, and though I'm your mother, and I love you, I know it's none of my business. However, I can't help but wonder if the two of you have taken the time to get to know each other? Do you know his hopes and dreams? Goals for the future? Does he know yours?"

Randi had her assumptions, but she really didn't know what Jason wanted, other than for her to not love him. "No." She huffed out a sigh. "Right now I don't even know what mine are."

Her mother squeezed her hand. "That might be a good place to start. The two of you might have more in common than you imagine. You could even want the same thing."

* * *

"I've test driven several motorcycles, but never pulled the trigger," Randal said, running a hand over the leather seat of the motorcycle. "This is a Black Hawk Chief, isn't it?"

"It is," Jason replied, leaning against his other motorcycle. "So is this one. I've had other bikes, but like the Indian the best. You can take her for a spin if you want."

Randal grinned. "I do want to do that. Take Jolie with me. She thinks they're dangerous, but I'm sure if she rode on one, she'd change her mind."

"You're welcome to it," Jason said. His breathing was finally under control. Making love to Randi had stolen every last breath in his body, and it hadn't returned before they'd both been running a marathon to get dressed before her parents arrived.

"Changing a woman's mind isn't an easy thing," Randal said. "Not my wife's or my daughter's. They're stubborn, opinionated, but also smart, savvy, and I wouldn't have it any other way."

"Not to mention beautiful," Jason said.

Randal chuckled. "So beautiful they can make a man lose their minds. I know, I've been there."

Jason could believe that. Randi got her beauty from her mother, and he'd lost his mind over her years ago. Never really got it back, either.

Randal folded his arm across his chest. "There was a time when I wanted to buy a small airplane company, knew it had the potential to be much more, but I needed something in order to buy it."

"Money?" Jason had always figured the man had been well-off, but the stories he'd heard could be wrong.

"No, I had that. I needed a wife."

Jason's head snapped up.

Randal nodded. "Neither Randi nor Joey know this story. Jolie's father had died a few years before we married, leaving the family somewhat destitute. She married me in exchange for me paying the taxes on her mother's home."

Jason grasped a hold of the handlebars on his motorcycle to keep the shock from knocking him off his feet.

"You've met Amelia," Randal said. "Randi's grandmother. She still lives in that house."

Still reeling at the information, Jason nodded. He had to believe the story, because Randal Osterlund was an honest man. He was proof of that. As soon as he'd learned the truth, Randal had gone to the judge to have him released from reform school.

"It didn't take long before I was head over heels in love, but I was too stubborn to admit it. There had never been a lot of love in my family. My mother died when I was young, and my father was bitter. He'd put his focus on making money, like his father had, and I followed in their footsteps. Thinking money, success, was all that mattered."

Jason shifted his stance, not sure he was ready to hear more. His mother wasn't dead, but she'd been gone, his father had been bitter and he'd been focused on making money since he'd left reform school. Because he'd never had any. That was a major difference between his past and Randal's.

"Coming from a man who has been very fortunate makes it sound vain, but the truth is, I would give up every dollar I ever earned, everything I own, for my wife. She is the root of my happiness, of my life, and I know she feels the same. That we could lose everything, but as long as we have each other, we won't have lost anything that matters."

Jason looked down at his shoes. A woman also had to be proud of her husband, and there was nothing in his past for Randi to be proud of. He'd gained a lot of respect for his father-in-law, and knew he could be honest with him. "You know my past. Randi and I are from two different worlds."

"As far as I know, there is only one world," Randal said. "I do know your past, and I'm proud of how you've faced challenges, overcome them. You should be, too."

"I am, but that's not enough."

"For what?"

"For Randi. She deserves the best."

"The fact you believe that, says she already has it."

Jason glanced toward the door that led out of the garage and scratched the back of his neck where it was tingling. That couldn't be true. She deserved love. The kind Randal spoke of. He shook his head.

"The airplane company that I wanted to buy was owned by Jolie's godfather, and when he told me that it wasn't for sale, I didn't know what I was going to do. There were other companies to buy, but I wanted the airplane company and he wasn't selling it because he was giving the company to Jolie. That knocked the wind right out of my sails. She'd married me because her family needed money. Once she inherited that company, she wouldn't. Therefore, she wouldn't need me."

Stunned, Jason didn't know what to say.

"Thank God it wasn't material things she needed, because they wear out. But the best of a person, that part of us that's brought out when we love someone deeply, it gets better. And when two people in love share the same goals, there's no stopping them."

The weight in Jason grew. He'd done nothing but stand

in the way of Randi's goal. Furthermore, they weren't in love.

Randal slapped his shoulder. "Tell me what I need to know about this motorcycle before I go get Jolie and take her for a spin."

Chapter Nineteen

All four of them ended up on the motorcycles. Randi was behind him and Jolie was behind Randal. Jason took it slow, just drove around a few blocks in his neighborhood. Long ago he'd fallen in love with the freedom associated with riding a motorcycle, and more than once had lived up to the reputation he'd built of being a daredevil. Right now, with Randi's arms around his waist, her body pressed up against his back, being a daredevil was the furthest thing from his mind. He was carrying the most precious cargo on earth. His wife, with his child growing inside her.

Pulling up beside them at a stop sign, Randal asked, "Could we go farther? Faster?"

Jason chuckled. "Sure. Any place particular?"

"We should find a café and have lunch," Jolie said. "We haven't eaten."

"Neither have we." Randi's arms around his waist tightened. "We know the perfect place. Mama's."

"You told me about that place," Jolie said. "Let's go there."

"It's half an hour away, in Downers Grove," Jason warned.

"Sounds perfect," Randal said, twisting the throttle to rev the engine of his motorcycle. "Let's ride!"

Randi's laughter echoed in his ear as Jason took off, leading the way to the highway and to Downers Grove.

The sun was out, the roads were dry and the company made it the best ride he'd ever taken.

"That was so fun!" Randi said, hugging him hard as he shut off the motorcycle in Mama's parking lot.

"Yes, it was," her mother agreed. "We are going to have to do this more often."

"We'd need our own motorcycle," Randal said. "We can't expect Jason to let us use his all the time."

Laughing, Jolie climbed off the motorcycle. "You've wanted one for years."

Jason waited until Randi was off the bike before he set the kickstand and climbed off. He took a hold of her hand and threaded his fingers between hers. "Your father might be hooked."

She leaned against him. "Might be?" Giggling, she watched her father climb off the motorcycle. "He is hooked, and so is my mother." She then looked up at him. "So am I. I've always wanted to ride on a motorcycle."

He searched her glowing face, her twinkling eyes, looking for a sign that she was faking it, saying that only because others were nearby.

She squeezed his hand. "I've also always wanted to ride in a red hot rod with a ball of fire painted on the hood."

Most days she looked like she'd just stepped out of a fashion magazine, so refined and beautiful that she took his breath away. Today, dressed in jeans, with her hair windblown, she still looked picture-perfect, and still took his breath away. So did the honesty in her eyes. "Why?" he asked, still skeptical.

"Because I like cars." She placed a quick kiss on his cheek. "And because it's yours."

"This place is adorable," Jolie said.

"It is," Randi replied, tugging him in her wake as she hurried toward the door. "And they have the best milk-shakes."

A moment later, as they walked through the door, Jason wasn't surprised to see several of his family members, including Rachelle.

She was still wearing her braces and using the crutches, but the speed at which she could move had increased substantially. Besides him and Randi, Rachelle included Randal and Jolie in her round of hugs.

"Sorry," Jason said after they'd managed to eat while visiting with several family members. "Everyone gathers at Mama's on Sundays as if it's Aunt Marla's private home."

"I think it's wonderful," Jolie said. "And the food was delicious."

"Yes, it was." Randal laid his napkin on the table. "If you will excuse me, I need to get some change for the jukebox because a little girl promised me a dance as soon as I was done eating."

Jolie slid out of the booth as well. "Excuse me, I'm the cheering section."

As they walked away, Jason asked Randi, "Do you want to dance?"

She set her napkin on the top of her plate, but said, "We don't have to."

He knew how much she enjoyed dancing, and how they were on shaky ground after the last month of barely speaking and then their amazing lovemaking. "I know we don't have to, but I want to."

She looked at him and tried hard to hide a smile. "You do?"

He took her hand and slid out of the booth. "Yes, I do."

A fast song was playing as they arrived on the dance floor. He twirled her under his arm, but just as her spin ended, so did the music. Pulling her toward him, he placed a hand on her waist and held their clasped hands close to his chest. It was complicated and he might be opening himself up for the worst hurt of his life, but if he didn't take the risk, he'd never know. He brushed his lips over her temple, whispered, "I've missed dancing with you in the kitchen."

She stiffened slightly. Looked up at him with a hint of insecurity in her eyes.

He touched the tip of his nose to hers. "And cooking with you, doing dishes, watching TV, folding clothes."

The music started, a slow, soft melody. She leaned against him as they started to dance. "I've missed all of that, too. Very much."

The ache in his chest that had become a part of him the past month, slipped away as they danced. Something took its place. Something light and bright. He didn't ever want to dance with anyone else. Just her, for the rest of his life, but what did that mean, exactly?

Pure happiness had filled Randi on the dance floor in Jason's arms, and that happiness remained until they arrived home and her parents left. Then a sense of panic slithered in to take its place. Her mother had told her where to start, but what if she discovered Jason's goals, the future he wanted, didn't include her? Could she live the rest of her life knowing that?

His fingers wrapped around hers, and his thumb rubbed the back of her hand. "I went to the courthouse a while ago, put your name on the land. You can build your washing bay wherever you want."

Her heart sank. "I don't want your land, Jason. That's why I went to California, to investigate building one out there. My father told me to put it off until next year, but I haven't. I asked Gus to recommend contractors he's worked with to bid the project without anyone else knowing." The frustration inside her doubled. "But the truth is, I don't care if it gets built or not. I don't care if Wayne Klein takes over for my father. Sam can, for all I care."

"That can't be true. Air America, taking over for your father, is all you've ever wanted. I'll help you. Whether it's here or in California, I'll help you build a washing bay."

She was touched by the sincerity in his voice, on his face, but would never expect him to do that. "You're already working night and day. I wish there was something I could do to help you. I'd rather do that than build a washing bay."

"I don't need help, and I know how much Air America means to you. It's the reason you went to college here instead of out east like your brother and cousins."

She blinked at the tears in her eyes, not sure which hurt worse. That he didn't want her help, or that he believed Air America was all she cared about. "Air America isn't the reason I stayed here." A full admission that he was the reason she'd never left town would leave her vulnerable, open for more heartache, and she was afraid of that. "It wasn't my dream. It's what was expected."

A frown had formed between his brows. "By your parents?"

"I was expected to have goals, to work toward them, so did Joe, but the expectations came from others. I was continuously asked which company I was going to take over.

Most assumed it would be JO's Dream Wear, and were surprised when they'd learned I worked at Air America. It became assumed that I wanted to take over the helm."

"You don't want to?"

"Yes and no. I'd be honored to continue what my parents started, but I'd also like to have something of my own. I've never had that. Whatever I've done, whatever I've had, is because of who I am, not my abilities." She hadn't meant to sound so selfish, so ungrateful. She wasn't. She was just being truthful.

"That's why you want to build the washing bay."

"I thought it would prove I could do something on my own. Instead, all I managed to do was trap you in a marriage you never wanted." She hadn't meant to say that. To point out the obvious. It was impossible to hold back her guilt. "I didn't set out to, but that's what happened."

Jason shook his head. "I never said I didn't want marriage, I said I'd never thought I'd get married."

She opened her mouth to say that was the same thing, but he spoke first.

"Let's grab some jackets and ride out to the land." He tugged on her hand, pulling her toward the bedroom.

"Why?"

"So you can see the land, see if it will work, and jackets because the ride home could be chilly."

She already knew the land wouldn't work because she wouldn't build a washing bay on it, but the excitement of riding on the motorcycle again had her walking into the bedroom beside him. "We're taking the motorcycle?"

"Yes."

She hurried to the closet. "I don't have a short jacket. They are all knee length." Scanning her wardrobe, she searched for something that might work. "Would a sweater be okay?"

He reached around her, to his side of the closet. "I have an extra leather jacket. It might be a bit big."

Her heart skipped a beat as he pulled out a leather jacket identical to the one he always wore. Being jacketed by him back in high school had also been a dream of hers. "That'll be perfect." She slid her arms into the jacket as he held it up for her, and the scent of leather filled her nose, as well as the spicy aftershave he always wore. Hugging the jacket to her, she spun around. "It's absolutely perfect!"

"It looks good on you." He gently flicked the end of her nose and grabbed his coat off the chair, hooked it on a finger and flung it over his shoulder. "Let's go."

With the wind whipping her ponytailed hair and leaning with him as he skillfully guided the motorcycle around corners, the ride to the property was wonderful. She couldn't help but hope that there was a difference between never thinking about getting married and not wanting to get married. It was a little thing in the overall scope of things, but perhaps it was a start. Her mother was right. Everything had happened so fast she and Jason hadn't had a chance to get to know each other. Not really. Maybe she needed to quit worrying about what they didn't have and focus on what they did have.

Chapter Twenty

Jason balanced the motorcycle on its kickstand and climbed off, took a hold of Randi's hand. The last thing he wanted her to see was the shack where he'd grown up, but he could relate to her wanting to create something on her own. He'd never considered how difficult things had been for her. All the expectations put on her, and truly wanted to help her with her washing bay. "The cars are in the barn. We'll take one of them out to the back forty."

"How many do you have besides the red one?"

He'd worked Ted Nash's gas station, changing oil and tires from the time he'd been twelve until he'd moved out of his father's house. Other than food for him and his father and other necessities, nearly every penny he'd made had gone back to Ted. First to buy the Chevy, then for the paint job. "There are two others in the barn."

She laughed. "Besides the one in town and two motorcycles, and several pickup trucks."

Three pickup trucks. Stu drove one, as did his cousin Steve, who was the foreman of another one of his crews. "Yes."

She was staring at the house and squeezed his hand. "Could we go look at the house first?"

"There's nothing in there but a few pieces of old furniture and other junk."

"I still want to see it."

"There's mice, and dust, cobwebs, spiders."

She started walking that way and tugged him along. "I don't care."

He was the one to bring her out here, so he complied. Found the key over the door, opened it. The sun was still out, but lowering in the western sky, casting shadows inside. That might hide how bad it was. "I had the power to the house shut off. Still have it in the barn."

She walked farther inside, peeking into the bedrooms. "Did you always live here?"

"Yes, my father built the house and barn before I was born. He farmed the land then, mainly corn. But the Depression hit, and the drought. Without money for fuel and water for crops, everything dried up." He hadn't repeated one of his father's stories, ever, not to anyone, but felt as if he had to justify the plight his parents had faced. "He'd never mortgaged the land, so didn't lose it like a lot of other people, but couldn't borrow against it, either. I was too little to remember any of it, not even him joining the army when the war broke out." He wasn't sure why he didn't remember that, because he did remember other things. Like how his mother had worked at Air America. She used to walk him all the way out to the highway to catch the school bus, and then cut across the field to go to work.

"How long was your father gone, in the army?"

"A few months, but most of that was spent in the hospital. The boiler on the troopship taking him overseas blew up and he was injured. The ship returned to New York. He never made it overseas." Which is why he'd never received any combat pay. That was what his father used to say.

"That's awful. How badly was he injured?"

"I don't know." His father never spoke about it unless he was drunk, hurting. "He had headaches, and would drink, said it was the only thing that helped the pain." That was often and when he'd complain about everything else in life, too.

"I'm sorry he was in such pain," she said softly.

A sense of guilt for never realizing what his father had been through washed over Jason. He'd blamed their being poor on his father's drinking, but never gave the reason his father drank any credence.

He hadn't come out here to walk down memory lane. The letter from his mother was still in the back of his mind; he hadn't had time to process that yet.

Randi was standing near the table, he held out his hand for her to take. "This place is full of mice droppings, let's get out of here."

"Mice droppings or not, I'm not done looking."

"There's nothing else to see."

She walked around the table, to the sink. "Yes, there is." Looking out the window, she asked, "Are the old ropes in that tree from a swing?"

"Yes, there used to be a swing in that tree."

"A big one?"

"Yes, like a porch swing. My father built it for my mother. She used to sit in it—" his throat locked up for a moment "—a lot." For a flash of a second, he'd seen his father and mother sitting in the swing, happy. Laughing. Hugging.

"I can believe she did. I would, too. It would be a lovely place to sit and watch the sunset." She turned around. Smiled. "It had to have been nice, living out here. It's so quiet. So peaceful."

"Quiet and peaceful can drive some people crazy."

She walked around the table, took a hold of his hand. "Show me your cars now. Are they all red?"

"No. Red, white and blue."

She giggled. "All American."

He locked the house after they'd walked out the door, as always, to keep the memories inside the walls. This time, though, while holding her hand as they walked to the barn, he couldn't help but think that he'd come a long way since living in that house. Maybe, with hard work and luck, he'd someday become enough for her. Become someone she could be proud of.

After unlocking and removing the padlock on the barn, he opened the double doors and clicked on the overhead lights.

"Shh," she whispered. "The cars are sleeping."

He laughed at her joke. "I cover them to keep from getting too dusty."

Taking in the toolboxes, metal workbenches and shelves of miscellaneous parts and tools, she said, "You must spend a lot of time out here."

"I do in the summer." He pulled the silk covering off the Chevy.

"It's exactly like I remember it." Walking along the side of the car, she looked in the driver's window. "Four on the floor."

He chuckled. "Yes."

"Do you still drag race?"

He was going to miss that, but her happiness would be worth giving it up. "Once in a while I run her on the track I built. Wally and his friends use it the most. I'd rather they were out here racing than in town where they'll get in trouble."

"Out here? You have a track?"

"I built it a few years ago." He pulled the covering off

the next car, a white two-seat convertible Ford Thunderbird.

"Cherry! I almost bought a bird," she said. "But the Bel Air's six cylinders get better gas mileage than the bird's V-8 would."

He was impressed with her knowledge.

She sighed. "And my father didn't think I needed a car with that much power."

Eyeing her, he asked, "Do I need to worry about your driving?"

"No." She laughed and pointed to the third car. "What's that one?"

He pulled the cover off that car, a blue Buick with a wraparound windshield and tail fins. The aircraft design of that one had reminded him of her. That was the only reason he'd purchased it.

"Man! You own all the best machines!" She roamed around the car. "I love the aerodynamics of this model. Joey and Gus would be drooling right now."

"Is that how you know so much about cars?"

"Maybe," she said, walking back toward the Chevy. She opened the passenger door. "Maybe not."

Chuckling, he walked to the driver's door. "It's loud," he warned once seated.

Her smile showed her pearly whites, and her excitement. "I remember that."

He turned the key and laughed at her glee as the powerful engine made the seat rumble. She looked adorable in his coat that was too large and her hair tied back in a ponytail. For a second it felt as if he was seventeen, taking her out on a date.

The car had get-up-and-go, but he took it slow, drove out to the strip.

"Is this where you're going to punch it?" she asked.

"You want to go fast?"

"Very!"

He knew the car like the back of his hand, and gave her a good run, but not nearly as fast as he would have if he'd been alone.

"Can we do it again?" she asked.

"Are you a speed demon?"

"I've always wanted to be, but never had the chance."

He put the car in Neutral and let it idle. "Do you want to drive?"

Her mouth dropped open and she shook her head. "No one lets someone else drive their hot rod."

That was the cardinal rule, but he was willing to break it, for her. "They do when it's their wife."

She squealed. "Do you mean it? I'll be careful. I promise."

He opened his door. "I trust you. Scoot over here." As he climbed out, he said, "But wait until I get in the passenger seat before you shift it into gear."

She was already in the driver's seat, holding on to the steering wheel and grinning like she'd just opened a gift that she loved. "I will!"

He ran around the car, climbed in.

"Ready?" she asked.

"Whenever you are," he replied.

She shifted into First and took off like a pro.

"Tight clutch!" she shouted above the engine. "I like it!" She advanced through the gears with skill and precision that impressed him, and brought the car to a smooth stop at the end of the track.

"Take her back to the other end," he said.

She bit her bottom lip and looked at him.

"You don't have to if you don't want to," he offered.

"I want to, but um—"

"What?"

"Could I do a moonshiner's turn when we reach the other end?"

There was nothing in the way, so he nodded. "Sure."

"Yes!" She revved the engine, dropped the clutch and spewed dust and dirt in their wake, grinning the entire time.

At the other end she performed a moonshiner's turn that would rival his. "I'm impressed," he said as the car came to a stop.

Laughing, she said, "I used to practice those in the parking lot at Air America, until I almost hit the building. Then my dad made me stop." She grimaced. "I probably shouldn't have mentioned the part about almost hitting the building."

He laughed. "Now I know why he didn't want you to have a V-8."

"I've never driven a car with this much power, it's addictive." She was glancing around the area. "And this is the perfect place for a track." Leaning back in her seat, she looked at him. "Is this why you said you had plans for this property? This track?"

"I have other property I could build a track on."

"It's already built here, why would you move it?"

"So you could build a washing bay."

She turned off the car so they didn't have to shout over the engine. "A washing bay will never work here. It's too cold. Would cost too much to keep it heated for the planes to dry during the winter. I understand all that now. California would work better."

He could see her point. "Is that why your father gave up trying to buy this land?"

"I think Dad just wanted it for expansion. I was the one who came up with the washing bay idea."

"From what you said, it's a good idea."

She scanned the area again. "Not as good of an idea as a drag strip." She gestured with one hand. "You could build a real one. Open it to the public. Have bleachers at the start and finish lines. An announcer's booth in the center. A pit area over there, and concession stands back behind the bleachers."

The hair on his arms stood at the way she'd described the exact plans he'd drawn up. He'd never shown them to her. "Have you been to a strip?"

"A couple of times in California, with Gus. There's not one near us. This would be a real draw." She opened her door, swung her legs out. "We'd have to bring in power, gotta have an electric scoreboard, and lights for night racing."

He climbed out, met her near the front of the car.

Rubbing her chin, she said, "Dirt track would work, but paved would be better."

Astonished, he was tongue-tied.

She turned, looked at him for a long moment. "Is this your dream? To build a drag strip out here?"

"I've thought about that," he admitted.

"And?"

He shrugged, grinned. "And, I have plans drawn up for one. Pretty much identical to what you just described."

She squealed and clapped her hands. "Can I see them? Can I help? Please? I know we both have our other jobs, but we could do this. We could really do this!"

"You'd like that?"

"I'd love it! Wouldn't you?"

Her excitement was rubbing off on him. "Yes, I would."

She squealed again and looped her arms around him, hugged him. "When can we start?"

They spent so long walking around, sharing ideas and

making plans that it was almost dark when they closed the barn doors after returning the Chevy to it.

The few lingering rays of sun were shining on the house, making the glass windows sparkle. Like the shadows inside, the sunset made the house look not so decrepit.

"Would you ever consider living out here again?" she asked while climbing on to the motorcycle behind him.

"No." A drag track out here was one thing, living here again was different. That would never happen again. There were too many memories.

After arriving home and making soup and sandwiches for supper, they settled in the living room to watch television. Randi wondered if he would sleep in the other room again tonight, and couldn't think of a good way to ask him to sleep in their bed instead.

Their bed. That was how she thought of it, just as she thought about the drag strip as theirs. The idea of creating something with him thrilled her beyond belief. She couldn't describe how it made her feel, but she didn't want to lose that feeling.

Lifting her head off his shoulder, she kissed his cheek. "I'm going to get ready for bed."

"Tired?" he asked.

"No." Her heart nearly beat its way out of her chest as she waited for him to respond. Then welled with happiness when he stood and held out his hand.

Much later, after a spectacular bout of lovemaking, she got out of bed to use the bathroom, and on her way back, noticed the envelope beneath the chair near the closet when she stopped at the vanity to remove her ponytail and brush her hair. "A letter fell out of your coat earlier, when my parents arrived. It's under the chair."

"I saw that."

He was lying on the bed, naked, hands behind his head and legs crossed at the ankles. The reflection of that in the mirror made her grin.

"It's from my mother."

The brush stalled in her hand. She turned around. "Your mother?"

"You can read it if you want."

She considered saying no, but couldn't deny that she wanted to read it. Setting down the brush, she walked to the foot of the bed.

"I found it this morning," he said. "At the house, my father's house. It's a sympathy card she'd sent when he died. It had been stuck in a magazine. I never saw it until the magazine fell on the floor this morning."

Being here for him, through the good and the bad, was what she'd promised, and would fulfill. She walked over, picked up the envelope. "What does it say?" She couldn't judge a woman she'd never known, but she knew his mother's leaving had affected him greatly.

"Not much. There's a check in there, too. For the funeral, or whatever was needed, or to go to Texas and see her."

Randi climbed on the bed, sat back on her knees, holding the envelope. "Texas? Not Florida?"

"That's what it says."

"Are you going?"

"No."

"Why not?"

He rolled onto his side, laid a hand on her thigh. "She wrote it four years ago, and I never responded."

"Because you just found it."

"She probably believes I don't want anything to do with her."

Her heart ached, for both him and his mother. "She probably does."

He took the envelope, opened it, handed her the letter. "It's short. Just says she's sorry, that my father was a good man and that she never stopped loving me or him."

She glanced at the letter, but didn't read it. Her heart was too busy breaking for him. "You could call her," she said, giving him back the letter.

He put it in the envelope, dropped it on the table and pulled her down beside him. "Or I could kiss you."

"Yes, you could," she whispered. He might not love her, but right now he needed her, and that was enough.

Chapter Twenty-One

Two weeks later Randi was sitting at her desk when her father walked into her office. "Hey, Dad, what are you doing here?"

Holding his arms out at his sides, he frowned. "That's the greeting I get? No, *It's good to see you*? Or, *I've missed you*?"

She laughed and met him in the center of the room for a hug. "It's very good to see you, and I've missed you." After kissing his cheeks, she added, "And Mom. How many cities did you hit this time?"

"I think it was twenty-three, in six days. Your mother is relentless."

She laughed, knowing that her parents were in this run together. As they'd been in everything. Lately, she and Jason had been, too. Not just in conversations about the drag strip, but in everything. They talked about all sorts of things. Childhood events, dreams, fears and life. They'd formed a connection like she'd never had with anyone.

But there was still something missing, and despite everything else, that weighed her down.

Rather than the chairs by her desk, she led her father

toward the leather sofa that sat along one wall. "Sit down and relax. Do you want some coffee?"

"No, I'm fine, but I do want to talk to you."

She knew why. "Okay." They sat side by side on the sofa.

"I came into the office for a meeting with Wayne this morning, and he told me you've met with him several times, have been instrumental in assisting him with the entire transition."

"I've just given him a few heads-up and some pointers."

"And told him that he can count on you for whatever he needs." He patted her knee. "You have no idea how proud that makes me."

She didn't need praise. In fact, she didn't deserve it. "It was something I should have done when you announced he was taking over." There was more she needed to admit. "You were right, Dad, as usual. I'm not ready to take over for you. I might be, someday, if it works in all aspects." Here and at home. She'd learned things about herself, about life, lately. Jason, the way he forged ahead despite things that had happened, made her want to do that, too. It was hard to explain, but she no longer felt trapped. No longer felt being her father's daughter was a burden. It was a privilege.

Her father grinned, touched the tip of her nose with one finger, before pulling up a more serious expression. "I just had a meeting with Sam, too."

Here it was. She drew in a deep breath and repeated the gist of what she'd told Sam. "I may be your daughter, but I'm also an employee here, and deserve the same amount of respect as everyone else. I'm willing to work on our differences, but he has to, too, otherwise one of us will be looking for a new job." Sitting a bit straighter, she added, "And it won't be me."

His serious expression remained. For a moment. Then it broke into a smile. "I told him I agree with you one hundred percent."

"You did?"

"Yes, I did. He's a great accountant, but I've considered firing him more than once, because of his attitude toward you, and Joe at times. I didn't because I knew if you took control of the situation, that you'd really have what it takes. Not only to run Air America, but to manage whatever life throws at you. Facing fear isn't always easy, but it has to be done."

He was right, in a sense. "I wasn't afraid of him."

"I know you weren't afraid of him. I would have gotten rid of him if that was the case, but you were afraid of what his reaction would be."

She nodded. "I was. I knew he'd tell you, and I was afraid that you'd think I couldn't handle things on my own."

"I've always known you could handle anything." He squeezed her hand. "It was you who needed to figure that out."

She could handle things, and it was time she took care of a couple more. Two significant things that were focused on Jason. She wanted a marriage where she and Jason not only desired each other passionately, but also loved each other openly, honestly, and had figured out how to make that happen. She just hadn't acted on it yet, because she was afraid of how he might respond.

"How is everything else going?" her father asked. "Anything new?"

"The washing bay project is on hold, but Jason and I will be flying out to California this summer to go to a drag race, and I might have discussions about it while there."

He chuckled. "I'd expect no less. Anything else?"

"Will you and Mom be home two weeks from Sunday?"

"We can make sure we are, why?"

The wheels were still turning inside her head. "I'll let you know as soon as I have it all confirmed with Jason."

"Fair enough." He patted the leather seat before standing up. "I have a luncheon, so have to get going, but keep up the good work, and stay happy, it looks good on you."

She gave him a hug goodbye, and walked to her desk, stared out the window. Jason had the ability to love and be loved. There was one hurdle that kept him from seeing that. It was a risk, but one she had to take. She sat down, picked up the phone and dialed the Texas number she'd gotten off the letter from his mother.

Keeping secrets had never been one of her best assets, but this one she would keep. At least part of it. A major part of it.

Jason was already home when she arrived, in the kitchen putting something into the oven. She dropped her purse on the table and walked over, hugged him from behind.

After closing the oven door, he turned, engulfed her in a hug. "How was your day?"

"Good. How was yours?"

"Good, even better now that you're home." He ran his hands down her back, cupped her butt cheeks and brought them closer, so their bodies pressed against each other.

He kissed her, an openmouthed kiss that had her insides swirling.

"If you keep kissing me like that," she said in between

breaths when the kiss ended, "I'm going to forget what I have to tell you."

He wiggled a brow. "Oh, what's that?"

Giving his chest a playful slap, she stepped away, otherwise she might take him up on his teasing. "Are you busy two weeks from Sunday?"

"I don't know, am I?"

She planted her hands on her hips.

He laughed. "What are we doing two weeks from Sunday?"

Dressed, her growing stomach wasn't overly noticeable because she wore loose-fitted dresses or positioned the waistbands of her skirts higher on her torso and didn't tuck in her blouses, but naked, the expansion was very noticeable. What she'd thought had been butterflies, because Jason set those off with nothing more than a look, had been confirmed by the doctor as movement. Baby movement, which was utterly fascinating. "Having a party. I think it's time we tell others."

Two steps brought him directly in front of her, and he laid a hand on her stomach. "People are noticing?"

She placed her hands atop his. "No one has said anything, but I want them to know."

"You want them to know?"

She nodded. "Yes, I want everyone in the world to know I'm having your baby."

"What about your father's campaign? We could put it off—"

"My father's campaign doesn't have anything to do with this. I want everyone to know that we are going to have a baby." She willed her heart to not pound out of her chest. "And that we are happy about it."

He stared at her for a stilled moment, then grinned. "All right. Where are we having this party?"

"At Mama's."

"Okay. Mama's it is." He cast her a hooded look that said his mind was turning to something else. "I have an idea for tonight."

"I'm listening."

"Let's go to the drive-in."

Taken aback because that had not been what she'd expected him to say, she asked, "The drive-in?"

"Yes." He kissed the side of her neck. "You know. Where we sit in the car and watch a movie."

"Yes, I know." She also knew they were called passion pits because there was often very little movie watching taking place. "What movie is playing?"

"I have no idea."

"Okay," she agreed.

The storm broke out halfway through the drive-in movie, making it impossible to see the screen, and a bolt of lightning struck so close the sky lit up at practically the same time the crack of thunder echoed through the air.

Startled, Randi let out a squeal and pressed closer to his side. "Goodness, that was a close one."

"It was." Jason rubbed her upper arm. The speaker hanging inside his window had gone silent and though they hadn't been able to see the movie, the screen that had been lit up was now dark. "Looks like it struck something. The electricity quit."

Horns started honking and car lights came on around them.

She lifted her head off his shoulder. "Aren't you going to start the car so we can leave?"

"No. The wipers can't keep up with this rain. Even if they could, it's too dangerous to drive when it's raining like this." He kissed her temple. When it came to her safety, he was the opposite of the daredevil he used to portray. "We'll just wait it out."

"Maybe you'll get to second base while we wait," she whispered while kissing the side of his neck.

There was no more pretending between them, not in public or private. It was all natural. He was even beginning to believe that he could learn to love. She was loveable, completely. He just had to forget all he'd ever known about it and start over. It was scary, because he didn't want to fail. Not in that. Not with her.

He rubbed her stomach, then slid his hand up to cup a breast. "I got to second base before the movie started. Remember?"

Putting her hand over his, she held it in place. "That's second base?"

"Yes."

"Then what's third base?"

Jason explained aloud, while showing her, and a few other things as they waited for the rain to let up. As soon as that happened, he rolled down his window and attached the speaker to the metal pole before starting the car. "We'll finish this at home."

"Where we don't have to worry about someone peeking in the window," she said while double-checking that her blouse was buttoned straight.

"Yes." He respected her too much to ever want to embarrass her.

She snuggled against his side. "Okay."

By the time they entered their neighborhood, the rain was little more than a drizzle and he eased his foot off the gas pedal at the plethora of red lights flashing.

Randi stiffened beside him, seeing what he did at the exact same time. "A house is on fire! It's not our house, is it? Tanner's home!"

He couldn't tell for sure, but the sinking in his stomach said it was their house. "It's all right," he said, trying to stay calm, yet hit the gas pedal. "He has the doggy door."

A police barricade stopped him before he could turn into the alley, before he could see exactly which house was on fire.

He threw the car in Park. Her hands were cupped over her mouth. He grasped her wrist. "You stay here. Don't get out. I'll be right back."

She nodded and frantically said, "Find Tanner. Please find Tanner. He can't get out of the backyard! The fence is too high!"

He shot out of the car and ran up to the closest officer. "My house is on this block."

The officer held his arms wide at his sides. "Three houses are on fire, sir, I can't let anyone past."

"What—"

"Lightning strike," the officer said. "Hit the electrical pole."

"My dog is in the backyard, it's fenced in, and—"

"I'm sorry, sir. The firemen..."

Jason heard barking and shouted Tanner's name.

As the officer spun around, Jason shot past him, ran. Firetrucks lined the street, pumping water onto his house and the two on the left of his place, but flames were still shooting high in the air. It stunned him for a moment, but another bark sent him forward again.

He ran through the neighbor's backyard, to the alley and to his garage. Throwing open a door, he ran through the garage, to the service door and wrenched it open.

Soaking wet, Tanner shot inside the garage.

Relief filled Jason as he slammed the door shut. Smoke filled the air, burned his nose, and the heat from the fire consuming the houses was intense. For a moment he thought about all the things in the garage. Not only the vehicles, but all of his tools. This is where he stored most everything for his company. There was time to get some out, but then he thought of Randi, waiting in the car. "Come, boy, we gotta go."

She wasn't in the car, she was on the street, arguing with the police officer when Jason ran around the side of the neighbor's house.

Tanner bolted forward, barking and running toward her.

Her squeal had other officers and bystanders looking and moving toward her, until they saw her and the dog united.

Jason wasn't sure if it was raining again or if the moisture in the air was from the water being pumped onto the flames—either way, he had to get her out of here. She was kneeling on the ground, hugging Tanner. Jason grasped her waist. "Come on, sweetheart, we have to go."

She stood, but shook her head. "Go? We can't go! That's our house!"

"There's nothing we can do. The fire departments are here."

"But—"

"Tanner's safe," he reminded, and knowing the only way he was going to get her out of here, save her from watching their home be completely destroyed, was for her to think she was saving someone else. "Let's take him to your parents."

"That's clear across town, our house…"

"I know, but we have to get him cleaned up, make sure he doesn't need to see a vet."

"A vet!" She ran to the car, with Tanner at her side. "Hurry! We have to hurry!"

Her parents had been in bed, but came running down

the stairs practically the moment he, Randi and Tanner walked in the door.

"What's happened? What's wrong?" they asked simultaneously.

"Tanner was home alone and our house is on fire!" Randi answered, dropping down to inspect the dog. "Jason had to rescue him from the backyard, and there were flames everywhere!"

Jason explained the situation, trying to remain as calm as possible, he ended by telling Randal quietly, "She needs to stay here. I need to go back." Everything he'd had to offer her was going up in smoke. If he didn't hurry, he'd have nothing left. Nothing.

"Of course," Randal said. "Give me a second to get dressed. I'm going with you."

Jolie seemed to comprehend how Randi might protest, and said, "Come. Let's get Tanner upstairs and into a bathtub. Get this ash washed off him so we can see if he needs medical attention."

Tanner was black with ash, but walking and acting fine, which gave Jason hope to believe he was uninjured.

The two women and dog were on their way up the stairs when Randal raced back down them. "Let's go, son."

Chapter Twenty-Two

It was odd to feel out of place in the home where she'd lived her entire life until marrying Jason, but Randi did.

Because they'd been constructed of brick, their house, as well as the other two, were still standing, but due to smoke and water damage, the interiors would need to be rebuilt and most of their belongings were beyond salvageable.

"Things can be replaced," her mother said. "People can't."

"I know." Randi drew in a deep breath. "I'm so thankful Tanner got out safely, that's really all that matters, I just... I don't know, feel sort of lost. Homeless."

"You aren't homeless. The three of you can stay here as long as needed. Forever would be fine."

She smiled, because she knew that was true. The forever part. Her mother and father had mentioned more than once that their big house was too empty now. She appreciated their love and their offer, but she and Jason had been making headway and she didn't want that to stop.

The fire had happened Thursday night, and it was only Sunday, but it felt like months had passed.

She lifted her glass of lemonade off the table between her chair and her mother's as they sat on the back porch.

Tanner was lying at her feet, completely fine now. All he'd needed was a bath, thankfully. Jason, along with her father, had left earlier this morning to see what they could salvage out of the basement and empty the garage before vandals realized the burned-out homes might be easy pickings. They'd said it was too dangerous for her and her mother to go over there again until they'd fully inspected everything.

A hopelessness filled her, and she didn't like that feeling.

"Don't fret so," her mother said. "Jason will be able to rebuild your house as good as new in no time."

"I know he can rebuild it," Randi replied. "But he has so many other jobs. People are buying his houses faster than he can build them, and he's looking at buying another apartment complex. The other one is full and has a waiting list."

"There is definitely a housing shortage right now. It's in all the papers and one of the main concerns that comes up at every town hall your father has spoken at."

Randi set her glass down. "I love you and Dad, but I don't want to live with you."

With one of her light, on-a-song-sounding giggles, her mother patted her hand. "I can appreciate that, dear. And your honesty."

"Jason and I cooked together, did laundry together, cleaned together and we can't do those things while we are living here. It might sound silly, but it felt as if we were building something together, the two of us, and I don't want that to stop."

"It's not silly, honey. I totally understand. You were building your lives together. We'll find a place for you to live, don't worry."

She couldn't help but worry, and couldn't get one possible solution out of her head, either. "Will you take a drive with me? There's something I'd like to show you."

"Of course."

Her car had been in the garage, and unharmed other than a thick coating of ash that Jason had already washed off. "We'll take my car so Tanner can come with us."

"All right." Her mother stood. "But Tanner is more than welcome to ride in any of our vehicles just as much as he's welcome to live in our house. He's family."

Tanner barked, as if in total agreement.

A short time later Randi turned off the highway onto the gravel road leading to Jason's land. "Now, don't judge it on first sight. Look at the potential."

"I won't, and I will," her mother replied. "I have a feeling your mind is already set."

"When we pull in, I want to hear your first impression before we get out of the car."

"Okay."

Within minutes she pulled up next to the house, with its sagging porch roof, and turned off her car. To her, the little porch looked cute, sagging roof and all. "Well?"

"First impression?"

"Yes. An honest one."

"I wouldn't give you any other kind. It reminds me of Dad Jansen's cabin. The one we used to stay in when you were little. His sons sold it, and your father has always regretted not being the one to buy it."

A chill rippled up Randi's arm, a wonderful sort of chill. "That's it. I knew I had happy memories of a place just like this, but I didn't know exactly what they were."

"You were only six the last time we were there."

Randi opened her door. "Let me show you the inside." Not tall enough to reach, she had to use a stick to

knock the key off the top of the door frame. Once unlocked, she pushed open the door, stepped inside.

Her mother was right behind her, and the first thing
she did was gasp.

Randi spun around, looked at her mother, who had a
hand over her mouth, giving her no idea if her mother
was surprised, or appalled.

There was a full-blown smile on her mother's lips when
her hand fell away. "Darling, we could have this place
cleaned up and you living in it within a couple of days."

Excitement filled her. "That's what I was thinking!"

Her mother started tossing out ideas of wallpaper, rugs
and curtains, and Randi could see every image in her
mind. A hint of concern, though, of how Jason might
react to the idea, had her suggesting, "Let's not say anything to Jason."

"Why not?"

"Because I want to surprise him. He has enough on
his mind with salvaging everything at the other place. He
feels like the fire was his fault, and it wasn't."

"No, it wasn't," her mother said. "I see a broom. Let's
roll up our sleeves and get busy."

As they worked, her plan grew. She would have the
entire place sparkling clean and filled with furniture,
curtains, rugs, and the cupboards full of dishes before
telling Jason a word about it.

That, however, wasn't to be. She and her mother were
still cleaning when Tanner barked, and a moment later
Jason's pickup, with the back of it heaped full, pulled
into the yard.

"Looks like our secret is out," her mother said.

Randi held her smile in place as she set aside her
broom and walked outside. Jason had already climbed
out of his truck and was walking toward her.

"What are you doing here?" he asked.

She hurried to him and tilted her face upward, for a kiss. He glanced at her, at the house, and then—as if he didn't want to, but felt he had to, to make her happy—he brushed his lips over hers.

He also grasped her arm as he repeated, "What are you doing here?"

"It's going to take months to rebuild our house, and with the housing shortage, we aren't going to find a house to rent or buy, so we'll either have to stay with my parents, or—" she planted on a big smile "—move out here."

"We'll stay with your parents."

"But this house is plenty big enough for us."

"No, it's not."

"Yes, it is." She gestured toward the barn. "And there's room to store all your work tools."

He shook his head. "You shouldn't even be inside there. It's dirty."

"We've already swept and dusted. We need to have the electricity turned on for the water—"

"Go back to your parents' house."

She drew in a deep breath, mainly to calm herself, to keep from telling him how stubborn he was acting. "No." Walking away, she said to her father, "Doesn't it remind you of Dad Jansen's cabin?"

"It does," her father said.

She hooked her arm through her father's. "And wait until you see the cars in the barn. Red, white and blue. A Chevy, Ford and Buick."

Jason barely looked at her as she and her mother helped him and her father unload the truck of things they'd salvaged from the basement. They put everything in the barn, where he also showed them his cars. Her insides were sinking deeper and deeper. He was pleasant, acting normal, but he was faking. She knew. She'd seen him do it before.

He faked his way through dinner later that day, too. Especially when her mother mentioned that the little house was well built and that it wouldn't take much to make it fully livable.

When her father mentioned that she could practically walk to work if she lived at the cabin, she saw Jason's jaw turn hard.

As soon as they entered her old bedroom back at her parents' house, he said, "We are not living in that house."

They were both wearing borrowed clothes, from her mother and father. Without saying a word, she turned her back to him, silently asking him to unzip her dress.

He unzipped it and walked into the bathroom attached to her room.

She looked at Tanner. He lay down and put his paws over his ears and eyes. "Thanks for the support," she said drily.

When Jason left the bathroom, she entered it. After completing her nightly routine, she clicked off the light on her way out, and climbed into bed, naked as always. Whether they made love or not, she loved curling up next to him, sleeping with their bare flesh pressed together. Tonight was no different, even if he was mad at her.

He was lying on his side, wearing a T-shirt and underwear. She curled up against his back, hooked a leg over his and an arm around his waist. "This has all been so upsetting. The fire, the damage, staying here, but let's not be upset with each other."

Jason held his breath, feeling the irritation that he'd been harboring slipping away. Randi challenged him in ways no one ever had. He rolled onto his back, slid an arm underneath her neck and held her close. Other than a few things in the basement and garage, everything was gone. Everything he'd had to offer her was gone. He didn't even have a home for them to live in. It was so infuriating. Life had been good. So good. Then, out of the blue, disaster. It was like life itself thwarted him at every turn when it came to her. "I'm not upset with you. I'm just frustrated that you lost so much in the fire."

"*We*, and we didn't lose anything in the fire that can't be replaced. We have each other and Tanner. I will live anywhere you want, as long as we are together."

He knew the *anywhere* she was referring to. "I don't want you living in that old, worn-down house, and I don't want you walking to work." He'd worked too hard to get out of that life. He wasn't going to go back, and wasn't going to take her with him. Wasn't going to watch her walk across the field to go to work like he had his mother. "I'll rebuild our house. It won't take that long."

She inched her hand under his T-shirt, ran it across his stomach. "I know you will rebuild it, and I'll help, but that little house would only take a couple of days and we could move in. I could do most of the work myself."

There was no way he'd let her clean that place up by herself, nor could he understand why she would want to live there. "This room is almost as big as that entire house."

"I know. That's why it won't take long to fix."

That hadn't been his point.

"You already have everything stored in the barn." She kissed his shoulder.

Jason could feel things inside him shifting. He wanted to give her whatever she wanted, but that house was a shack, especially compared to the mansion they were in right now.

She scooted closer, was partially lying on his chest, looking at him eye to eye. "I understand that you might have some bad memories of living there. But that's all they are. Memories. We could make new ones. Good ones." She shrugged. "I have bad memories of this house. It's where I got my first spanking. Where my great-grandfather died. This is the room I locked myself in when my father wouldn't buy me a pony."

He brushed the hair away from her face. "How long did you stay locked in?"

"A couple hours. Until I got hungry."

He loved her honesty. "When did you get the pony?"

"Never. I got riding lessons instead, and that's when I started working at Air America in order to pay for them. A portion of them." She ran a finger along his jaw. "This is also the room I spent hours, weeks, months, crying in because I'd laughed when you asked me to go out with you."

His heart tumbled in his chest. He felt bad for assuming what he had back then. She had a heart of gold, was the sweetest, kindest woman on earth.

"I don't blame this house for any of that, and we can stay here for as long as we need, but it'll be so different from what we've gotten used to. No cooking together, no dancing in the kitchen." She kissed his chin. "No home runs while watching *I Love Lucy*."

Certain things would be hampered while living here, he'd already thought about that, and had wondered if he'd ever get used to sitting down at the table and having the food served to him. He also knew she was working her magic on him. "It would take more than a couple of days to get that house livable."

Her eyes lit up. "I'll help. My mom will help. My dad will help."

"You really want to live there?"

"Yes."

"Why?"

She bit down on her bottom lip, a sure sign that she didn't want to answer.

He ran a finger over her lip. "Tell me."

"Because I don't want you to feel trapped, and you might, living here."

Once again, he wished he'd never said that. "I won't feel trapped."

"You might, the dinner parties alone can do that to a person."

Thinking of her sneaking into her mother's office, and hoping he wasn't making the biggest mistake of his life, he said, "I'll have a crew start working on the house tomorrow."

"You will?"

"Yes, but we'll need furniture and—"

She planted a kiss on his lips, then several across his face while saying, "I'll start shopping tomorrow."

He rolled, flipping her onto her back so he could explore her bare skin, inch by inch. "Right now let's give this room some new memories."

"I like that idea."

So did he, and they made memories deep into the night.

By Thursday Jason had to admit that the little house he remembered was hardly recognizable. He'd pulled men off every job site to work on the place. The front porch was now twice as large, and there was a back porch off the laundry room he'd also added to the back of the house. That door was where he installed a doggie door for Tanner. He'd also installed a new-fangled automatic dishwasher where the old clothes washing machine had been in the kitchen. The addition also provided for the bathroom to be expanded. The entire place had been painted, inside and out, and a new swing hung in the tree where the old one had been.

All in all, the place looked good, but he still wasn't seeing it through Randi's eyes. She was in love with this place. That was written all over her face, and reason enough that he'd live here. Bad memories and all.

He pounded in the last nail on the hook she'd asked him to install on one of the porch pillars so she could hang a pot of flowers, and dropped the hammer into the loop of his carpentry belt as a car pulled in the yard.

"Place looks great," Randal shouted as he climbed out of his Cadillac.

"It'll do," Jason replied, walking down the steps of the porch as Randal opened the back door on his car and Tanner leaped out.

"The women are grocery shopping now," Randal said. "Tanner and I were given the job of bringing out the items they bought this morning."

A silent chuckle rumbled in Jason's throat. The house was full of furniture, the cupboards were full of dishes, pots and pans. The bed was made, curtains hung on every window, even the closet and dressers were full of new clothes.

"I was told to put it all in the bathroom," Randal said, opening the trunk.

Jason lifted out a couple of bags. "That's the only room not full yet."

"I have a feeling you are never going to get Randi to move back into town." Randal closed the trunk after lifting out two other bags. "Can't say I blame her."

"I think you're right," Jason admitted. "Once I get

caught up on other jobs, I'm going to start building a house on the other side of the barn, near that grove of trees. A brick one. Modern style."

"Well, when the time comes, and if you decide you want to sell this one, I'm first in line."

"Why?" Jason asked as he opened the door to the house.

"I've always regretted not buying Carl Jansen's cabin. Jolie and I loved going there, both before and after the kids were born. It was small and we liked that. Sometimes I spend what seems like hours searching our big old house for Jolie. I considered buying Carl's place, but it was too far away. We could never have gotten there often enough, but we could drive out here whenever we wanted, and when the baby is older, you and Randi can just open the door, and tell him or her to go see Grandma and Grandpa."

"I guess we could." Jason set his bags on the floor in the bathroom, and took the ones from Randal, set them down as well. Once again, he was surprised that all he'd once assumed about the Osterlunds hadn't been close to the truth. They had money, but they were good, honest people. People he liked.

He also was amazed by how he could tell Randal things, and not be judged. "I just want Randi to have the best of things."

"I appreciate that." Arms crossed, leaning against a wall, Randal looked around, then back at him. "And I think she does. She has you. I could never have asked for someone to love my daughter more than you do. I see that every time you look at her."

Chapter Twenty-Three

Everything was backfiring on her.

They'd been living in their little house for over a week, and Randi feared she'd made a huge mistake. The biggest mistake she could have made.

Jason was faking it again.

He was kind. Considerate. Caring. And distant. More distant than he'd ever been.

The house didn't leave much room for actual physical distance. It was more like he'd built a wall around himself.

She'd thought living here might open his heart to love, but the opposite had happened and she was to blame.

They were sitting at the table, eating lunch, after he'd spent most of the morning clearing the last of the items out of the basement and garage of the old house. "Do you want to cancel the party tomorrow?" It was more than the party she was worried about canceling. That had seemed like the perfect place for him to see his mother again, but now it didn't.

He looked at her, frowned. "No. Why? Do you?"

"No, but—"

Tanner barked, several times, and trotted to the front door.

Jason pushed away from the table. "But what?" he asked on his way toward the living room to see who was pulling in the yard.

Without answering, she stood, followed. The curtains were open, showing the car that had parked in the driveway.

"What is a taxi doing here?" he mumbled.

Her heart crawled into her throat as the driver got out, opened the back door for a woman to exit.

The sound of his intake of breath told her what she feared was true. It was his mother.

He turned, looked at her.

"I called her," Randi admitted. "Invited her to the party tomorrow."

"Why the hell would you do that?"

Her fears hit a high she'd never known, and all she could do was tell the truth. "Because I was afraid."

"Of what?"

She couldn't tell him. Not with his mother walking toward the door. She gestured at the door and turned, walked back into the kitchen.

The opening of the front door was quiet, but echoed in her ears like thunder. Thunder from the storm she'd seen on Jason's face. She wanted to run into the bedroom and cry, but that wouldn't relieve the pain in her chest. He'd never forgive her for this. Never.

How could she have been so wrong?

Because she'd been desperate.

Desperate for his love.

Forcing herself to move, she cleared the table, rinsed the dishes and put them in the dishwasher, all the while wishing she didn't need love. But she did. She'd known it her entire life and couldn't bring a baby into a home where there wasn't that kind of love shared with everyone.

She was wiping the table when footsteps on the front porch had her looking up, watching Jason walk through the door. Alone.

"Where's your mother?" she asked, barely sounding like herself.

"Outside."

It was hard to look at him. He was everything she ever wanted, yet he couldn't give her what she needed the most. Love was a need. Stronger than desire. Stronger than passion. And she couldn't live without it.

She turned, carried the dishcloth to the sink. "Aren't you going to invite her in?"

"No."

"I'll go to the bedroom, stay there, or leave. Go to town."

"No, you won't."

She closed her eyes. Her heart felt open at both ends, raw. To the point, when he touched her arm, she flinched.

His hold tightened and he forced her to turn around, to look at him. "You aren't going anywhere until you tell me what you're afraid of." He was frowning. Deeply. "Is it me?"

Her first instinct was to say, "No." But then she had to correct it. "Yes."

"Which is it?" He released her arm, stepped back. "Why?"

Instinct again had her stepping forward, closer to him, but she stopped herself after one step. "It's not your fault. It's mine. I tried to convince myself that for the baby's sake, it would be enough. Whatever you were willing to give would be enough, but—" She had to stop in order to swallow.

He cursed.

She pressed a hand to her lips, knowing he didn't want

to hear it, but she had to say it. Explain it. Fast, while she could. "But then we'd pretend. Act like we were so in love. It hurt, knowing it wasn't real. It hurt more when we stopped pretending, because then I had hope. And I shouldn't have. I know that. I know it's not what you want. But I couldn't help it. Every day I fell deeper and deeper in love with you. I couldn't stop it from happening. I told you I didn't expect you to love me, and I honestly thought I could live like that. But I can't. I was afraid that it was going to slip out, that I was going to say it and I was afraid of how you'd respond. I thought, if you saw your mother again, found out that she still loved you, then maybe you wouldn't mind so much if I love you, too."

He ran a hand through his hair, shook his head.

Her entire body was trembling, and her heart pounded so hard it was echoing in her ears. "I understand why you can't love me in return. I do. Truly. My entire life I've had people expect things from me, but you never did. I had to try so hard to make you notice me in high school. Then, when you did, I behaved foolishly, and then my brother let you take the blame and my father sent you to reform school, and then, years later, I show up on your doorstep and end up pregnant. I haven't done anything to make you love me, ever. But you, you've given me so many reasons to love you that—"

He moved so quickly, silencing her with his lips, she was stunned at first, couldn't respond. But that didn't last. Her passion for him was too great. Her entire being responded to his slightest touch. And did so now. She melted against him even though she knew she shouldn't because passion wasn't enough.

Still, she drank it in, because their passionate times were when she could let her true emotions reveal themselves. She'd slept with him the first time because she'd loved him then, too. Just like she had for years before then.

When his lips left hers, she was more afraid than ever. What if that had been a goodbye kiss? She couldn't bear the thought and a sob escaped.

He cupped her face, forced her to look up at him. "I love you. I've loved you for years."

Her vision was blurred, her hearing muffled. Her mind momentarily blank. She could barely get out the word, "What?"

"The reason I said that I'd never thought I'd get married, was because you were the only woman I'd ever want to marry. The only woman I'd ever love."

"Love? Me?" Stunned, shaken, she shook her head. "You can't."

Jason had never been shot so close to death and back again as the roller-coaster ride his emotions had just gone through while Randi had been speaking. From fear to ecstasy and everything in between. Biting back a grin, he asked, "Are you trying to talk me out of loving you?" He caressed her cheeks with his thumbs. "Because it won't work. I already tried that."

"When?"

He'd made an unspoken pledge to himself as a child to never be vulnerable again, but it was time to break that pledge. Actually, he'd already broken it. "Since the first day I saw you. You were walking into the school building, wearing a pink skirt, white blouse, red sweater and black-and-white shoes. I didn't know your name, but knew you were the one." He huffed out a breath. "As soon as I did learn your name, I tried to fall out of love with you. But couldn't. Everything I've done, from motorcycles to hot rods, to building houses, I've done because I wanted you to notice me. Including trying to stop Joe and his friends from breaking into the Air America building."

"You have?"

"Yes, but I was convinced that you could never love someone like me. Someone with a shady past and bad reputation. When you became pregnant, I knew I couldn't live without you, without our child, and decided that I'd do everything within my power to make sure you had everything you wanted. Then I met your parents and was afraid that I'd never be able to love you the way you'd always been loved. I'd never known that kind of love, never seen it." He shook his head. Shrugged. "Never believed it was inside me. But you found it, forced it to come out, and when I realized that, I was even more afraid, because I knew I needed it. Love. Had needed it for years."

Randal had made him face the fact that he loved Randi every time he looked at her. Every time he thought about her. Day in and day out. Up until this moment he'd been in hell trying to figure out how to tell her that he loved her, but that he also needed her love. People had been expecting things from her for years, and he didn't want her to feel obligated to give him anything. Especially not her love.

Tears were trickling from her eyes, and he wiped them away. "The harder I fought it, denied it, the deeper my love for you grew. I was pretending, but it wasn't what you think. I wasn't pretending to love you. I was pretending that I didn't love you, and it was the hardest thing I've ever done."

"It was so hard for me, too."

It was ludicrous that they'd both been fighting the exact same thing. He pulled her close, held her tight. "I didn't want to hurt you, to disappoint you, but that's what I've done, and I'm so sorry. So very sorry."

She lifted her face, looked at him with those amazing blue eyes. "No, you haven't. You've made me the happiest person on earth. Given me everything I've ever wanted."

"I thought I had to give you material things." Her living in this tiny, old house had eaten away at him the past week. "The best of things."

"I've had the best of things my entire life. My parents loved me for myself. Somehow, years ago, deep inside, I knew you could give me that, too. Love me for myself. That was confirmed when I saw how you loved Rachelle at her birthday party. I fell in love with you again that night, and have loved you more every day since, but I didn't know how to show you that was all I wanted. Not your land. Not a big house. Not a big diamond. Just you. Your love. I love you, so much. So very much."

He now understood how precious love was, and how fragile it could be, and why people would give up everything for it. "You have it. I love you. Always have, always will."

Capturing her lips with his, the rush that filled him was like none other. All the love he'd kept locked inside him was now free to flow without any barriers or limits. It was incredible, freeing, and a happiness he'd never experienced filled him. Laughter bubbled inside him.

Their combined laughter parted their lips and he picked her up, twirled her around as their happiness filled the room. Filled the house.

Her laughter stopped abruptly. "Your mother! Where is she?"

He set her down, kissed her forehead. "Tanner is showing them the barn."

"Tanner is a dog!" Her eyes grew wide. "What if she left?"

"She hasn't. I sent away the taxi." With his mind fully on Randi, not greeting his mother and her husband affably, he'd excused himself. "I told them we were in the middle of something."

"I'm sorry."

The grimace on her face made him smile and kiss her. "It's fine. Everything is fine. Better than fine."

"Go get her. I'll put coffee on. I made cookies this morning, and—"

He stopped her from saying more with another kiss. One that left her breathless. Him, too. "I love you." Later he'd show her how much he loved her. Right now he needed to show his mother his greatest accomplishment— his wife.

Hours later Jason wrapped his arms around Randi from behind, and relished in how easy it was to love her. It had always been easy. He just hadn't wanted to accept that he deserved love. Everyone did.

Including his mother.

She and Scott, her husband, had left moments ago, borrowing a car to use during the time they would be in town. If he hadn't married Randi, the visit may have gone differently. He may still have been too full of himself to listen, to believe that things hadn't been exactly as he remembered.

"You didn't know, did you?" Randi asked quietly. "About the shrapnel embedded in your father's skull."

"No, I didn't." There had been a lot of things he hadn't known, including how that shrapnel had changed his father. How kind and loving he'd been before his injury. How, when his father had told his mother to leave or she'd regret it, she'd believed him. She'd left him behind, with his father, because she'd feared that alone, his father would never have survived. Jason believed that, too. Without him, his father would never have eaten, never had food to eat or fuel to heat the house. Even after he'd moved out, he'd continue to bring groceries to his father, pay the utility bills.

"He didn't want to be injured, didn't want to be in pain, and she didn't want to leave," Randi said.

Jason now had empathy where loathing and embarrassment had once lived. The knot that had lived for years inside him was gone, but it hadn't left all on its own. Randi was the reason it had disappeared. Her love, her actions, had dissolved it piece by piece, without him even knowing it. "I know." He kissed the side of her neck. "Thank you for inviting her here." He was glad he knew the truth and had the opportunity to know his mother again.

"You're welcome." She twisted in his arms, looked up at him. "I love you."

He'd been so foolish. He'd had all he'd ever wanted and had still been so blindsided by his past that he could have lost it all. "I love you, so much, and I swear I'll be here every day, building a life, building a family, with you, every step of the way."

"That's all I want." She poked him in the ribs. "Along with a racetrack." Giggling, she said, "I guess I do want your land, after all."

He laughed. "Our land." Touching her hair, he said, "There is one thing I'd like to know."

She frowned slightly. "What?"

He wasn't sure if she even remembered, but he'd always been curious. "When I got out of reform school, there was a letter waiting for me. From you."

She nodded.

"What was in it? I wanted to open it, but thought it was probably telling me to never ask you out again, so I wrote return to sender on it and put it back in the mailbox."

She ran a finger along his jawline. "It was the opposite. I apologized and asked you to please ask me out again and said that I thought you were a very special guy. I still do."

He picked her up and realized there was something to be said about a small house, because within a few steps they were in the bedroom.

The old pride he'd held on to so tightly transformed into one he'd become honored to carry. That of being married to *the* Randi Osterlund-Heim.

Their love grew with each passing day, and Jason could hardly believe how fast summer passed and fall descended upon them. What he could believe was that he was the luckiest man on earth. His favorite thing to do was lie in bed beside her, with his hand on her stomach, feeling the baby move and talking about if it would be a boy or a girl. He didn't care, as long as they—the baby and Randi—made it through the delivery with no problems.

Dr. Spencer said there was nothing to worry about, that Randi's pregnancy had been perfect right from the start. He had to agree with that, but he was still worried.

The crib and cradle he'd made were set up in the second bedroom, along with a rocking chair he'd made, and there were so many toys, clothes, blankets and bottles from her baby shower that he'd had to build a set of shelves along one wall to hold everything.

Her due date was only a week away, and there were a large number of people who hoped they'd still be in town when the baby was born. Others, as well as her cousin and brother, had arrived yesterday, because today was Election Day.

He reached over and laid his hand on Randi's stomach. They were on their way home after standing in line to cast their votes, in the Thunderbird because it was a warm, sunny day for the first part of November. She looked adorable, wearing a pair of big sunglasses and her hair held back by a blue-and-white polka-dotted scarf that matched her dress. "How are you feeling?"

"Wonderful." She laid both of her hands atop his. "I'm going to make oatmeal cookies as soon as we get home. There's time before we have to be at the hotel."

Everyone who had worked on Randal's campaign was meeting at the hotel downtown to watch the votes being announced. Then, to celebrate the win.

"We can stop and eat if you're hungry," he said.

"No, I just want oatmeal cookies."

He chuckled. "I love you."

She let out a big sigh. "I never get tired of hearing that."

"You never get tired of oatmeal, either." Giving her a wink, he added, "I'll help you make the cookies as soon as we get home."

At the house, once the first batch of cookies was in the oven, he went out and pulled the Thunderbird into the barn. While he was at it, he pulled the Chevy out. Joe and Gus were on their way over to take it out to the track. They always did that when they were in town, and normally, he and Randi would go with them, but not with her due date being so close now.

He was walking back to the house when Joe and Gus pulled in. "Keys are in her," he told them. "Total her and she's yours."

"Don't tell him that," Joe said, pointing at Gus as they climbed out of their car. "He'll total her on purpose."

"Not if he knows what's good for him." Jason leaped up the steps and entered the house, which smelled like cinnamon.

Randi met him at the door. "You can go with them."

"I'd rather stay here with you."

"Baking cookies instead of racing?"

"Yes."

She rubbed her stomach. "If my belly still fit beneath the steering wheel, I'd be out racing with them."

He steered her toward the kitchen. "I know you would be." She loved racing as much as he did. "But then you wouldn't have oatmeal cookies."

The cookies won out, and when they brought the Chevy back, Joe and Gus enjoyed them almost as much as she had.

"By the way," Joe said, taking another cookie off the plate on the coffee table. "You are now looking at the director of the art department for JO's Dream Wear."

"Art department?" Gus asked. "Man. Leave it to you to get a job doing what you've been doing your entire life."

Jason looked at Randi, but she shrugged. "What's he been doing his entire life?"

"Drawing pictures of naked women," Gus answered.

Randi threw a pillow at him. "Will you ever grow up?"

"Why?" Gus asked. Having caught the pillow, he acted like he was going to throw it back at her.

Jason gave him a warning by simply shaking his head.

Gus dropped the pillow in his lap.

"Brat," Randi said to Gus as she scooted to the edge of the sofa.

"What's wrong?" Jason asked.

"I have to go to the bathroom."

Jason helped her up, walked her to the bathroom.

"I gotta get back to town," Gus said. "Put on a monkey suit for the party."

"I told him that I'd catch a ride with you and Randi," Joe said. "Mom's bringing my suit to the hotel."

"That's fine," Jason answered, noting he'd have to change clothes soon, too.

"Catch you on the flip side," Gus said, heading out the door.

Jason stood in the kitchen, talking to Joe and glancing at the bathroom door, wondering what was taking Randi so long until he couldn't wait any longer. He knocked on the door. "Are you okay in there?"

The sound was muffled, but he heard enough to throw open the door. She was crouched down, holding on to the bathroom sink with both hands. Hands that were so white, they looked as if no blood was flowing into them.

He shot into the room.

She was huffing, panting. "My. Water. Broke." She let out a low growl while squeezing her eyes shut. "The. Contract—"

He heard no more, picked her up and ran out of the room. "Her water broke!" he shouted at Joe while running for the door.

She let out a groan and laid her head on his shoulder. "I think it stopped. I think the contraction stopped. It wouldn't in the bathroom. I couldn't even shout for you."

His heart was pounding. He'd read about labor and delivery, accompanied her to every doctor with lists of questions, and this was not how early labor had been described.

"What car?" Joe asked, running beside him. "I'll get the door."

"The hot rod," he answered. It was the fastest, and

from what he'd read, she needed to be at the hospital already.

Joe opened the door and Jason slid her in.

While running around to the driver's door, he told Joe, "Take whatever car you want." Jumping into the car he added, "And grab her suitcase out of the bedroom."

"My parents, Dad's party!" She let out another moan and arched her back, grabbed a hold of her stomach. "Oh, no, it's another contraction!"

"And call your parents!" Jason shouted, hitting the ignition, shifting and stomping on the gas in swift order. The hot rod held the record of zero to sixty in less than eight seconds on the strip, and he was trusting her to beat that record now.

After they hit the highway, Randi swiped the sweat on her forehead. "I don't think it's supposed to be this hard, this soon."

He knew it wasn't, but said, "Dr. Spencer said every baby is different. It's all going to be fine. We'll be at the hospital in no time."

"I hope so, because, oh, no, here it comes again!"

His foot couldn't press on the gas pedal any harder, and he was trying just as hard to remember everything he'd read. "It's going to fine, honey, just keep breathing. Don't hold your breath!"

They'd no sooner hit the city limits when a siren sounded. Usually, red lights in the rearview mirror had people stomping on the brakes. Not him. Not today.

"We can't stop!" Randi shouted. "Unless that cop knows how to deliver a baby, because this one is coming out soon!"

"We aren't stopping and that baby's not coming out until we get to the hospital!" Jason hoped by saying it, it would be true. "The hospital is only a few blocks away. Just keep breathing."

"I am breathing! You just keep driving!"

"I am driving!"

"Go faster! Or let me drive!" She doubled over, holding her stomach again. "Oh, here we go again." Between groans, she added, "There's another cop!"

Jason saw them, and the third one.

Minutes later he slid to a stop so fast in front of the hospital, the tires were smoking. He jumped out, ran around and lifted her out of the car. "We're having a baby!" he shouted at the man near the door as he ran. "Open the door! Now!"

Randi's face was red, and she was letting out growls of pain.

Jason shot through the open door. "Get a doctor! Get a doctor!"

A nurse rushed forward. "Calm down, sir."

"She's having a baby!"

"I know. I know," the nurse said, walking down a hallway. "This way, we'll get her on a gurney."

"Jason, Jason, don't leave me. Please don't leave me alone."

He kissed Randi's forehead. "I'm not going anywhere, honey."

"Right here," the nurse said, entering a room. "Put her right here and we'll wheel her down to maternity."

Jason slowly lowered Randi onto the sheet-covered cot on wheels, and held her head because there was no pillow. "She needs a pillow."

"We'll get one. You can leave now, go check her in at the front."

Randi was doubling up in pain again, groaning and clutching his arm.

"I'm not leaving," he told the nurse.

"Sir, you can't—"

"It's coming!" Randi shouted. "It's coming!"

"It just feels that way," the nurse said.

"She said it's coming!" Jason shouted. "Check!"

The nurse lifted Randi's skirt and immediately started shouting, "Doctor! We need a doctor!"

The room filled up and though several people told him to leave, they were too busy to make him, because within minutes his son was born.

Randi was sore in places but was too happy to focus on that. She had a son. A beautiful little boy, who, just like his father, was already setting records in racing to the finish line. It seemed as if it had been hours since they'd made Jason leave the room so they could clean her and the baby up and transfer her to an actual room rather than an examination station.

Dr. Spencer walked into the room shortly after the nurse who had wheeled her into the room left. "I believe that was the fastest delivery this hospital has ever had. You don't mess around, do you?"

"Only with my husband," Randi answered. "Where is he? And our son?"

"Your son is in the nursery. I just checked him, and he's perfect. Jason will be up here in a little bit, and I've made some special arrangements considering the circumstances."

"What special arrangements?"

"Adjustments to visitors and visitation hours. This is a private room—Jason's orders—so don't worry about that bed on the other side." Dr. Spencer folded back the sheet. "I need to give you the once-over, make sure all's well."

After some poking and prodding, Dr. Spencer assured her that all was fine. "I'll find Jason and send him in."

"Thank you, and our son?"

"I'll let the nurse know that he can be brought in, too." The doctor left, closing the door behind her.

Within minutes it opened again, and like always, her heart skipped a beat at the sight of her husband. He had flowers in one hand and a huge stuffed bear in the other. Setting them both on the table, he arrived at the bed and engulfed her in a hug.

"I love you so much," he whispered. "So, so much."

"I know you do." She knew that sounded conceited, but she was conceited when it came to him. "And I love you."

He kissed her forehead.

"John Jason Heim," she said. Jason's middle name was John, and she was set on flipping them around for their son.

"J.J. Heim," he said.

"Yes." Happiness filled her all over again. "That's a good name for a drag racer, don't you think?"

Jason kissed her again. "Cars and airplanes, you are a special woman."

A knock sounded and the door opened. A nurse entered, wheeling a bassinet. "I have a precious little bundle for you."

Jason lifted J.J. out of the bassinet and laid him in her arms while sitting down on the bed beside her. They spent several quiet moments just holding their son, before the nurse entered again.

"I have a few people waiting to come in. Dr. Spencer approved it."

"Yes, please, let them in," Randi answered.

Her mother and father entered first, and after a few

minutes Joe joined them. Next came Stu, Lottie and Rachelle, and following them came others, until the room was practically bursting.

"You should all be at the hotel." Randi looked at her father. "Especially you."

"This is more important than election results," her father said, kneeling next to the chair where her mother was holding J.J. "My first grandchild."

"What time is it?" Randi asked Jason, having long ago lost track.

"After nine. The results should be coming in soon."

Now that her mind wasn't fully occupied with their son, she asked, "What about the police?"

Jason glanced at her father.

Catching a look between them, she asked, "What happened?"

"When Joe called and said Jason was taking you to the hospital in the Chevy, I called the police station and told the chief that you needed an escort to the hospital," her father said. "They had an officer waiting at the edge of town, but he couldn't keep up. Neither could the other two."

The room erupted in laughter that only stopped because the phone rang.

Her mother handed her J.J. and then wrapped her arms around Randi's father's arm. "It's the election results."

Cradling J.J., Randi looked at Jason. "You answer it. Please."

He picked up the phone, and the smile that appeared said it all, even before he told her father, "You won! You won!"

Cheers were still filling the room when the door opened again and—carrying a child's pedal car, red, with a ball of fire painted on the hood—Gus entered the room. "Never fear, Uncle Gus is here!"

Jason leaned closer, whispered, "He's from your side of the family."

She giggled. "I know, but you love me, anyway." Then, not caring that the room was full, she kissed him, let him know she loved him, too.

Epilogue

"Look, J.J., there's Daddy," Randi said, pointing to the starting line where Jason was lined up on the asphalt quarter-mile strip.

Twenty months old, and completely enthralled with his father, J.J. jumped up and down in her arms, clapping. "Da-da. Da-da!"

Family members surrounding them laughed and clapped with him, and Tanner, never far away from J.J., let out a bark.

The flag dropped and the cars took off, speeding to the finish line. It was over within seconds, with Jason winning. As she knew he would. Yet, it still thrilled her every time. He loved racing that car, and she loved watching him. She also loved driving the car, and did so regularly.

The racetrack was as much of a success as his construction company. People had come from surrounding states, and sometimes farther away, to race during the months since they'd opened it.

"We'll keep J.J.," her mother said. "Go join Jason."

Randi kissed her son's forehead. "Mommy will be back." She hurried down the bleachers and ran over to where Jason was turning his car around to drive back past the bleachers.

He stopped the car, pulled off his helmet. "Hello, beautiful. Want a ride?"

She opened the door. "Are you picking up chicks?"

He winked. "Only one."

With a laugh, she climbed in. "Congratulations!"

"Thanks. I'll expect a kiss as soon as I park this old girl."

"Only one?"

The announcer came through the loudspeakers. "There he is, ladies and gentlemen, Chicago's own Jason Heim. He's not only the winner, he and his wife Randi are the owners of this fine new racetrack. How about a round of applause for them?"

She and Jason both waved out their windows as they drove past the bleachers full of cheering race fans.

The announcer continued, explaining the races that would happen throughout the day, and where concessions could be purchased, as Jason drove the car off the strip and around a fence into the pit area.

She scooted across the seat, hugged his arm. He had built them another house, a bigger one on the other side of the barn, and tonight she was going to tell him that in several months one more bedroom would have an occupant. Baby number two.

He'd be thrilled. As thrilled as she was.

"My parents have to be back in Washington next week, so they are staying at the cabin all weekend. And your mother is arriving on Tuesday to stay for two weeks."

"When do we fly back out to California?" he asked.

He'd helped her with the washing bay by overseeing the construction. "Three weeks. Sam's out there, counting nails to make sure we don't pay for any extras before the washing bay can be officially opened."

Jason grinned. "He is good at what he does."

"I know." She and Sam had worked out their differences, and she agreed that his accounting skills were a real asset. The washing bay was only one of her projects that had come to fruition. Someday she'd completely take over for her father, but not until she was ready.

Who knows, maybe someday she'd even run for office. Or maybe Jason would. He'd be a shoo-in.

Or maybe they'd create a division for female drag racing at the Heim track.

Whatever they did, they'd do it together.

Jason stopped the car and shut off the engine. "I'm ready for that kiss."

She looped her arms around his neck. "Me, too."

He was everything she'd always wanted and that would never change, but what made her even happier was knowing he felt the same way about her.

* * * * *

If you enjoyed this story,
be sure to read the first book in
Lauri Robinson's
The Osterlund Saga duet

Marriage or Ruin for the Heiress

And why not check out her other miniseries
Twins of the Twenties

Scandal at the Speakeasy
A Proposal for the Unwed Mother